n inventive--and highly believable--biblical revisionist
e... The authors go right to the heart of one of the
reat unknowns of Christian history: the role of women
n the early church. The journey is ultimately more
thoughtful and satisfying than a mere holy grail."

— *KIRKUS REVIEWS*

"The narrative is well written, intriguing and inspiring...this story blends an ancient conflict with present
day debate in a fictional yet eye-opening manner...Just
when you think all has been unearthed and exposed,
you realize there is much more to this story. The
Mystery of Julia Episcopa is a great beginning to a
promising conspiracy series."

— *READERS' FAVORITE (5 STAR REVIEW)*

"This was an unexpectedly moving mystery. I hope to
hear more of the Vatican Chronicles! I cannot recom-
mend this audio book enough - truly an awesome
listen. Not a dull moment!"

— *AUDIO BOOK REVIEWERS - ABR REVIEWER*
CHOICE AWARD WINNER

THE ANONYMOUS SCRIBE

JOHN I RIGOLI
DIANE CUMMINGS

THE
ANONYMOUS
SCRIBE

To the memory of my wife Delphine ... Mizpah
For Scott and Jordan

CHAPTER ONE

Israel Museum, Jerusalem
Present Day

SUSAN BAUER EMPTIED A THIRD CUP OF COFFEE AND SET HER MUG down with a thud, thankful that the caffeine was kicking in. She shivered. On a gloomy day like this, Susan's cramped corner of the dimly lit museum basement felt like a cave. She reached for her heavy, gray cardigan, drew it around her shoulders, and began the mind-numbing chore of fitting together ancient scroll fragments.

Susan landed this job after seeing a post on the college bulletin board that a Dr. Samuel Gold at the Israel Antiquities Authority needed an assistant. Within two weeks, she found herself on a long economy flight to Jerusalem. She had jumped at the chance for numerous reasons, none greater than she wanted to put some distance between herself and a bossy mother, a milquetoast father, and a spoiled, demanding younger sister whose all-consuming wedding had been on the brink of devouring her too.

Her job, though, had turned tedious, and she wondered

why she had ever signed on. As she clamped down on a yawn, she spotted something unexpected on her screen.

Normally, Susan's work on the scrolls referenced rules, traditions, and teachings of the Essenes, an early Jewish sect from the second-century BC. But these fragments were different. Her brown eyes narrowed and, as she leaned in, shiny, chestnut curls fell forward about her face. She looped a lock behind an ear to clear the view.

"Dr. Gold, come have a look," she called out to the middle-aged, watery-eyed scholar who sat across the room engrossed in his own work.

Dr. Samuel Gold was a prominent paleographer appointed by IAA to interpret ancient writings. An unmarried solitary soul, he was interested only in his current project, the Dead Sea Scrolls, discovered in 1946 in the Qumran Caves on the north shore of the Dead Sea in the West Bank. Making sense of the large find had claimed his undivided attention since the nineties, when IAA made a great push for their translation.

Dr. Gold frowned. Susan had broken his concentration. He had never gotten used to interruption when he was absorbed in the fascinating details of ancient history.

Heaving a sigh, he rose, adjusted his baggy pants, and ambled over. "What is it, Susan?"

"Look," she said.

Dr. Gold stooped over her shoulder and squinted through small, round, metal-framed glasses at the fragments of parchment on the computer screen. His eyes locked on the words *temple scroll* written on two pieces that Susan had fitted together. "'During ... the rule of Vespasian ... on the ninth day of Av ...'" he began, scanning the words carefully. "'The house of Israel ... destroyed ... looted ... treasures taken from priest's library ... secret temple scroll stolen.' Hunh?!" Dr. Gold barked. "How old are these pieces?" he asked.

Susan referred to her log. "Between 18 and 69 CE."

Dr. Gold frowned. "This reference to the destruction of Herod's Temple is odd. I mean, odd that it's showing up here. It's out of the time frame you're working in. *secret temple scroll?*"

"What should we do with these fragments, Dr. Gold?"

"I'm not sure. I just don't know," he repeated as he wandered away.

Susan looked over at Dr. Gold. That was all she was likely to get out of him for the day. She saved the fragments to her desktop and headed to lunch, unaware that what she had found would turn her world—*the entire world*—upside down.

CHAPTER TWO

Jerusalem AD *30*
The Fifteenth Year of the Emperor Tiberius
The Twelfth Year of Caiaphas, Jewish High Priest in the Jerusalem
Temple

FROM HIS CAPACIOUS, OVERHEAD, TERRACE VIEW, THE HIGH PRIEST Caiaphas relished the early evening breeze as he watched the young man seated on a stone stool in the courtyard below drop a few coins into the frail, weathered hand of an old farmer. The farmer bowed, which didn't take much given he had the spine not of an olive or fig but lifelong wheat picker. As he turned away, a fisherman—Caiaphas could smell the peasant from his high post—stepped forward. The young man on the stool smiled at the newcomer. This tickled Caiaphas almost as much as the newly potted cypress caught in a cross breeze, teasing his shin. The young man dipped his stylus into an inkwell that sat upon a low, hand-carved stand made of the finest Lebanese cedar and curled over the sheepskin papyrus spread across his lap. As the fisherman spoke, he wrote.

Caiaphas noted with satisfaction the line behind the fisherman. Citizens from as far away as Sidon and Tyre were here to give their testimony. They had come by boat, on horseback, and arduously on foot, all in the name of civic duty.

On completion of the testimony, the young man wiped an index finger, chalky and stained with diluted charcoal, on his linen *chiton*. Then, he retrieved coins from its deep and weighted pockets and dropped them into the open, eager hand of the fisherman.

"Quite a crowd," Theophilus noted as he approached his brother-in-law.

Caiaphas nodded.

"For what purpose?" Theophilus knew his brother-in-law had put out word that any Jewish citizen who supplied testimony about the man who was attracting followers in Galilee would receive coins for speaking out, but he wanted to hear him say it.

"The scribe is taking their testaments," Caiaphas said.

"I see. Of course, they are poor and will say anything for bread."

Caiaphas pressed his lips together in annoyance, a common byproduct of talking politics with the man to whom his sister was wed.

"This so-called new leader hasn't caused us any trouble, dear brother."

"He's gaining followers."

"A bunch of rag tags," Theophilus said with narrowing eyes.

"This Yeshua's teachings are outside our law."

"But they are not. This Yeshua teaches the Torah," Theophilus said.

"Not exactly." Caiaphas, as high priest, oversaw the correct observance of Jewish worship. "The rites and rituals of Jewish law must never be compromised. Yahweh is God of the Universe, and these new factions must stay in line. It would be gravely unwise for them to miscalculate our response should they migrate to Jerusalem with any new notions. I do not want trouble." Any disruption in the smooth running of events at the Temple would bode ill for Caiaphas. Jews had much freedom, both civil and religious, if they did not trouble Rome. The slightest disturbance, however, would bring Roman soldiers bearing down on Jerusalem, to unleash death and destruction.

"You will avoid this trouble how?"

Caiaphas gave a sharp nod toward the young man below. "His writing is our safeguard."

CHAPTER THREE

Sepphoris, Galilee AD *30*

THE YOUNG SCRIBE SAT DOWN ON A LARGE, FLAT ROCK IN THE small hills of a grassy knoll and stretched his woolen bundle across his lap. He dug through it until he found his goatskin canteen. The fluid swished faintly as he shook it. Flipping the top off, he drank a little. With time still to go, he wished he had refilled it when he passed the well outside Nazareth.

He put his canteen back in his pack and resumed walking. The leather straps of his sandals dug sorely into his ankles. *The next time I make this journey, I will have a mule carry my belongings. I will have plenty of water and an extra covering for the cold nights.*

Only the wealthy could travel with mules or camels but, as a scribe, he hoped to rise to the ranks of Jerusalem's elite. The scribes were the most influential, their wisdom revered throughout Judea and Galilee. Even the Romans treated them with respect, knowing most scribes understood their language.

He heard a soft bell-like sound to the east and turned. A

young shepherd was shaking an instrument. The sheep behind him stopped grazing and followed. Looking up, the shepherd waved in greeting. "Where are you coming from?" The shepherd ran a few paces to catch up.

"Nazareth. Well, I'm coming from Jerusalem. I have been working at the temple school." The young scribe proudly displayed his scroll and then put it in his bag.

"I am impressed." Then he asked, "How is it in Jerusalem?"

"The same. Each day there are more soldiers, but they do not bother us much. Of course, I was too busy to notice most days."

"You are traveling back to Sepphoris?"

"Yes, I have not seen my family for some time. And you?"

"I am continuing north to Ptolemais. They now ask a rather fetching price for wool."

The young scribe studied the shepherd. He knew the young man was not much older than he was, but his craggy face feathered with deep lines and somber eyes showed of a hard life.

The young scribe looked at the deep green of the farmland along the roadside. "I had forgotten how truly beautiful the land is here."

"Oh yes, Galilee is truly the most beautiful land. I do not care how elaborate are the spires of Jerusalem." He laughed. "Here, in Galilee, a man belongs to the land in a way one never could in the city."

"I know what you mean. I have thought about these fields often when the noise of merchants along the street continues well into the night. It is a different place entirely."

The two parted ways wishing each other well.

The young scribe's ankles were starting to bleed. *When I arrive in Sepphoris, I will have Raphael stitch together a new pair of sandals.* Prices for such things were high in Jerusalem and he did not trust anyone to know his feet as cobbler Rafi did.

He came to a familiar grotto of carob and pomegranate

trees. He took a deep breath and relaxed, knowing home was but a *mil* away. As the young scribe passed by the orchard, he saw two women collecting fruit and stocking their baskets. "Hello!" he called out. "I suppose you could not spare a pomegranate for a traveler at the end of a long journey."

The younger one smiled a wide, engaging, lopsided smile.

The young scribe walked to the edge of the grove. As he approached the girl, catching a better view of her face, his breath caught. Her deep blue eyes, a rare sight in the holy land, sparkled against her dark skin.

Her smile grew nervous, and she gathered her linen hood around her face. Gingerly, she chose a large pomegranate and handed it to the young scribe. Indeed, she could see he had been traveling. His shawl was dusty gray and stained with grunge. "So, where do you come from?"

"Jerusalem. I have completed training and am now ready to work as a scribe." He wanted everyone to know of his achievement and once again retrieved his scroll from his bag as proof.

The girl raised her eyes to meet his. "How wonderful. Are you home on holiday?"

"In part. I shall have work here as well."

The older woman set her basket down. "Rebecca," she called. "Hurry along."

"Much fortune with your work and travels." Rebecca nodded, managed a small, feeble curtsy, and ran toward the older woman.

The young scribe dug into the pomegranate. The juice-filled beads spilled onto his wrists. He sighed at the deliciousness and wished he had offered the girl many thanks. After all, they sold these in town for a price.

Then, Rebecca returned.

The young scribe offered no words to the girl, simply cocked his head.

"I have heard of a man who is talking of matters I have not

heard before. Supposedly, he comes from Nazareth. He has been traveling all around Galilee ... with followers. They call him a holy man."

"Oh, yes? Do you know his name?" Perhaps the young scribe could learn something more before he set out on his mission.

"I heard it only once, and now I cannot think of it. Have you by chance come across anyone like this? I am burning to hear what he says. I am asking everyone I meet. Sorry if I've held you up."

"No matter." The young scribe certainly could not disclose the fact his recent work had only to do with the so-called holy man. He discarded the rest of the fruit peel and dropped a handful of seeds onto his tongue. "I have not met such a man. I am journeying from Judea, not Galilee." The young scribe walked away, the buildings of Sepphoris in his sight.

Just outside the city walls, he passed by an abandoned, moss-covered hut, tilted and wobbly, looking as though it might blow away in a puff of breeze. It reminded him of the history of this place. Before he was born, shortly after the death of Herod the Great, a peasant named Judas the Galilean acclaimed himself a messiah and sacked the treasury of Sepphoris. The Romans killed Judas, burned Sepphoris to the ground, and slaughtered its inhabitants. His grandfather had been beaten to death publicly in that battle.

The young scribe entered the city through the Southern Gate, relieved that tall, cement walls shielded him, briefly, from the sun. Narrow steps led him to the center of town. His heel slapped down onto a cobblestone street, which was wider and flanked by two-story stone buildings. First floors opened into the street where merchants sold everything from fruit to cloth to books. People crowded terraces outside apartments above the stores. The whir of wheeled carts spinning over the grooves of the stone streets punctuated the voices of the people who stopped to bargain. The young scribe could not believe how fast these buildings had gone up. When he had left the city for school, the street was a narrow dirt road boasting one-story mud, brick, and reed buildings. The new buildings were three stories tall.

"You're back!" a familiar voice rang out.

He squinted, his eyes sore from the sun. "Adriel!" A girl he had grown up with stood on a second-floor terrace of one such newly erected building that overlooked a fresh fruit shop. A protruding belly told him that her life had changed, just as his had done.

He patted his own belly. "When?"

"Soon. I married Micha last year. He's down there somewhere seeing to customers."

His gaze lowered to the colorful fruit displayed in the shop. Micha was bargaining in his animated fashion with a prospective buyer. On spotting the young scribe, he waved. "Hey, carrot top, you're back! I can see they didn't put much meat on your bones. And you're still pale as a snowflake."

"Well, I guess I haven't changed much then," he shouted back to Micha, annoyed with his observations. The young scribe hated references to his uncommon rust-colored hair. He yelled back up to Adriel, "Congratulations!"

"Are you finished with school?"

"Indeed, yes." Again, he fished for his goatskin parchment in his shoulder pouch and held it up like a trophy.

Adriel shouted, "Well done! When are you going to settle down and find a wife?"

The young scribe laughed, overjoyed to be back. He had not made any friends in Jerusalem. They laughed over the way he spoke and called him *vlácho*—peasant—whenever the masters were not around. It never changed no matter how he worked to excel and fit in. "When my father says so," he replied. His training had come at a price. It cost his father dearly in fees and bribes to send him there. Now, at nineteen years of age, it was over, and a bright future lay before him, but one that he owed to his father.

"You'll need a wife if you want to join the *booshy* on the hill," Adriel added.

At this, the young scribe bristled. *Booshy? Is that what she calls the ruling class?* Open disrespect for the elite was dangerous. Yet Adriel was speaking for all to hear.

"What woman would have me?" he responded in jest, but anxiety crept in. He hoped his father had not arranged a marriage in his absence.

Adriel leaned over the railing. "What next?"

"I've already completed my first assignment, and the priests are pleased. They've let me come home to visit my family."

Adriel waved him on, and the young scribe disappeared farther into the city, finding himself on the main street, newly named the Forum. His eyes met those of a Roman soldier as he passed a fig and vegetable stand. He looked blankly ahead, pretending he did not see him, before continuing. At the end of the street, he advanced to a large aqueduct fueling a fountain and pulled out his canteen. Dumping out the swish, he refilled it with fresh, cool water. Holding the nozzle to his lips, he sucked the cool liquid. When his thirst was sated, he poured water onto his hand and splashed it over his bloody ankles.

The graceful arches of the aqueduct intrigued him. He wondered how long it had taken to build this curtain of arcs. Like arms, they extended from the eastern hillside into the center of town. From where he stood, he could see the aqueduct thread through the large spread of homes in the eastern quarter. These were the homes of the wealthy, Romans mostly, with a few merchant Jews thrown in. The merchants did quite well with the Romans, since they could always pay more than what was due at tax time. It was either that or risk being crucified.

As the young scribe approached his house, the low murmur of a crowd grew louder. Standing outside the spacious, one-story, stone structure, it sounded like a small party was going on.

CHAPTER FOUR

Sepphoris AD *30*

HE SLID THE LEATHER LATCH BACK AND SWUNG OPEN THE DOOR, brushing past his uncle who was pouring wine for a man he recognized as one of his father's clients.

"Son, you are home at last! Come in, come in." His father rushed forward and embraced him.

The entire family accosted the young scribe with hugs and kisses. Their enthusiasm overwhelmed him, and he felt emotion flush his face as tears wet his eyes. Fortunately, his uncle, in his rich baritone, yelled out that they should stand back and give him air "lest he fall to his demise by smothering." That brought a round of laughter, and the elders unhanded him and resumed their prior conversations, while the children scampered off to play.

His mother had redecorated in his absence with new carpets, curtains, and divans. While the house was spacious, a home to be proud of, it seemed somehow smaller, probably because of the enormity of the Temple, where he had trained.

"Where is *Ema*?" Steam and smoke rose from the open

14

stone ovens across the courtyard. He could only assume that his mother was busy near the kitchens, no doubt ordering the cook and the servants about. She would never settle for anything less than perfection, particularly on the Sabbath.

"My dear," his father yelled out. "Your son is home."

His mother scurried across the courtyard. Her dark-brown eyes glistened as she reached up to embrace him. Her head-scarf hid her wavy, black hair but highlighted her clear, olive skin. Tiny lines at the corners of her lips hinted that he had been away too long. His mother kissed him and, without giving him a moment to speak, ordered him to go wash off the dust from his journey. She bade his sister to fetch him something clean to put on and set the servants to warm the *mikveh* for his purification bath and see to him in his ablutions.

After all the dirt from the road was washed clean, he climbed into the fresh pool and immersed himself, saying the prayers of purification. Once, twice, seven times. He felt clean, refreshed, and ready for Seder.

The table was set for fourteen. His mother's servant carried a silver tray and placed fresh slices of bread on each plate. His sister set down a bowl filled with figs, grapes, and dates, while his mother and aunt stepped in from the courtyard carrying more trays laden with steaming food, including his favorite succulent lamb.

His father sat at the head. After the blessing, he stood. "We are thankful that my boy has made it home safely after such a long journey. I'm sure he will be the finest scribe in all the land, one worthy of all the rewards, opportunities, and respect his title warrants."

His father's words were humbling indeed.

"Hear, hear," his uncle said, clapping a hand on the young scribe's shoulder and giving it a squeeze of affection.

"Look, he's embarrassed," his sister teased. "His face is red."

The young scribe gave her the most hateful look he could

muster, while his mother drew on her sternest tone. "Daughter."

His sister had unleashed a collision of emotions within, and he struggled to hold in his tears.

"I didn't realize how quickly you would begin your work," his father said, redirecting the young scribe's attention. "Tell me of your first assignment?"

"Copying texts, no doubt!" his uncle bellowed.

The temple leaders had warned the young scribe to be cautious about speaking of his work, and, when everyone simultaneously stopped eating to hear his words, he had to think fast. "I cannot discuss it too much as it hasn't begun yet, but it's nothing of import. If it were, they would have assigned it to a more seasoned scribe, for certain."

That seemed to appease everyone, his father excluded.

After supper, the guests retreated into the open sitting room as the servants cleared the table. Eventually, everyone left, and his mother and sister withdrew to their bedrooms.

"Let's go to the roof," his father said, reaching inside a cabinet and pulling out two woolen blankets.

The young scribe followed him up the ladder onto the rooftop. The sky was clear and dressed in a million sparkling stars. They unrolled straw mats and situated the blankets, then stretched out and pulled them over their legs.

"It is not even cool tonight," the young scribe's father said.

A star leapt across the sky, sketching a limb across the blue-black night.

"Oh, Father, there is a shooting star!" The young scribe sat up and pointed.

"One second of life. To be so restless and so stunning."

The line of the shooting star, which curved to resemble a lip, still clung to the sky. The moon was in quarter, its long white body arched in a sitting position. He'd studied the stars in school, but often had difficulty locating Andromeda or

16

Mercury, the star figures the Romans and Greeks could spot with such ease.

His father reached over and touched his arm. "We've missed you. Your mother is finally at peace."

His words fed the young scribe's soul. Weary from his trip home, sated by his mother's luscious meal, his eyelids began to droop. He was nearly asleep when his father spoke again.

"Sepphoris is looking more and more like a Roman city," his father commented. "I had hoped that one day the Romans would grow bored with our town and leave. But they believe the Galilee is the birthplace of insurrection and rebellion, and they are clamping down."

"Well, it is true." The young scribe had learned as much away at school. "It's always been that way with our town being so centrally located."

Sequestered at the Temple for the past four years, the young scribe had not given thought to such things. He was finding his first voice on the subject. "It seems that as long as we do nothing to threaten Roman rule, we can live freely, don't you think?"

"Son, do not kid yourself. The soldiers are always every-where. They remind us every day that we Jews live under the watchful eye of Rome. Even in our own homeland, our influ-ence is limited."

He thought about that, as he did about all the teachings of his father. However, his father was a man from a different time, and the young scribe had more experience now. It was thanks to his father that he had his own edification but, still, he certainly did not want any discord on his first night home, so he kept those sentiments to himself.

"Keep your distance," his father cautioned, as if he could sense the young scribe's obstinate brain at work.

Was this conversation supposed to lead to why his father had called him to the roof? He could no longer tell, but the sky was only getting blacker as midnight approached. "My first assignment is to document a young man called Yeshua of Nazareth. He has started his own religious sect, and the Sanhedrin is quite disturbed."

His father drew in a breath. "I have heard of this one, though I have not seen him." He let out his breath. "We certainly do not need another trouble-making prophet here."

The young scribe knew his father was referring to John the Baptist, the apocalyptic and charismatic rabbi famed for his baptisms in the Jordan and for his outspoken criticisms of Herod Antipas, who ruled in the Galilee. When John the Baptist dared call Antipas's marriage adulterous and his wife a whore, Antipas took off his head and served it to his guests on a silver platter. It was an ugly business.

"What do they intend to do about this Yeshua?" his father asked.

"They're moving on him already. Caiaphas had pilgrims from Galilee rounded up, those who had heard him speak," the young scribe told him. "He offered silver half-shekels to any who could testify about the man. Being from Galilee, the priests brought me in to translate and record their words. The priests in Jerusalem do not speak Aramaic, and they certainly don't know the different dialects spoken in our lands. I translated their stories from Aramaic to Hebrew as they spoke."

His father beamed. "You see, being a country boy isn't all bad. It made you of use to your masters. What did they say of him?"

"Their stories differed some. A few insisted that he'd healed them with a touch of his robes. Most said that Yeshua was performing exorcisms and magic tricks and trying to get people to revolt against the Temple, even against the Romans. A few swore he was a prophet and a man of God."

"Ah. What did the priests have to say to this? They must

have been some comforted." His father didn't look comforted. He looked worried.

"Father, I am only a prentice scribe. No, a journeyman now. The priests don't speak freely in my presence, but I imagine they argued. They always dispute each minor matter. In the end, they decided to send a scribe to follow Yeshua, watch him, and listen to what he says. I'll send them my report and they'll determine whether Yeshua is really a prophet, just another roadside rabbi, or someone who should worry them."

"And *the someone* they are sending is a wide-eyed boy?"

"I'm not so young, Father. Besides Greek and Aramaic, I speak Hebrew and Latin, and I understand the dialects in our lands. I know the territory. Who better to send?"

His father sat up and bellowed, "I'll not have it! You are my son. They have no right to order you and no call to be meddling in the affairs of the Galilee. We have our own tribunal, our own priests, our own scribes and elders. Our high court here decides what is right and what is wrong. I do not want you to be a spy for Caiaphas and his court. It is a sin, and it is against our laws!"

The young scribe let this sit for a moment. "Father, I am not to spy on him. My masters simply want to know more, nothing else."

"And report back to Jerusalem," his father added. "Son, getting involved in the affairs of the Temple ... I like it not."

Not once did my father ask me what I want. I am a man now, not a boy caught throwing stones at the sheep. But I will not try him. "Again, my job is to find out more about this man. That is all. I do not mean to cause him harm. I admit the Sanhedrin probably wants to put a stop to his preaching. But from what I hear, Yeshua appears to be a peaceful man."

"You do not really know what kind of man Yeshua is."

"You're probably right," the young scribe said, tossing water onto the flames of their debate.

"Is he in Nazareth, this Yeshua?"

"I was told to seek him in Cana."

"The Galilee is filled with wandering rabbis, some honest and some just intent on fleecing gullible fools. What's so special about this one?"

"I don't know, Father."

"I'll not have you used as a weapon against your fellow Galileans. We'll find this Yeshua together."

"What?"

"You will listen to him and make your report," his father said with finality. "If I have to, I will bribe those who insist that they can have none other than you, a simple peasant! Then, you will turn in your scroll and come home for good. Your mother will have it no other way."

The young scribe fumed silently.

CHAPTER FIVE

Paris
Present Day

THE OLD PRIEST STEPPED OUT OF HIS ANCIENT RENAULT AND approached a pawnshop set in a posh shopping district between *Ladurée Chocolatiers* and *La Femme Clothiers* on the bustling *rue Riquet*. Hesitating at the door, he looked right and then left. Seeing no one of interest, he shuffled through. The hem of his ankle-length, black *soutane* kicked up in the backdraft and nearly caught in the door. Relieved no other customers were present in the stuffy, little place, he moved to the counter and pressed the call bell.

Emile Bird, a slim man of average height, appeared from the back between two floral curtains. "*Monsieur le curé*, you return once again." M. Bird noted that this was the priest's fourth visit to *La Vieille Collection* in as many months, and always on a Thursday.

The priest regarded the proprietor vacantly. He reached into the slit that served as a pocket for his vestment and withdrew a small box. He set it on the counter and removed the lid.

M. Bird lifted an eyebrow. "More?"

The priest murmured, "How much will these bring?"

"They are as ... ah ... the last time, the same, *oui*? From your late aunt?"

The elderly priest nodded.

The proprietor snapped up the goods and disappeared behind the floral curtains, returning to the counter minutes later with an empty box. He handed it back to the priest and paid him.

The cleric pocketed the box and the euros.

"Will I see you again?" The proprietor's hooded eyes housed a mixture of suspicion and hope. In his line of work, one needed to be cautious, not ask too many questions. It was always a balancing act.

His customer evaded the question and turned to leave. "*Merci.*"

The shopkeeper scooted out from behind the counter and took the old priest's elbow. "*Laisse-moi t'aider, mon père.*" He ushered him out the door, then lingered, watching him wobble to a rusty, red car that looked prehistoric.

The old priest got in, started it up, and headed north.

That was all Mossad operatives Philippe Gaston and Anna-Marie Mannes needed. Philippe pulled out, causing chaos in midday traffic, and headed in the direction of the Renault. In fact, the only person who didn't take notice of the scene he'd created on *rue Riquet* was the old priest.

It was certainly enough to spook Emile Bird. He made a snap decision to close shop early. He made his way inside and flipped the sign on the door from *Ouvert* to *Fermé*. But, before completing the quarter turn on the dead bolt, a tall, fit, refined-looking gentleman pushed his way inside.

He might have appeared cultured, polished, but Jacques Ignatius had fired quite a few arrows with precision into targets over his twenty-year career with Mossad. However, one would never suspect it when he stood before his French history class at American University.

"*Desolée, monsieur, nous sommes fermé,*" M. Bird said, looking up at Jacques and pointing to the sign.

"Closed? At this hour?" Jacques asked, voice steady.

Noting how well-turned-out the man in the tweed jacket looked, M. Bird did not consider he might be a mob enforcer or another kind of threat. He had entertained those men in his shop before. He couldn't count the number of crooks looking to get hands on a valuable ancient artifact. It was big business. Yet this man's tone said otherwise. "How can I help?"

With a mild smile in place, Jacques said, "I want to see the coins."

"I don't know what you mean, monsieur." Fear clouded the proprietor's eyes. "Who are you?"

"I am not police, but I will notify police if you do not cooperate *toute de suite.*" Jacques had no doubt the proprietor would move fast to turn over the coins to black marketeers, which was why timing was everything.

Weighted by fear, the shop owner slumped.

Perfect. Jacques opened his tweed jacket just enough to reveal the Ruger in his chest holster.

"One minute," the proprietor conceded. "I need to retrieve them."

"From your pocket? That should not take a minute."

"They are ...."

"Monsieur, *s'il vous plaît.*"

With that, the proprietor pulled a single silver coin from his pocket and opened a shaky hand. The coin glistened with perspiration.

"Turn it over," Jacques instructed.

He did.

"Who's the priest?"

M. Bird raised his eyes to Jacques'. He stared for several seconds, until he decided that further delay would land him in trouble. "Father Claude Fullier."

"*Merci*," Jacques said, and left.

CHAPTER SIX

Pilsen, Czech Republic

Yigael Dorian had just closed the annual meeting of the European Association of Archaeologists with a talk that had inflamed the bulk of attendees. He'd claimed the dramatic rise in the number of dig sites in Israel and beyond, coupled with twenty-first-century technology, would uncover artifacts believed lost forever and shed new light on the famous Yeshua, proving the gospels to be nothing more than bedtime stories passed down through the ages.

Despite Yigael's standing as the world's leading archaeological scholar, his critics shouted him down during the question-and-answer period, contending that the Holy Spirit inspired the gospels, and nobody must question them. Those on Team Dorian were quick to bite back, insisting that no one could dismiss Yigael's ability. When the ruckus went into overtime, Yigael withdrew from the stage unnoticed. He made a quick exit from the main university campus and pressed ahead to catch a shuttle back to Parkhotel.

On returning to his room, he kicked off his shoes and lay

down to unwind. When his phone rang, it instantly energized him. *Fast work*, he thought, even for Jacques. But, on reaching for the device, he deflated. "Herschel."

"You never learn, do you?" Professor Herschel Banks had just finished giving a dreadfully dry guest lecture on ancient cities to a graduate class at American University in Paris.

Yigael could hear the smile in his colleague's voice. "And how would you know?"

"Live stream. Apparently, my attendees left me for you. Thanks for upstaging me. Listen, I would've waited for us to meet back in Jerusalem, but, well, we lost our funding."

"I'm not surprised."

"They think we've spent too much time on it already. To them, it's a cold case."

Herschel was referring to the Israel Exploration Society, an archaeological research nonprofit. Yigael and Herschel had received an IES grant to look for the long-lost Jewish treasure stolen when the Romans destroyed Jerusalem and sacked Herod's Temple in AD 70, the events that ended the Second Temple period in Jewish history. Less significant pieces of the treasure had turned up over the centuries, but it seemed the priceless artifacts had simply vanished. Their most recent dig was just outside Rome.

"Who else can we see for funding?" Yigael asked. "IAA can't do it, won't do it." Even as a higher-up for the Israel Antiquities Authority, he'd failed to convince the other board members to fork over more capital. Road to nowhere, he'd heard more than once.

"And the government turned us down."

"Twice."

"Right. I guess that's it, then. For now," Herschel said.

"Not for me, it isn't."

"We had our window."

"It's not closed yet."

Yigael had been on edge more than ever these days. It was no longer just about finding the treasure and returning artifacts to Israel, though his country was the rightful owner. He hoped for something more, something to give to the Jewish people.

His phone rang again. He moved it away from his head to get a quick glance at the caller. "Herschel, I need to run."

"Okay. Dinner, next week? The usual?"

"Yep. See you."

Herschel shook his head. *He always hangs up mid-goodbye.*

"Philippe," Yigael said in lieu of a salutation. "What do you have?"

Yigael had been watching the movement of the coins in Paris from the start. The ancient silver coins weren't rare. However, they usually didn't turn up so frequently, and they rarely turned up outside Israel.

On leaving the Mossad, Yigael had taken care to keep regular contact with several associates—allies, actually—still with the agency. When the coins began showing up in a pawn-shop regularly, Yigael got word from his contact at the Paris police. It took but one phone call to get operatives Jacques Ignatius, Philippe Gaston, and Anna-Marie Mannes to swing into action.

The three knew each other and Yigael well, and each held a conventional job as cover. Anna-Marie, a slightly manic redhead, lived in Paris and worked for an ad agency. Thirty-two-year-old Philippe taught art history while finishing his doctorate at the University of Paris. He was as attractive as they come, with sparkling, blue eyes and sandy-brown hair perfectly tousled. His looks were distracting in a way that made him strangely more effective in his undercover work for Mossad. In fact, he was so successful exposing terrorist groups that Mossad demanded more, which had disrupted his studies, shelved his graduation, and, more recently, wrecked his young marriage. So, Yigael asked him to track the coins, mainly as a way of keeping him busy and out of his own head.

"Jacques spoke with the shop owner," Philippe started. "They're Second Temple."

"Who brought them in?"

"You'd never guess. A priest. A Father Claude Fullier. Been at the basilica in Saint-Denis for years. He has two living relatives. One, a niece, lives in a modest apartment in Chatou. Makes one hell of a blueberry scone, by the way. I didn't see any sign of coins or other artifacts of interest."

"You were ... I don't need details."

"And a great-niece. I didn't get a chance to see her. Cooks for the diocese, lives on site." Philippe paused, then added, "This priest is old, Yigael."

"Meaning?"

"Meaning, I can't imagine the coins are worth pursuing. The old man's probably saving up for a new car. You should see what he drives."

"Noted, Philippe, thanks." Yigael hung up.

Who knew where the coins might lead? Yigael thought he knew. Worth a shot anyway.

CHAPTER SEVEN

Beit Aghion, Jerusalem

YIGAEL SHIFTED IN HIS SEAT IN THE WAITING AREA OUTSIDE THE prime minister's headquarters. The door finally opened to a tall, dark usher in a black suit. "He's ready for you now, sir."

Yigael entered the sparsely decorated office in this 1930s-era government building. Prime Minister David Golman sat at his desk. He stood and offered his hand.

"Hello, Yigael. Please, sit down."

Yigael and Prime Minister Golman had crossed paths during the past twenty-five years. The first time was when Yigael picked up a special commendation for uncovering information on the Iraqi missile attack during the Gulf War, and twice in the last two years when he'd turned him down for funding.

"Good to see you, Excellency."

"Please, Yigael, David." Prime Minister Golman peered through the spectacles at the end of his nose at the letter before him. "Second Temple coins in Paris?"

Yigael nodded. "Yes, that's correct."

"What's so special about these coins that you think they'll lead you to the treasure you've already uprooted three continents to find?"

"It's not just about the treasure, David. Herschel Banks and I have a theory that a document written about Yeshua during his lifetime may be part of the treasure."

"What kind of a document?"

"One that predates the gospels by a couple of decades, and, unlike the gospels, it was written in the presence of Yeshua."

"Oh? Since when are the Jewish people interested in Yeshua?"

"I take your meaning, but this document is believed to have been written during Yeshua's lifetime and to contain written accounts of his personal life and teachings."

"Ah, I see." Golman knew Yigael Dorian well. "You're hoping this document will place Yeshua unfavorably among Christians."

"I believe this document will reverse some of the beliefs held by Christians, yes."

"Why have I never heard of this?"

"Um, well, it's more lore than fact, honestly. But, as the old rabbis handed down their convictions about it, someone somewhere down the line gave it a name."

"What name?"

"The *Secret Temple Scroll.*"

"Rumored?" Golman's eyes nearly crossed. "Do you really expect me to fund an escapade based on old stories, name or no name?"

"Prime Minister," Yigael said, reverting to formality, "Herschel and I believe this document does exist."

"Based on what? Lore?"

"Lore often proves out."

"And what is its connection to the coins?"

"These coins were circulating in Jerusalem when Rome

destroyed the city and carted away the spoils. It is reasonable to consider that any number of them went with the treasure. The coins might lead us—"

"—to the treasure, and to the scroll, you hope. Yigael, you and your never-ending quest for the treasure, which now includes a rumored scroll, I don't know." Prime Minister Golman, weary of hearing an add-on to the same conversation, shook his head.

Yigael, aware that he hadn't presented many facts, added, "A lot of what I do is on instinct."

"While I appreciate that gift, Yigael, most of what I do isn't."

"Look, Prime Minister, it's worth the search. When this scroll is revealed to the world, the mighty Roman Church will no longer be able to give out their biased and distorted version of religious history. The publication of eyewitness testimony will tie their hands. And you'll be able to tell your children, with documented facts, who this man really was, and who he wasn't." Yigael inched forward in his seat. "This mission will vindicate our forefathers and compensate for the blame we've borne from those who've accused us of killing their so-called Messiah. It will put an end to the persecution Jews have suffered over the centuries."

"Sounds like you want me to fund a personal vendetta."

"No, I'm just a hot-blooded man."

"You're a decorated Mossad operative," the prime minister said, reminding Yigael of what they both knew. "Who allegedly penned this scroll?"

"No one knows." Yigael's mood sank. He was half-tempted to get up and leave. Damned instinct.

"It's just not enough, Yigael. I know this is disappointing, but I'm not getting into the ring with the Vatican based on Second Temple coins in Paris and rumors of some secret scroll written by some anonymous scribe. That's like skating on a lake in May."

"No, no, of course. I get it." Yigael relaxed a little, at least it was over. And then he exhaled, and, with it, a laugh escaped.

"What's so funny?"

"Skating on a lake ... here in the desert?"

"Well, see what I mean?" The prime minister stood. This talk was over.

CHAPTER EIGHT

New Artist Colony, Jerusalem

NEAR TO THE ISRAEL MUSEUM, IN THE ARTIST COLONY WHERE some of the world's most beautiful artwork was displayed, Yigael, his assistant, Josh Reznick, and Herschel waited at the famous Eucalyptus restaurant for their colleague and old friend, Sam Gold. With its mixed Arab-Jewish staff and an eclectic offering of kosher food, along with Middle Eastern cuisine, the ambiance truly reflected the two cultures. Sam had commented often that the place was a real treasure, so Yigael and Herschel decided a few years back that, when Sam was free to join them on their Monday night outings, they'd do it here.

"Sam. About time," Herschel said.

He took a seat next to Yigael.

Moshe Basson, the owner, approached and, with a fourth stomach in attendance, suggested they sample from the eleven-course tasting menu, a feast prepared with fresh herbs, fruits, mushrooms, and lamb to mimic dishes that originated during biblical times. They readily agreed and ordered a round of Goldstar on tap.

Dr. Gold caught the attention of Moshe Basson before he left the table and said he would like his favorite drink, instead, which was an infused concoction of asparagus, flowers, and *Arak*—an anise-flavored alcohol. He could never remember the name of it.

"Sure thing," the owner said. "Don't fill up on bread now, gentlemen. The first course will be out shortly." Moshe Basson dipped his chin and left.

"Fancy drink. Is it your birthday, Sam?" Yigael chided.

Herschel laughed but then began dominating the conversation, as he often did, this time regaling his colleagues with a summary of a recently published article in *Biblical Archaeology Review* with the intimidating title "Cyber-Archaeology in the Holy Land." Noting Dr. Gold appeared quieter than usual, Herschel said, "Earth to Sam."

Dr. Gold refocused. "Pardon me. Work. You were saying?"

"What could possibly be new about the Dead Sea Scrolls?" Yigael interrupted.

"Those old writings examined ad infinitum," Herschel added with a grin.

A server dropped off three Goldstars and the cocktail.

Dr. Gold spread fig jam on a piece of pita, revealing a hint of a smile as he did. "Matter of fact, I found something new just last week."

"Right," Herschel teased.

"I did."

"I'm interested, Dr. Gold. What is it?" Josh asked.

"You ever heard of something called a *secret temple scroll?*"

Herschel and Josh glanced at Yigael, stock-still, his beer a statue in midair.

"Actually," Dr. Gold went on, "the words were sandwiched between information about the destruction of Herod's Temple."

"What did you just say?"

"Are you listening, Yigael?"

"Of course, I am. How old is this fragment?" he asked, attempting to temper his excitement.

"Fragments. Several. Susan says between 18 and 69 CE."

"Who's Susan?"

"My assistant."

"What else?" Josh asked.

"Yes, go on," Yigael demanded.

Dr. Gold closed his eyes, envisioning the text verbatim. *"During ... the rule of Vespasian ... on the ninth day of Av ... the house of Israel ... destroyed ... looted ... treasures taken from priest's library ... secret temple scroll stolen."* He opened his eyes. "That was it."

Herschel nodded in the direction of Yigael. "We need to see it."

"Now." Yigael stood.

"What?" Dr. Gold took a quick sip of his drink and pushed his chair back.

"It's after nine, Yigael." Josh knew if he didn't step in, they would all be out the door and working till midnight. "We could wait till morning, if you want to, boss." He did his best to sound noncommittal. "We *did* already order."

"Yes, of course," Yigael said, sitting back down, though he did not like waiting. "Okay, then. Let's eat." He hoped to tame his impatience for the long wait.

35

CHAPTER NINE

Cana AD *30*

THE MORNING AFTER SHABBAT, THE YOUNG SCRIBE WATCHED AS Raphael fashioned a new pair of sandals. He added a thin, extra sole at the young scribe's request and left a small slit, so he could hide *shekels* he might need one day. He had seen one of his classmates, one of the privileged locals, take a coin from a slit in his sandals when a cart was selling sheep tail on skewers. That's when he made note to add the extra sole to his sandals.

The wounded skin around his ankles still burned, but the new footwear was comfortable and did not dig in where the flesh was still tender. Then he and his father set out east on the narrow, dusty road for Cana.

With appealing green fields and a mild, morning breeze, it was neither a long nor cumbrous venture. But the sun did not rest for long in the early days of spring, and he and his father found themselves sticky with sweat and thirsty after the hour-long jaunt. They headed for a well and drank to their satisfaction.

"This town has changed little," his father commented.

One could hardly call Cana a town. It barely qualified as a village. Small shops, set up under awnings in front of a few homes, served as the town center. The merchants were just opening for the day.

A fruit cart beckoned from across the road. His father recognized the merchant standing behind it as the same man from eighteen years back, when the young scribe was but a toddler just finding his legs. The young scribe chose some golden-brown, sweet dates, his father a plump, deep-purple fig.

They entered a quaint pottery shop, where a man was working behind a wooden counter, hands thick with clay from the potter's wheel. An array of jugs, some pieces exhibiting intricate, painted designs, decorated the shelves behind him. The potter looked only middle aged, but years spent bent over his wheel had already caused his back to hunch.

"I will speak with you in a minute," he said, as his fingers deftly pressed on the spinning clay, shaping it into a large serving dish before their very eyes. He worked his way to the edge of the plate, stopped spinning the wheel with his free hand, and then leaned over to rinse his hands in the wooden bucket at his feet. Wiping them on a woven piece of cloth, he walked over. "Would you like anything in particular?"

"Actually, we are not here to purchase."

The young scribe was glad his father had started the conversation, since he felt awkward luring the potter away from his work when they did not intend to buy anything.

The potter frowned but said nothing.

"We are trying to find some information about a young rabbi."

A wrinkle appeared between the potter's brows. "Where are you from?"

"Sepphoris. My son has attended school in Jerusalem. He is now, I am proud to say, a scribe for the Temple. He's been sent to detail the exploits of a certain Yeshua of Nazareth."

"Of course," the potter said, "a self-taught rabbi, not formally trained by the Temple. Nice, young man. Speaks softly. You have to move close to hear him." His mind seemed to wander for a stint, then, he added, "He healed my daughter."

"Your daughter!" Surprised, the young scribe said, "Is he some kind of physician?"

"He is not a physician, but no physician could find what was wrong with her. For weeks, she could not rise from her mat. The light hurt her eyes, and she cried often from pain. My wife and I feared she would die." The potter looked back at the thin door that separated the shop from his home. "I sought young Yeshua. I heard he had cured a man—one touch and his pain disappeared."

"And you believed that?" His father's eyes narrowed.

"Not really, but I was desperate. Yeshua was living in the wilderness at the time. People said he was running around with that odd John the Baptist."

"Oh, I see," his father said. "Like the Essenes."

"Now there's a crazy group," the potter said. "I've heard they abstain from everything: food, drink, even pleasures of the physical nature. Nobody owns anything, and everyone owns everything. They do not swear, sacrifice, or trade. Very strange." The potter laughed. "They don't even own slaves. Yeah, they keep to themselves."

"So, Yeshua actually came to see your daughter?" his father asked.

"Yes. Someone sent word to him, and he came."

"How did he examine her?"

"He did not examine her, not that I saw. He sat next to her and spoke so softly I could barely hear, something about the light living inside him lived within her, as well. That her soul and mind were both pure and free, filled with the Father's love. Then, he kissed my daughter on the forehead and left." His eyes widened. "After that, she sat up and said, 'Papa, the pain is gone.'" His eyes filled with tears. "The next day, she went outside and greeted the light."

The young scribe and his father exchanged unconvinced looks.

"Directly following this episode, the elders asked the rabbi Yeshua to speak here in the synagogue."

"Oh, yes?" The young scribe's father stood straighter. He was eager to hear him tell of this.

"Well, we expected him to tell us stories of his travels. Instead, he spoke like a great sage, talking about the prophets and the laws, as if he hadn't grown up a simple peasant like the rest of us. When we objected, he got angry."

The young scribe nodded. *This story is not the unfavorable type the Temple seeks, but it shows how Yeshua fancies himself some kind of healer and a prophet.* He was so grateful for the information that he reached into his money purse and came up with coins to buy a jar for his mother.

Then, he and his father left and found a small grove of almond trees with two cement benches under the shade of their street-side branches. The young scribe removed his new sheepskin scroll, unrolled it, and found a patch of flat earth by his ankle upon which to set his inkbottle. He dipped the wick of his new reed pen into the diluted charcoal solution and began to write with vigor.

When he finished the potter's tale, he and his father set off for the weaver's shop. The weaver occupied the largest building near the western end of town. In a front workroom, two weavers threaded layers of flax through long strips suspended from a ceiling pole, a step on the way to producing linen.

The young scribe and his father stepped inside and watched the activity for a moment. His father then rang the clay bell for service.

One of the weavers looked up and came to greet them, a lad

about the young scribe's age. "I am afraid I do not recognize you," he said. "How can we help?"

His father introduced himself and his son and explained that they were looking for information.

The weaver claimed to know little about Yeshua but offered to retrieve his father.

An older man appeared, coughing uncomfortably, and said in a gravelly voice that his name was Joel. "If you don't mind, I would like to sit down." Joel flipped up the hinge of the counter and walked to one of the stools. He gestured for them to sit, as well.

"So, everybody seems interested in Rabbi Yeshua," he said. "I have lived in this area my entire life, and I know all the stories. They circulate about the Galilee, changing here and changing there." Joel paused and then lowered his tone. "You know, Yeshua was born a bastard. Back then, his father shamed Mary, and the two had to leave for some years. They stayed away. Egypt, I think, until the little boy was a toddler. Then, they came back married, settled for good in Nazareth, and seemed respectable enough. People have a way of forgetting when a man turns into as fine a craftsman as Joseph was."

Joel's candor startled the young scribe. "Are you saying Yeshua was born before his parents were married?"

The older man nodded. "These stools you sit on are his work, and they have lasted through many seasons. Yeshua was as fine a boy as comes along: smart, gifted, sincere. I guess those are the ones you really have to watch out for."

"You mean you have changed your mind about him?"

Joel coughed again and pounded his chest. "My oldest son is running around trying to spread God's word, or so he calls it. He thinks of Yeshua as the anointed one. The young follow him like starved bunnies and call him *rabbouni*. The older ones, Pharisees and the like, they come asking questions about him. If Yeshua is such a leader, why are we still under Rome's thumb? If he had supernatural powers, the Romans would be out of here, perhaps on a boat somewhere capsizing."

The young scribe's father nodded. "So, your son no longer lives at home."

"Well, my youngest is still here. I suppose they mind the easiest. I don't know who this Yeshua thinks he is. He travels with riffraff, troublemakers. And there's my oldest, right along with them, preaching to peasants and acquainting himself with filth. I think they're drunk on wine and howling at the moon. He says he is caring for the poor! Am I not poor?"

The young scribe touched Joel's arm. "The Sanhedrin is aware of Yeshua and not pleased. The temple priests did not teach him, and they do not want him teaching God's word when he was not chosen to do so."

"To my eyes, he is trouble." Joel's voice suddenly cleared. "But he is a gifted speaker. He grew up beside his father, swinging a hammer. Though, when I think on it, my impression was always that of a boy who spoke beyond his years."

"Yes," the young scribe's father said. "I *have* seen him. Oh, I remember the calm solitude of the boy's eyes now that you mention it. Joseph worked on my home in Sepphoris before we were blessed with our own son here. Those are not eyes one can easily forget."

"Father? How ...?"

"Son, be still. I did not know that this was the same Yeshua until this very moment."

Joel and the young scribe's father exchanged half-grins.

"I, too, remember his eyes. Like something from another world." Then Joel shrank in his chair.

"My son is here to help people like you, to document Yeshua's activities, so that the Sanhedrin can expose him for the fraud he is. Even if he is a nice, young man, he cannot claim to be the divine agent of God. It is not right."

"My son is convinced this Yeshua is a divine prophet."

The man's hopeless resignation saddened the young scribe. "Do you know where Yeshua is now?"

Joel shrugged. "Somewhere around Capernaum, I think."

Capernaum. The fishing town in the Upper Galilee on the edge of the sea. An idea formed.

"Are you ready, son?" his father asked.

The young scribe pulled coins out and purchased a small jug for his mother as a thank you.

They wandered to catch a moment of shade under a sycamore tree.

The young scribe, sitting on the grass, unfurled his scroll to take copious notes from which to draw upon later.

"The Sanhedrin will be pleased with what you have found so far." His father beamed. "Your mother will be expecting us soon."

The young scribe did not wish to oppose his father but felt there was no other choice. "Father, I know you want what's best for me, but the priests have tasked me with a great mission. If this Yeshua is truly a prophet—"

"He is but a peasant rabbi. Like the Baptist before him. And we all know what happened to John. I'll not have you caught in the middle of this."

His father could not understand. This mission could allow him more years of freedom and adventure. After all, he had been locked up for four years, toiling over scrolls. He decided to try a new tactic. "Father, my report would only be a few sentences at most thus far. If I send them this, they may be angry."

His father raised his bushy eyebrows. "You will spend tomorrow reworking the testimonies, expanding them for your masters in Jerusalem. And then we'll put an end to this."

"They might see that I was intentionally giving little attention to the task. You want me to establish a good reputation, yes?"

"Of course."

"You called in many favors to have me educated. You might need their goodwill in the future. But if I fail them—"

His father stopped him short with a grunt. "Son, I have neglected my own work since you returned home." He seemed to look past the young scribe, searching his mind for a solid excuse.

"Father, you venture home to Mother and let me go to Capernaum. I must meet and hear Yeshua, just once, to make these writings complete."

His father's stillness unnerved him. But then, the young scribe saw the tightness in his shoulders drop. "It would do no harm, I suppose. But be back in time for dinner on *Shelishi*. Your mother will be roasting fish with capers and dill."

"Thank you, Father. I will."

They kissed and departed, his father heading south back to Sepphoris, and the young scribe going northeast to Capernaum. He made sure to fill his waterskin at the well before heading out.

I wonder what he's like, this Yeshua. Does he lure one in? Does he sound like a flute or a desert lark when he speaks, singing his stories? Does his voice soar like an ibis? Is that it? Does this Yeshua have hypnotic power? The weaver said that an outsider with the power to influence the thinking of others could be dangerous.

I agree.

CHAPTER TEN

Capernaum AD *30*

THE YOUNG SCRIBE FIRST LAID EYES ON YESHUA SITTING ATOP A rock in a wheat field, beams from the afternoon sun serving as his spotlight. At one glance, he knew this was the man he sought. It mattered not that his ankles were sore, his waterskin drained, or his belly hollow. A power outside his control had transfixed him. Although he expected Yeshua to be a man of striking appearance, nothing prepared him for his uncommon physical beauty. He was tall and slender, taller than most Galilean men, even from a seated position. The rock he sat on kept his visibility clear, despite being surrounded by his *disciples*—the word of the day for his followers.

His hair was black and unruly, his eyes honey brown, his skin dark and weathered from the sun, and he had a thick beard. His features, though attractive, were broad and large, indicative of a man of this region.

Men, women, and children had gathered around Yeshua. They were partaking of a meager meal and laughing at whatever he was saying.

The young scribe shook the spell and approached, and, just as a shepherd gets caught sneaking up on his flock, the gathering took notice and turned as one.

Yeshua stopped speaking. With eyes that sparkled, he said, "Welcome, Young Scribe."

The young scribe's mouth dropped open. Both he and his father had taken pains to wear their homeliest clothing, leaving any signs of rank or position at home in Sepphoris.

Yeshua let out not a mocking but a mirthful chuckle at the young scribe's dismay. "I was a follower of the Baptist. Surely, you do not think that you are the first scribe the priests have sent to catch me out." He looked down at the young scribe's hands. "With soft hands unused to manual labor and ink staining your fingertips, I am no soothsayer."

On that, the crowd laughed again.

"You are a stranger to Capernaum. Sit and join us. Have you eaten?" He nodded toward a girl bearing a jug of fresh water and a basket of fruit.

She scurried over.

The young scribe chose two figs that clung to a single forked branch and opened his waterskin. The girl poured in a splash of fresh liquid, enough to wash down the meal. Then, she ran back and joined a group of young people sitting on a straw mat.

"If you have ears, hear this."

On that, the gathering quieted, as Yeshua regaled them with *The Parable of the Three Sons*.

They used to recite this to the boys at shul, so the young scribe knew it well.

He saw from the start that Yeshua was a master storyteller, unlike the high priests who seemed fatigued at the retelling of these old tales. His audience, most of whom had likely never been so far as Sepphoris or seen so much as a single, silver *drachma*, sat rapt in this tale of adventure and wealth.

At the story's climax, Yeshua paused and shook his head. "All three sons were given coins. Two of the sons grew rich, dripping in silk and linen, stuffed fat from lamb and wine and bread. But the third son? He did nothing with his coin whilst his father was absent. He tended the fields. He kept the servants fed. He cared for his elderly mother." He looked at his small flock, his eyes resting on one and then the next.

"Which son do you think most pleased his father?" Yeshua asked.

At this, the babbling began. Some argued that the eldest pleased his father most, as he had grown richest. Others fought for the middle child, for he had begun with less. The audience finally calmed, realizing it was the only way to get their answer.

"With boots covered in manure and robes creased with sweat and dirt, the father addressed his third son. 'You alone have done what I asked. You kept my coin safe. You worked my land. You cared for your mother. You are my only son.'"

Yeshua fixed his eyes on the young scribe. "And then the father repossessed the riches gathered from his first and second sons and awarded them to his most obedient one. 'My other sons have already enjoyed their reward. The last shall be first, and the first shall be last, as to the Law of Moses.'"

The quarreling erupted once again.

But Yeshua kept his eyes trained on the scribe. Though he had presented the story better than the young scribe had ever heard it spoken, this was a lesson taken from any school in all their lands, a lesson received by Jewish boys in every synagogue, a reminder that obedience to one's father—and to God—was more important than all the gold in heaven.

Surely, the priests had no reason to be concerned, and the young scribe's report would say as much.

Amid the discord, Yeshua rose from his perch upon the rock and walked toward the young scribe.

"So, have I taught anything that is not the Law of Moses?"

The young scribe flushed. Yeshua taught the law with all the authority of any teacher he had ever served. He shook his head.

"Report to your masters what I have said here. Perhaps it will allay their fears." With that, he walked away. Then he stopped and ventured a look back. "And when you tire of serving men, consider serving God instead."

CHAPTER ELEVEN

Israel Museum, Jerusalem
Present Day

WHEN SUSAN RETURNED TO WORK IN THE MORNING, SHE FOUND Dr. Gold closeted in his office with three strangers. One of the men looked familiar. The world of archaeology was small, Hollywood small, but it didn't come with paparazzi, so you could hardly ever put a face to a name. Dr. Gold motioned her over, then instructed her to send the file they were examining the other day.

"Hurry," he said.

Is he referring to those curious temple scroll fragments I pieced together last week? Susan wondered what had him so antsy before 8:00 AM. She headed for her computer and sent the file in a snap. "You should be able to open it now."

Remembering his manners, Dr. Gold invited Susan into his office and introduced her. "Susan, this is Herschel Banks, an old friend of mine. He teaches here at Hebrew University, and he's extremely interested in the fragments we discovered."

We? Susan thought.

"Indeed, I am." With lanky arms extended, Herschel reached for Susan's hand with both of his and began pumping up and down, crushing it in the process. "Some detective work! Quite amazing,"

"Nice to meet you, Professor Banks."

"Herschel."

Dr. Gold gestured toward the other two. "This is Yigael Dorian and his assistant, Josh Reznik."

Susan gave a start. *Yigael Dorian. Of course.* He was no stranger to her. His work was legendary. The legend was smaller than she had imagined, and entirely baldheaded. *They're always smaller in person. Built like a bullet, though.* "Dr. Dorian, an honor."

"Yigael will do," he said with a sharp nod.

Wow. Susan was smitten. All she could think about was getting a selfie with him. *Would he agree?* Then, as an afterthought, she nodded in the direction of the great-looking, younger guy. "Nice to meet you, too, Mr. Rezneck."

"That's Reznik," Josh said, emphasizing the *nik*. "But, please, I'm Josh," he added with a lingering gaze at the pretty girl with the knockout figure.

"Now, about the fragments." Yigael was all too eager to get down to business.

The three newcomers bent over the computer screen and buried themselves in concentration.

With eyes still fixed on the screen, Herschel asked Susan, "How did you come across this?"

"It was just simply part of the group of fragments I've been working with."

"Amazing," Herschel said.

Yigael's steely, dark eyes bore in on her. "It is. Please don't mention this find to anyone. His intense stare lasted for two extra seconds."

"Of course, Dr. ... Yigael."

Dr. Gold echoed Susan's next thoughts with, "Can somebody please tell me what all this is about?"

As Josh fetched folding chairs from a corner in the basement, Susan left for her desk.

"You stay," Yigael ordered her.

Susan, noticeably intimidated, followed Dr. Gold to his sofa, sitting next to him, where she felt more secure.

Josh placed three chairs in a half-circle in front of them.

Herschel, as he loved to do, nominated himself the storyteller. "Okay, here we go. In the late first century, in year 70 to be exact, as you know, Herod's Temple was destroyed by the Romans."

"Set on fire, the Jews were slaughtered," Dr. Gold broke in, "and the treasure was taken to Rome. Everybody knows that!"

"And some believe that when the treasure was taken, a document known as the *Secret Temple Scroll* went with it."

"The reference to which, we found on these fragments?" Dr. Gold questioned.

"Right."

"Well, what is this magic scroll?" Dr. Gold asked. "How have I never heard of it?"

"Because you split your time between your dungeon and board meetings. This type of stuff, you gotta go into the jungle to find," Yigael said.

"It's one of those stories, Dr. Gold, that's like aliens landing in Roswell in the forties," Susan tried to clarify.

"What she means is, to some people, it's like the quest for the Holy Grail," Josh said, mostly to catch Susan's eye.

"That damn thing," Dr. Gold commented.

"At any rate," Herschel said, "there's been no trace of it."

Dr. Gold still looked bewildered.

"Okay," Herschel said, a mild expression showing his patience. "Let's back up a bit."

"Please."

"As the rabbis tell it," he continued, "when Yeshua began to speak openly in Galilee, the high priests at Herod's Temple saw red. He was undermining their religious rules, usurping their power, and drawing attention in Rome, which was dangerous because the Romans were tracking down more and more Jews and imprisoning the ones they didn't kill outright."

"Herschel, get to the point."

"It's a long and winding road to get to any point with Herschel, as you well know, Sam," Yigael reminded him. "Be grateful he didn't go grab his *simlāh* from the trunk of his Hyundai and put that on to set the mood."

Herschel shrugged. "Okay, so, Joseph Caiaphas, Jerusalem's high priest, decided to build a case against Yeshua by hiring this wet-behind-the-ears scribe fresh out of school to take testimonies against this rebel rabbi."

Dr. Gold raised an eyebrow. This, he did not know.

"As the legend goes," Herschel went on, "it wasn't long before this young scribe had documented scores of testimonies."

Susan slid a sideways glance at Josh to let him know she knew his eyes were on her.

"Testimony in exchange for coins," Josh said, getting his head back in the game.

"Exactly," Herschel said. "These were peasants, after all. They had next to nothing. Now, it is said that Caiaphas hid the records in the Temple, waiting until the time was right, and that time would be when Yeshua caused them trouble."

"Let me guess," Susan ventured. "Passover."

"Yep." Herschel gave her a slight bow of approval. "When Yeshua began to speak at the Temple and word got around that he was a holy man, a riot broke out, and that was all Caiaphas needed. He showed the testimonies to the Roman Governor Pontius Pilate. And we all know what happened next."

"So, you believe it was on the basis of this secret scroll that

Yeshua was crucified?" Dr. Gold asked. His brows were working overtime. How could this crucial, if true, piece of information have bypassed him for the better part of forty years?

"There are certainly those who believe that." Herschel shifted position.

"From that time on, all was quiet on the topic of the *Secret Temple Scroll*. Then, with the destruction of Herod's Temple, the subject came up once again. Was the scroll stolen along with Herod's treasure? Was it destroyed in the fire? Did it ever exist in the first place? Many scholars concluded the story was a myth. Others, like Yigael and me, believe the scroll did—*does*—exist, somewhere."

The room became quiet.

"Look," Yigael said, leaning forward, arms dropped on his thighs, fingers clutched together. "This scroll is believed to contain eyewitness accounts of Yeshua speaking against the Temple, even instigating an insurrection. There has never been such a document. There has never been even *one* firsthand account of Yeshua preceding the four gospels. Can you imagine the worldwide reaction if we came up with Yeshua's own words?"

"I can," Susan said.

"We're not referring to Facebook, Susan."

"Dr. Gold, neither am I." *Facebook?* Susan stifled a chuckle and came up with an actual rebuttal he could understand. "The New Testament is full of firsthand accounts, all due respect. The four gospels are treated as though they were eyewitness accounts."

Herschel countered, "I think you cannot assume historical accuracy in the gospels, and many scholars agree. They were compiled thirty to forty years after Yeshua's death. Stories change over time. They become altered, perhaps distorted, at least full of hearsay. No document has surfaced showing that it was written during the time Yeshua was teaching. This would be the first and only one."

"The lore handed down asserts the scroll contains documentation of questionable activities on the part of Yeshua that will turn the religious world upside down," Yigael said. "It could undermine the very foundation of Christian teachings."

"That was fairly strong," Susan said under her breath.

The scholars were silent for a moment.

Yigael couldn't contain himself. "The Roman Church has placed Yeshua on a throne and called him God. Never mind that Christendom, but especially the Church, blames the entire Jewish population for what a handful of misguided priests may have done. And the Church has the gall to make all other religions irrelevant by claiming that theirs is the only pathway to God. It's time to stop all that nonsense!" He took a breath and stared down at his shoes, mindful that what he really wanted was fair dealing for his people. "Look, Yeshua is largely irrelevant to Jews. Perhaps he was a healer, perhaps a minor prophet who had some novel ideas, but nothing more. This scroll would undermine Christian teachings and cast doubt on Yeshua's purpose."

"*Could*," Dr. Gold and Susan said in unison. Dr. Gold looked at Susan. Maybe he'd taught her something after all.

Susan dared to ask, "Why are you so sure this scroll exists? It's all just, well, rumor."

"It is not only upon old documents and inscriptions that scientists base their search," Yigael said. "Centuries-old folklore has value, too, as a starting point. We view the possibility that these stories are rooted in the historical past, and that's why I, *we*, never discount them. The fact that the *Secret Temple Scroll* has survived scrutiny down through the ages is enough. It's worth looking into."

"But where might it be?"

"The big question. When we meet next, I believe we'll have something to reveal on that score."

"Hersch?" Clueless, Yigael asked, "What in the devil are you talking about?"

Herschel gave Yigael a wink, which meant keep quiet. "With this reference, reference to the *STS*—how we refer to it—I think we can really press Israel for funds. Yigael?"

"Yeah, my specialty. Getting refused by the PM." Yigael cracked his second smile of the morning, for show. "I think we're done for today."

Dr. Gold couldn't get up fast enough. Back to his precious Qumran caves by the Dead Sea.

"Let's all meet in my office a week from today, 9:00 sharp," Herschel said. He handed Susan, the only one unfamiliar with his office, a business card.

Meeting next? Susan wondered. *What on earth for? Why am I even here now?* After all, she was neither religious nor into interfaith disputes.

Yigael needed to keep an eye on Susan, but he couldn't say that. "You, too, Susan. You have a skillset that could come in handy."

Susan had degrees in both archaeology and ancient languages like the dozen other applicants Dr. Gold interviewed, but her savviness with technology was what won him over. A former intern, who had helped weed down the candidates, commented on her *"Insta"* following, which caused Dr. Gold to inquire whether that was a reference to coffee. Then, the intern explained to Dr. Gold that Susan had a small following on social media because of her archaeological posts.

Dr. Gold knew how riveting decoding a single Hebrew character on a lava-encased scroll could feel, but he had always assumed the circle of people who shared that sentiment was indeed a small one, and they weren't uploading "pics" and "quips" and "tweets" about their findings. If Susan had a following in this focalized area of study, that had to mean something, not to him, but in general. One must keep up with the times, even when studying ancient history. And so, she was hired.

"She's my tech geek," Dr. Gold said.

Susan went back to her computer.

Josh paused at her door, leaning on the frame. "Hey, how about a quick coffee? My treat. Talk about the scroll?"

"Ah, I don't think so, Josh. I can hardly believe the scroll you're all so excited about even exists and, even on the remote chance it does, why would anyone care about an ancient parchment that recorded the testimony of paid witnesses? Wouldn't it be worthless? Paid informers? Sounds like fake news to me."

"Sure, but this is something that might affect the lives of people all over the world. It could change everything where believers in Yeshua are concerned."

"I suppose there will be those who think these are the workings of some kind of antichrist and others who'll think it's a hoax."

"Well, then, dinner? This sounds like a bigger conversation."

Susan laughed. "The job has been fairly monotonous. Until today." That was all she was ready to divulge, intense blue eyes or not. "I don't think so, thanks." Josh sauntered off, and she refocused on her never-ending quest.

As Yigael and Herschel exited the museum, Yigael said, "Okay, what is it? You're wound up tight as a corset."

"Come with me."

"Where?"

"To my office."

"Why?"

"Just come."

"Okay, and I have my own bit of news."

CHAPTER TWELVE

Hebrew University, Jerusalem

"WHAT'S UP?" YIGAEL TILTED HIS HEAD, READY TO LISTEN. "AND why haven't I heard about it yet?"

"Geez, how about one moment of peace, please. You haven't heard about it because I just figured it out. So, relax."

"Well, you knew it in the meeting. So, go on."

"Okay, after we lost our funding," Herschel said, "I decided to begin at the beginning, ignore everything we've done so far that hasn't turned up anything, and approach this thing new. Kick-start it."

"And so?"

"I had been working it from so many directions and coming up only with roadblocks, reasons why my theories wouldn't work. Then last night, after Sam told us about the scroll fragments, I just saw it. I got it. So, want to have a look?"

"Let's get to it." Yigael clasped his hands behind his head.

Herschel leaned in. "There are so many researchers who believe that the Vatican has the treasure and refuses to give it up, and others who think the treasure is hidden in caves in

Israel. Nothing has ever come from those two theories, and I think the treasure is somewhere else entirely."

"Where?"

"Come on over here."

Yigael stood and looked around. He was always amazed when they met in Herschel's office. With no windows and a single ceiling light, the room glowed yellow. Bookshelves covered two walls, and stacks of folders, books, and papers made his old, wooden desktop invisible. As fastidious as Yigael was, he could not imagine how anyone could work in such a mess.

He took two steps and joined Herschel in the center of the room, where books opened to marked pages covered a rectangular table.

Herschel pointed to color-coded maps of Europe and the Mediterranean. "This map shows the Roman Empire from 31 BC to 565 CE." The image was an elevated perspective above Spain looking downward across Europe with Asia fading off to the right. Multi-colored arrows starting from different points in Eastern Europe and Western Asia crisscrossed Europe, North Africa, England, and Ireland.

"Okay, here we are. These arrows show the migration of tribes from Asia and Europe in early times. He pointed to Rome where several colored arrows ended. "So, here we are, in AD 70, with the treasure stored in the great treasury, Rome."

Yigael nodded.

"So, the treasure stays in Rome for a few hundred years. Here's where the tale gets tricky. Scientists have it veering off in different directions. But there's one place they don't consider. Nobody has ever looked at it, based on my research, even though it's kind of obvious."

Yigael was engaged. If Herschel had a theory, Yigael knew it would be worth listening to.

"So, look here. The Visigoths sack Rome in 410. They move

on, to Aquitania—modern France." His finger traced the route. "They take the treasure with them. There isn't anything firm on this, but they'd hardly leave it behind!"

"So, we have the Visigoths in France, southern France."

"Yes, but not for long. Remember, the Franks are spreading out all over Europe and, in 507, they defeat the Visigoths and get control of Aquitania. The treasure is now in the hands of the Franks. It transfers from one king to the next and the next. The last Frankish king is Dagobert I in 634. He sets up shop in Paris." Herschel stopped for a breath. "Consider this: There is no word, written or otherwise, on that treasure since Dagobert got his hands on it. Nothing. So, isn't it reasonable to speculate that he takes the treasure there?"

Yigael was beginning to extrapolate. "So, you figure it has to be stored, buried—I don't know—somewhere in or around Paris."

"I think it's certain."

"You'd have to narrow that down to have any chance of finding it."

Of course, but think of this: Dagobert built the church in Saint-Denis. That huge basilica. He's buried there."

Yigael became still. He returned to his chair and sat down. *I can't believe it could be this easy.* "I can tidy up your theory a bit."

"How?"

"The coins turning up all over Paris? The ones you're not very interested in. 'Too common,' did you say?"

What? No, I'm interested. If they have to do with the treasure."

"Yeah?"

"Yes."

"We know who's hawking them."

"Well, who, for God's sake?"

"A priest."

"Come on ... a priest?" Herschel said. "So, you're hoping

that this guy, uh, priest, with the coins will lead us to a bigger part of the treasure, yes?"

"Find the source for the coins and find whatever else. Perhaps the golden candelabrum?" Yigael said, referring to the pure gold menorah, a symbol of Judaism from ancient times, stolen during the Jerusalem heist and so far, not found.

"Does this priest have a name?"

"One Father Claude Fullier."

"Ha!" Herschel said.

And that's when Yigael hit him with the punchline. "Father Claude Fullier is assigned at the Basilica of Saint-Denis."

"The priest?" and then softly, he said, "You don't mean it."

"I do, and he is."

"You know what that suggests, don't you?" As excited as Herschel was, one might have expected to see him do a little jig.

"I do. So, Saint-Denis? Have our intrepid team poke around a little? See what they can find?"

CHAPTER THIRTEEN

PRIME MINISTER DAVID GOLMAN WAS INTRIGUED WHEN YIGAEL hit him up for another meeting, citing new evidence about the errant scroll. The PM figured it must be hot or Yigael would not have dared to ask to see him again. When he heard it all, he hid his excitement but said, "Go on."

"Herschel and I have planned the operation down to the last coin, shall we say. And, you know I'm rather good at this." He dared a slight smile.

"Yes, on the ones publicized, but it's the ones where you disappear for weeks on end that worry me."

Yigael winced and then forged ahead. "We send our team into France, to Saint-Denis, to find the treasure and, all being well, the scroll. When we find the scroll, we grab it, take it out of France."

"But how will you know you have the real deal? It seems very iffy, and you say you won't be on site there to assess it."

"Okay, hear me out. From France, we move it into Italy, where two experts on first-century documents authenticate it."

"Italy," Golman barked. "What on earth?"

Yigael put up his hand. "Just a minute. Patience, sir." He added a smile. "Once the scientists give the go-ahead, we take it to southern Italy near Mount Vesuvius. Ercolano, to be precise ... and bury it. This site makes sense because so many active digs are going on there now and so many first-century artifacts turn up. We won't look suspicious. Also, I have a couple of people there now who fit into my plan."

"Where precisely do you bury it?" Golman asked.

"I've got a guy with a spot of land near there. My team comes in and begins an excavation. We find the scroll. After that, the translation and then, when the time comes, publication of the scroll's witnessed testimony and its return to Israel."

"Why not just bring the scroll directly to Israel? It seems logical, safer, and cheaper. You wouldn't risk having another country take control of it."

"If the scroll were to be unearthed in Israel it would lack credibility. Some would say we forged it for our own purposes. We can make up any number of stories about why the scroll would be in such a place. The truth about how we retrieved it will surface, but down the road after the smoke clears. Also, and just think about this, the symbolism of Italy returning a treasure stolen so long ago would be enormously powerful. This would gain much more world attention than if it were just another artifact found by Jews in Israel." Yigael was beginning to feel as convivial as Herschel, so he wrapped the oration in an elevated tone. "This mission must succeed at all costs."

Golman wasn't quite ready to quit. "Who's this so-called landowner you have in mind?"

Yigael wished he hadn't asked. "I, uh, I've got a syndicate guy lined up."

"What? No. This is ludicrous. Your, er, discovery in Italy could give ownership of the scroll not only to the Italian government or the Roman Church but, worse yet, the Mafia?"

"Which is exactly why we have to involve the, uh ... them. Since the scroll will be in the hands of a syndicate landowner, the Church and the Italian government can't make claim to it."

"You're up to date on your Italian law? You're sure about that?"

"Of course."

Prime Minister Golman laughed. "That leaves us to deal with gangsters then, eh?"

Yigael smiled. "My guy isn't interested in an old scroll."

"He'll want something in trade for his cooperation."

"And he'll get it." Yigael prayed Prime Minister Golman would not want to hear more.

Golman turned his chair around and grabbed a book off the shelf behind him on Western Civilization. He leafed through it, laid it on his desk facing Yigael, and pointed to a picture with a caption underneath it. "The Arch of Titus in AD 70 showing the triumphant Emperor Vespasian with booty seized from the Temple of Jerusalem.

"When my father was a boy studying history in school in Germany," the prime minister began, "his teacher showed this picture to the class. She elaborated on the idea that the Romans knew how to handle the Jews by destroying them and their Temple. My father was the only Jew in the class, and his class-mates delighted in taunting him." He closed the book.

"That happened years ago, but to hear my father tell it, to hear the pain in his voice, the injustice. It's still fresh. That picture has always haunted me." He swiveled and put the book back, then turned back to Yigael. "As long as there is the slightest possibility that such a document exists, we must find it first, no matter where it is or how difficult it might be to retrieve. And we must bring it back to Jerusalem and the Jewish people. Let's move on this."

That was the shot of adrenaline Yigael needed.

"But with so many uncertainties here, the funds must not

trace back to Israel. We need to keep our good relations with France and Italy. In case this blows up, we simply cannot risk making enemies of our allies."

"Understood."

"You may have to claim support from wealthy patrons who wish to remain anonymous." He added with a sardonic smile, "You can claim privacy of the confessional."

Yigael was flush with pleasure.

"We'll set up a fund for the mission in France and for the research post-mission."

"Thank you, David."

"But government money will not mingle with the Mafia. You need to manage that outside the scope of this conversation."

What Yigael obtained from PM Golman was more than he could have hoped for. He stood, the prime minister stood, and they shook hands.

Then Yigael left, muttering, "Now all I have to do is find a 2,000-year-old scroll hidden in a basilica in Paris, steal it, hand it over to the mob, find it again, and convince the Church, the Italian government, and the Mafia that it's not theirs."

CHAPTER FOURTEEN

Capernaum AD *30*

THE YOUNG SCRIBE HAD PLANNED TO SPEND TIME BY THE LATE afternoon sun scribing his first meeting with Yeshua. He changed his mind, though, and decided it might be best to start the journey home at once. He would not forget his encounter with Yeshua any time soon. That he knew. He found Yeshua to be gracious and charming. He could not draw any conclusions based on their brief encounter, but his first impression of Yeshua was that he was a decent, honest, and kind man. Maybe once he laid his observations to rest on a fresh scroll, the high priests would be satisfied, or even grow bored, and find a more ominous target.

The young scribe headed south.

Capernaum stood along the shores of Lake Tiberias, also called the Sea of Galilee. He got his first whiff of the lakeside village as he crossed a meadow where lambs grazed. Along with the scent of fish and damp earth came a memory of coming here once on holiday as a child. In the mornings, his father taught him to fish. He had loved the cool, dewy wind and the surprise of lowering his hands in the water and touching a jiggling fish. In the afternoons, they swam in the freshwater lake. He recalled wanting to grow up a fisherman just so he could live by the water. He remembered how the color of the sea overawed him. He loved the feel of the wet sand scrunching between his toes. The scribe decided to walk along those shores on his way home, for he had time to spare before tomorrow's dinnertime, especially now that he was not bent over a scroll.

The shores were majestic indeed. And they got his mind stirring, as nature does.

So far, he had gathered testimonies but nothing extraordinary. Nothing to prove his worth in the field. After his sleep this night, he could make it past Sepphoris to Nazareth, the birthplace and homeland of Yeshua. There, he would find the tales with the most meat. It was extra kilometers, but his sandals had proven secure thus far. *Thank you, Raphael.*

He would still be home for Mother's roast fish, and Father would be none the wiser.

That is what I will do.

CHAPTER FIFTEEN

As the shadowy, gray light of morning greeted the young scribe, so did the warmth of the day. His skin was already damp with sweat, so he pushed away the shawl he'd used as a blanket and rolled it tight to fit inside the satchel until he would need it to stave off the heat of the noonday sun. He always thought it funny how the shawl served both purposes.

As he closed in on the village of Nazareth that afternoon, the fragrance of sweet-smelling bread drew the young scribe toward a small mud-and-rock hut off the town square. He had bought a handful of blackberries off a street cart back in Cana and told himself to save his appetite after that, but he could grow hungry again on the road home. He was young, after all.

Outside the hut, an older woman kneaded dough in a trough as she kept one eye on the opening of the earthen oven behind her. The scribe watched until she tossed her ball of dough into the small, round opening. She picked up two loaves, already baked and cooling, and turned, stopping short when she saw him. "Goodness, and who would you be?"

"I'm sorry. I should have made my presence known." He gave her a big smile, hoping that he wouldn't put her off. "I am from Sepphoris, and I'm seeking news. However, the delectable aroma of your bread is what led me here."

She laughed. "Yes, everyone loves my bread. What are you asking after? Maybe I can help."

"It is about Yeshua."

Her wide smile soured. "Are you looking to become a follower or cause trouble for him?"

"Neither. I am a scribe. I simply seek to learn more about Nazareth's famous son."

She considered his words. "Yes, I do know Yeshua. Of course, I do. Used to change his swaddling cloth when he was just a *yalad.*"

It was clear this woman had held Yeshua in some affection. "He's made quite a name for himself, preaching and teaching all around the Galilee. He must have been a remarkable child."

"That he was. Always kind to everyone, always helpful. We all loved that boy."

The young scribe wondered what would cause them to repudiate him. This communication would complete the testimonies. He could sense it. "*Savta,* what happened to Yeshua that the entire village turned on him? Why, when he returned, did he cause so much upset? I would think the village would have been proud that one of their own had become a man of such note."

With a deep breath, the woman turned and pulled her bread from the oven. Setting it to cool, she brushed her hands on her apron and bade the young scribe to sit beside her. "Aye, you'd think they'd be proud. When Yeshua returned, his students in tow, the whole town rejoiced. We have little cause to celebrate in such a poor place, so, we threw our arms open in welcome and set a feast."

"What changed?" The scribe pulled his scroll from the satchel and peeled the wax from his inkwell. "Do you mind?"

She waited until he dipped his reed pen, and began, "He'd changed. In a place like this, that is sin enough. Some said he was holding himself over us. Others didn't like the way their sons and daughters were following him about, hanging on his every word."

"But to drive him out of town? Why so much anger?"

"'Wasn't anger. It was fear."

"Fear? Did he threaten you? Curse?"

"No. Nothing like that. It was the Sabbath, and Yeshua was to leave the next day. We assembled in the synagogue, and our elders invited him to speak. However, when he did, it was all riddles. It made no sense. Then—and this is what did it—he asked an elder for our scroll. Then, he opened it and read from our holy book. None of us has learned to read or write past signing our names and reckoning our figures. Yet, here was one of our own, reading like a temple priest or scribe or noble. Not even our elders can read from that scroll."

"Ah, I see." *I do not see. We Jews are the people of the book. Surely, if a man taught himself to read it, that spoke well of him.*

"One of the elders, a jealous, old coot, claimed he must be possessed. Others called Yeshua insane. Ill feelings that had been building up for days exploded and it was mayhem. Yeshua just stood there, smiling, waiting for a moment of silence. When all had had their say, he threw kindling on the fire. He quoted that prophets were never welcome in their own home. He meant to shame us, but some of the men took him literally. They interpreted his words to mean he was claiming to be a prophet. They worried that next he'd claim to be a messiah, and then the Romans would come and slaughter us all. They chased him and his followers out of town, and a few of our young ones tagged along."

With this, the woman tore at one of the still-warm loaves of bread, breaking it in half. The young scribe got a waft of mint. He didn't care for mint in bread with a meal, but alone as a treat, it was quite fine.

The young scribe capped his inkwell, rolled up the scroll, and took the bread, bowing in thanks. The two sat side by side, eating in silence, each lost in thought.

"Provincial, backward, and small-minded as the people of Nazareth may be," the old woman said, "they are not without wisdom." Shivering, she drew a shawl around her shoulders. "Should they start muttering the word *messiah*, no one around him would be safe," she reiterated. "The memories of Judah of Galilee and the terrible retribution that followed are still fresh in our minds. A man who can attract so many followers and gather the unwashed is indeed a danger to the peace. Another uprising in these lands would bring Rome's soldiers to our doorsteps."

A perfect sunset formed as the young scribe left Nazareth. Tangerine peach, lemon yellow, and petal pink tints lay lightly in the sky. Soon, as the sun slipped below the horizon, a purple haze, just becoming visible, would make this symphony of colors invisible.

The young scribe was halfway to Sepphoris before he knew it, lost in his imaginings. The Yeshua he'd encountered yesterday? To chase that man from town sounded absurd. *Yet a number of them did turn their backs on their fathers to follow him. Maybe that evoked much of the anger. Yes, that seems more logical.*

These musings about Yeshua had so engrossed him that he did not notice that the skies had turned dark, lit only by the stars and the crescent moon. Likewise, he did not hear the pounding of footsteps behind him. As the thumping grew closer, he turned to extend a greeting, but his smile faded when he saw two Roman soldiers closing in.

He forced himself to keep a passive face and addressed them politely.

The soldiers nodded but their eyes were cold.

He turned, determined to focus on the road, but his breath was shallow, and his pale skin felt aflame with panic.

Roman soldiers roamed the streets of Jerusalem and Sepphoris, and the citizens lived safely for the most part, per Antipas's orders. But in the smaller villages throughout the Galilee? On the open, desolate plains is where Roman animosity toward Jews tended to turn violent, where it was unlikely they'd get caught. The young scribe remembered a schoolmate who'd decided to travel south to Idumea. He never returned. Most believed the Romans killed him. Still, as with many young men, the young scribe believed he'd never find trouble. His class and status would protect him. Except, this time, he was dressed down.

"You," one of them said, poking the young scribe in the kidneys. "Turn around."

He could pretend he didn't understand Latin, but the Romans would know better.

The young scribe turned.

"Just look at him." The bigger soldier appraised him from head to foot. "A weakling. You off the teat yet, Jew? And what do you call those useless patches on your face? Huh?"

Noting the soldiers' clean-shaven faces, the young scribe looked down at his feet, embarrassed. It was true. His beard was developing in thin clumps. He so wished to grow a beard as thick and coarse as his father's. Yeshua boasted a beard worthy of praise too. He hated that a couple of brainless soldiers reminded him of his very private concern.

"Why do you grow this beard at all, half-dick?"

"Maybe he's better off without it." The second soldier piped in, withdrawing his knife and reaching for the young scribe's chin.

Fear shot to his throat. The young scribe felt his stomach heave. He knew if the Romans saw him vomit, they would pounce on his weakness. He felt dizzy, his feet like hot metal against the dirt. But he would not slow his pace.

"Put that away," the big soldier said. "You trying to scare this little boy?"

The two sprouted fake grins.

"Where do you travel to, Jew?"

"Sepphoris," the young scribe responded in Latin.

"Oh, look, he's a smart one."

"Well, see here, Jew, Antipas is in town. We've been charged with getting you undesirables off the road. So, come along now and do as you're told."

The two burst into honking laughter.

"And you're in luck," the guard with the knife said. "Sepphoris is just where we're taking you."

They might have decided to attack the young scribe, a bony man of small stature, where he stood, and he would have no chance against these muscled creatures. They could fell him in an instant with a chokehold or an arm lock or worse, their daggers.

The soldiers took places on each side of him. As they walked, they mocked and disparaged Judea and Galilee as a wasteland of sand and rock filled with ignorant Jews. The young scribe's anxiety made his shawl feel heavy over his arms and his tongue swell with thirst. He swallowed often, fighting to keep moisture in his mouth, afraid to sip from his canteen. He was seething with fury but dared not show it.

The southern wall of Sepphoris appeared in the distance. The young scribe wanted to run to the gate, but he kept a pace steady between them.

"Why do you go to Sepphoris?"

"I am traveling to my parents' home."

"Where did you come from?"

"Nazareth."

The soldier with the dagger poked the young scribe in the ribs. "What were you doing in Nazareth, Jew?"

"I told you about that weapon," the big soldier said. "This Jew here won't cause any trouble, will you, Jew?" Then, he yucked several times.

"My mother asked me to go."

"Why would she ask you to do this?"

Thinking quickly, he said, "She wanted me to take a pie to a friend."

"A pie to a friend?" The soldier cracked up once more. It seemed the funniest thing he'd ever heard. "I guess this is all he can do—walk about with a pie."

"This friend is incapable of baking her own pie?" the knifed guard questioned.

"The family is in mourning. The woman's husband died recently." How the lies were slipping out as if oil from a pressed olive had greased his tongue.

The soldier slipped his dagger back into its leather holster. "Let me see your money."

The young scribe reached into the leather purse attached to his girdle and gave him coins.

The soldier studied them, and then dropped the coins into his companion's open palm. "What else do you have?" He grabbed the young scribe's wrists and jerked them behind his back.

"Nothing of worth."

"We'll see about that."

The big one rubbed his hands over the young scribe's waist. Finding a pouch folded under his shawl. He tore it from his shoulder. Its contents, a canteen and tablet, tumbled to the ground. The guard released his arms, picked up the tablet, and looked at the scrawl.

"What is this?" he asked, studying the letters. "What is this writing?"

"It is just a story."

"About?"

"It's a children's story about two talking rabbits." *I cannot believe I uttered such words. When they realize I'm making fun of them, they will kill me instantly.*

The soldier snorted and tucked the tablet under his arm.

The weaver, the potter, the baker—I'll have to rewrite their testimonies. He was relieved he hadn't scribed about meeting Yeshua, as that story would have taken the longest to redo.

Then, the guard with the knife bent down to grab the young scribe's canteen. He paused when he noticed his shoes. "Say, maybe he's the one. The bandit."

They knew very well that the young scribe was no bandit. Even with the old robes, bandits were generally not of the linen-wearing kind. They were setting him up. But for what purpose? If they planned to ransom him back to his father, it wouldn't do to tell them who he was, that of a solicitor. Ruling class, yes, but royalty they were not.

"I think he is the bandit. The robes are dingy and those sandals, they look new."

You caught me. I'm a sandal-stealing bandit.

"Why are your shoes so new and your robes so worn?"

"Take them off," the guard with the knife said as he batted at the young scribe's feet.

He removed his new sandals.

On inspecting them, the soldier then took his dagger and slid it into the slit between the soles. As he pried the space open and discovered a coin, he gave the young scribe such a sinister look of delight that he knew this could very well be the end.

"I am not a thief." The young scribe managed to get to his knees. "I am a scribe, tasked with writing testimony on the rabbi Yeshua." In his panic, he made the mistake of speaking in his native tongue, Hebrew. He started again in Latin, "Please understand, I am a scri—"

The soldier with the knife punched the young scribe in the stomach.

The big soldier yanked the young scribe's arms over his head, while a hobbed boot slammed into his gut and he doubled over. Another kick straight to the groin sent him tumbling to the earth, and both men began stomping him. He curled into a ball, trying to protect his head from blow after blow.

One soldier yanked the young scribe back up, and both dragged him, nearly unconscious, to the city gates, where a cohort of Antipas's soldiers stood guard. Fear consumed the young scribe wholly.

With a nod, his captors marched him over and pushed him to the ground. "We don't know his name yet, but we caught him with stolen money and this." The first soldier held up the tablet, while the other handed over his torn and tattered sandals.

"You can go now," the guard said to the soldiers. "We'll take over with this one. Hold him until the priests decide what to do."

"I am not a thief." The young scribe managed to get to his knees. "I am a scribe, tasked with writing testimony on the rabbi Yeshua." His explanation hadn't worked the first time. He didn't know what he was thinking trying to explain himself again.

The guard laid into him with a kick to the stomach and a blow to the head.

The young scribe grunted and fell, hitting his head on a stone. He reached up and felt blood. He was trying to get up on all fours again when he got a heavy kick to his genitals. He screamed in pain as the guards laughed and kicked him savagely, ceaselessly.

"Preaching about Yeshua. Stealing money! The priests will

have a time with you!" Then the main guard's boot met the young scribe's face.

He disappeared into a cloud of pain. As he was drifting into oblivion, as if from a distance, he heard, "Put him with the others."

CHAPTER SIXTEEN

THE GUARDS DRAGGED THE YOUNG SCRIBE THROUGH AN IRON GATE that opened into a dark cave. Hurling him inside, he landed sharply on his back. The stench of festering sewage invaded every pore of his torn body. He prayed to pass out so that he could escape it. As his eyes adjusted, he made out a blurry picture of humans crowded into this black hole. They were heading toward him.

Then they were upon him—a million hands tearing at his tunic until they stripped him naked. The young scribe screamed like an animal in terror, lashing out in the wildest way. He scooted back, crouching against a wall, stretching out his arms and extending his hands—a cornered cat with claws ready to kick, scratch, and bite until the end.

Abruptly, the assault ceased.

A man came forward and looked him over. "Son, how did you get yourself in a fix like this?"

The young scribe squinted. It was Ori the roofer. He had

worked on his uncle's home. "Ori, I might ask the same of you," he said, before passing out.

When he came to, Ori was crouched beside him, and the men who had attacked him were crowded on the other side of the vile dungeon. He looked down and saw that his tunic, torn and filthy, covered him now. But the horror of it all—the filth, the stench, the numbing cold, his dry, aching mouth and the over-riding pain—caused him to cry out, and then he sobbed, quietly.

Ori placed a palm on his right cheek, the only part of him that was not bruised or bleeding. Though he surely had the calloused, cracked hands of a builder, his touch stirred up an image of *Ema* from back when he was young.

Then, he lost consciousness again.

When he came to again, Ori was gone.

A bit later, a guard arrived and ordered the young scribe to follow him, but he couldn't stand. The guard jerked him to his feet. The young scribe faltered and fell. The guard called for aid. The two soldiers hooked their arms under the young scribe's shoulders and dragged him out of the revolting pit and into the burning light of day.

Outside, another guard studied him. "Let him go."

The young scribe figured the guard must have recognized that he was of the ruling class.

As a final warning, the guard in charge said, "Stay clear of the roads."

Not far outside the gates, the young scribe found himself on the ground, unable to get up. *Perhaps a passerby will take pity on me and offer service.* But, even in his haze, he doubted it. Nobody wanted to associate with a criminal, and here he was lying in the dirt, filthy, half-naked, near dead.

He heard the far-off clatter of wheels on the stone road. The cart accelerated, the rattling grew louder, and then it ceased. The young scribe glanced up through swollen eyes. The blazing sunlight framed a figure but blinded him to any features.

He heard a woman's voice, and then felt a wet rag on his lips. He sucked and sucked, trying to wring the wetness into his mouth by biting down, but he didn't have much strength. Moments later, he felt an unusual lightness. It made him dizzy, and he wanted to cry out, but he didn't have the energy for that either. The pain was unbearable, made more so as someone hoisted him onto a cart. Then everything went dark.

Sometime later, the rattling of the wheels slowing down jogged the young scribe awake. His body screamed in pain as the cart came to an abrupt stop. His eyes opened to slits but the light pierced them, causing tears to distort his vision. Still, he could tell that it was his sister rushing toward him. She put the rim of a metal cup to his lips. *Mother's silver drinking cup? That is for celebrations only.* What an odd thing to pop into his head, the young scribe thought as he took a few sips.

"We need to get him inside at once," he heard his father say.

He awakened inside the house to hushed sounds, the worried whispers of his parents speaking to a man whose voice seemed familiar in the way an aroma from the courtyard *foúrnos* can.

"He needs water, but if they've broken him inside, it could kill him. Has he vomited blood?"

"Who would do this? Who would hurt my boy?" his mother cried.

"By the bruises, I would say he ran afoul of some Roman soldiers. Look here. These are nail marks from the bottoms of their boots."

"There is blood on his tunic." His father's voice was gruff, angry.

"He vomited, then, at least once," the physician noted.

Thick, cool fingertips pressed into the young scribe's abdomen, prodding. "He isn't swollen. The only bruising I see are the marks made from the *caligae*. Look here. See the pattern the iron cleats made? His ribs are broken but he's young and they'll mend. If he were bleeding inside, his belly would be blackening. Watch for that. Though I see no sign of it. Treat the swelling as you can. Wrap his torso when you can roll him to do so. Otherwise, keep him still and quiet. Increase water and broth as he can stomach it."

The young scribe felt the physician rise from beside the bed.

"And pray," he added. "Send for me if something changes."

Just after the physician left, he heard clanking and hurried activity. It sounded as if his mother was moving furniture, opening cabinets and chests, gathering linens and wool blankets. Oh, how he longed for her gentle touch.

SOME DAYS LATER, maybe a week, the young scribe recognized the footsteps of his mother entering the room with a bowl of broth. He could smell the garlic. She spooned in several mouthfuls. He could not think when anything tasted so good but was incapable of saying "thank you." He heard her put the bowl down by the bedside table she had pulled in. Then, she touched his arm and whispered, "Thank God you are home."

His eyes opened to those slits again. He noted that someone, thankfully, had closed the shutters to keep out the light. He saw his mother's sweet face and watched as she blinked away tears.

His father entered.

"Husband, get his tunic off," his mother said, then rose and left.

She returned with his sister in tow. They carried in a big bowl of soapy water, a jar of oil, and items from her medicine chest. They laid their implements down, and his mother said, "Daughter, please go to the neighbors and ask if they have any henbane seeds to spare. Tell them we will replace what we use the next time we go to market."

After his sister left, Mother said to Father, "Take off his undergarment, please."

Father sucked in his breath. "But surely ...."

"We do not know the extent of his injuries."

"*Ema*, please."

The young scribe felt mortified at the thought of lying naked in his mother's presence. He closed his eyes to escape.

"No, you cannot. It will shame him, and me."

"Husband, my son has been in a jail. Can you imagine what they subjected him to?"

Her words were enough to put his father to action. The young scribe felt him untuck the linen from the waistband and peel off his *'ezor,* to his utter humiliation.

The young scribe knew what they would find. His sore testicles had swollen from the beating he had suffered.

"Love, hand me the towel, please, and then you may go. Make yourself useful in the kitchen."

His father must have frozen like the bronze statue of Baal at the sight of his genitals. Given that, his mother added, "Your son will be all right. Now go."

He heard his father say, "They will pay," as his steps faded away.

His mother covered his private part with the linen towel and got to work. She bathed him with the warm, soapy water, having decided that oil and a scraper would be too harsh in his current state. When he was dry, she applied honey to his head wound and a salve of henbane seeds to the cuts and sores on his skin. To the young scribe's shame, she removed the towel and applied her salve to his scrotum. Then, she replaced the towel.

"That will relieve the swelling," she murmured, intuitively aware of his conscious state. She bathed his puffy eyes in a warm liquid that she referred to as her secret remedy. When she finished, she covered him with a clean, white linen.

"You do not need your tunic now, but it is folded over the chair for when you are ready. I will fix you some willow bark tea in a bit. Now, you must sleep."

Just being clean and cared for made the young scribe feel better, but exhaustion dictated sleep.

Though his eyes were closed and his thoughts flickering, the young scribe did not drift into the black space of unconsciousness. Instead, an image of the sea came into focus. In his mind's eye, he was in a boat, traveling he knew not where. He felt no pain and wondered if he were on his way to the Promised Land.

He was not afraid.

CHAPTER SEVENTEEN

Parioli, Rome

"What a horrific year," Valentina Vella muttered to herself as she stepped listlessly into her tidy, little kitchen and poured herself a glass of Pinot Gris. Moving to the sofa in the *salotto,* she set the glass on the coffee table and picked up a stack of bills. Sorting through them, she gave up, tossing them back down. She tucked her long legs beneath her and reached for the wine, taking a long swill as she stared out the window into the piazza below. There was a mother wiping gelato from the face of a toddler with the hem of her lemon-printed wrap skirt. Two *nonnas* seated on a bench in animated conversation. A teen in need of a trim on a skateboard. It all reminded Valentina that Italy was on the brink of summer and, life went on, unaware of her problems.

What had taken her and Erika Simone nine years to build, the Church had destroyed in as many months: *Valeri Laboratorio di Conservazione.*

After Erika's ex-partner, Paula Kirkpatrick, betrayed the two scientists at Oxford in front of 1,200 of the world's top historians, theologians, and archeologists, Valentina and Erika had fielded one uncomfortable phone call after another from peers and longtime colleagues, all with a variety of excuses to cut ties with them. Long-standing contracts were pulled from their lab, leaving them with no income except for the occasional request for a minor translation.

Their crime? What landed the two prominent archaeologists in hot water was the discovery of a first-century bishop of the wrong gender.

Under the authority of a red cap, they found the grave of a first-century Roman noblewoman who rose through the ranks of the early Church to become a bishop during the reign of Clement, the fourth pope. The noblewoman, Julia Lucinia, had been murdered and erased from the annals of history, until Valentina and her team dug her up. The discovery troubled the Holy Office. No longer could the cardinals lay claim to Church doctrine that "no woman had ever been called *priest*—therefore, only men can be priests." No longer could they claim irreversible, free-from-error infallibility. No longer could they rule out, unequivocally, the possibility of ordaining women.

The only man that seemed to understand the upside of the existence of Julia was Pope Augustine himself, the one man they needed. And, for a moment in time, elation had set in as a rumor began to circulate that the pope was about to issue an encyclical that would lay down a radical transformation in doctrine by promoting women to full equality in the Church. For the first time, they would be able to enter the priesthood. Then, just when their future had never looked brighter and the liberal wing waited with excitement for this letter, Pope Augustine was found dead in his quarters. With little fanfare, he was buried, not in the Vatican as expected, but far away in a cathedral on the other side of the city, far enough away to be forgotten.

The Holy Office breathed freely. With Augustine dead, it

would be easy to stash Julia and the so-called encyclical under a far-flung Persian carpet. If there was anything the Church was good at, it was deflecting, digressing, and making excuses.

But Cardinal Carlo Lavoti, the new Holy Office prefect, and his team of cardinals knew how tenacious "those infuriating women" could be, and they weren't sure the message was crystalline. Under his direction, they sent Valentina and Erika an injunction, hand delivered, which prevented them not only from publishing their findings about Julia, but of even speaking about them. While most likely illegal under Italian law, if appealed, it would take years and tens of thousands of euros to wind its way through the courts.

A month later, dinky articles in the right-wing press accused the women of fraud, heresy, and mismanagement of funds. Those soon mushroomed into forgery, apostasy, and embezzlement by the mainstream media.

The attacks had been even worse for Erika, as charges of feminism twisted into sexual perversity under the wet blanket of media truth. They used her sexual orientation as a gay woman for their *raison d'être*. And, somehow despite twenty-first century authenticity, it worked. Valentina felt terrible that she couldn't share in that heartbreak too. Except that, while Erika seemed to be recovering, she was barely holding it together. Maybe the same sexual status that made Erika a target also made her stronger.

Even their fans, those who'd pushed hardest for the Vatican to rescind its rules on women, those who'd held vigils and distributed leaflets, turned against them. They felt as if Valentina and Erika had betrayed them by not fighting back. Thanks to the gag order, they had no way to defend themselves. They'd been tried in the court of public opinion and prosecuted by an enemy with endless resources at its disposal.

Valentina fingered the amazonite balls on the beautiful crossover bracelet gifted to her by Luca. She still had him, her longtime beau and stalwart defender. She'd thought more than once that perhaps she should take up his offer of marriage, move to Switzerland, and vanish. The agony of defeat more than anything prevented her from pulling that trigger. And maybe she didn't want to abandon her business partner. They'd known each other since grad school.

A single rap on the front door signaled Erika Simone's arrival. They were meeting to come to a final decision about Valeri, the place they'd worked so hard to acquire. Valeri had become a top-ranked home for scientists around the globe. They depended on Vella and Simone for translations and data analyses, all to bring stories of lost civilizations alive. Valeri symbolized their high status in the field of archaeology and the endless possibilities for women in this new technological era. Mostly, Valeri was their identity. Neither woman had married. Neither had children. And together they had birthed Valeri. Valentina couldn't speak for Erika, but she'd lost all sense of self since the richest, most powerful institution in the world expelled their "baby" from the community.

Erika stepped inside Valentina's flat, phone to her ear. "Okay. Yes, of course. I understand. *Ciao.*" She tossed the phone on the sofa, gave Valentina a knowing look, ran her fingers through cropped, blonde hair, windblown from the ride in on her motor scooter, and headed for the kitchen.

"Archaeosearch?" Valentina asked.

"Yep. Luigi Panella himself. They have to 'put their attention elsewhere' now." Erika took the hand-blown wine glass that was sitting on the counter and filled it, noting the larger, red wine glasses were now in fashion, at least in this house, for all shades of vino these days. She grabbed her glass and the bottle and joined Valentina on the sofa.

Valentina's phone rang.

"You going to get that?"

"Nope."

Erika raised her glass and gulped a good measure.

The phone rang again.

"Aren't you curious who it is?"

"Nope." Valentina poured the rest of the bottle into her glass. "Well, I guess that's it then."

"You're out of wine?"

"No, God no. Relax. I mean with Valeri."

"Let the bank just have it? A buyer might be around the corner."

"The last buyer that could afford it just pulled."

Erika rested her head on the sofa back. "The Vatican can afford it. It'd be the perfect off-site lab for them. They're jammed with lab apps, and wait times are forever."

Valentina smirked. "Yeah, let's ask those guys for a favor. Why would those old geezers buy anything from us, anyway? I doubt they'd flip a coin into our basket if we were wearing rags and selling oranges at the door to St. Peter's. Matter of fact, it would be like them to wait for foreclosure and then pick it up for a song."

AND THAT WAS JUST what happened. In the blink of an eye, the bank took Valeri, and, in the next, Cardinal Carlo Lavoti bought it for a song, as Valentina had predicted.

CHAPTER EIGHTEEN

The Vatican

IF CARDINAL CARLO LAVOTI HAD EVER FELT CLOSE TO FAINTING, now was the time to get it over with. Just as he was chortling over the big buy that would certainly leave Valentina Vella and Erika Simone in a perpetual lurch, he was handed the Monday morning paper. There, above the fold, in Italy's largest newspaper, the headline read: "WOMEN WIN EQUALITY IN THE CHURCH."

So, before his death, Pope Augustine had indeed written that encyclical, the one Lavoti had dreaded to think could exist. He had been hoping for a pistachio *biscolatte* from *Panificio Mosca* to go with his latte, but no. Another fire to put out. *If I ever find out who had his hands on this thing and sent it to that vile reporter Michael Levin, I will personally put a bullet through his head.*

After Pope Augustine died in those uncertain, mysterious circumstances, Cardinal Lavoti lobbied hard, using everything in his extensive tool kit—payoffs, threats, extortion—to get elected to the white cap and lead the Church's more than one billion followers down a path of conservative, autocratic rule. But the College of Cardinals decided on the younger, more moderate Julius Africanus, handing Lavoti the consolation prize of heading the Congregation for the Doctrine of the Faith, CDF, as prefect. The defeat crushed him. *But the show must go on.*

Styling himself after Pius XIII, Lavoti called for a return to traditional values and pledged to purge the Church of dissidents, feminists (translation: heretics), and rebels against the princes of the Holy Mother Church. First, he'd spearheaded the venomous acts against Valentina and Erika and, second, squelched the rumors of an encyclical. And life was bearable, until five minutes ago when that irritating, ballooned tick of a man Father Orio Rinaldi put a latte in one hand and *La Carta* in the other, his inflated pink face sporting, no less, a knowing grin as he did it.

This was not going to be the status quo in his new, consolatory position, oh no. He was not going to spend the rest of his days as a dutiful disciple of the Lord God Himself, always on defense. Somebody had to take the world by the reigns and keep it on track in the name of Christianity. This encyclical, he told himself, would be the last mistake to make it past his good sense and into the public domain. The very last or may God strike him down.

Cardinal Lavoti rose from his armchair, stormed through his suite of rooms festooned with the finest frills and trimmings, into the common office of his new secretary. He rushed the priest's desk, locked eyes with him, and scowled. His plan? He had none. Then he remembered how much he wanted to get rid of the officious, fussy, little pest who snooped continuously for the latest gossip. He shuddered to think of the cost to him should his most-recent treachery be revealed.

Father Rinaldi looked up through eyes that appeared dwarfed by blubber. "Cardinal, can I do something for you?"

He wedged a heavy torso out of his chair in a show of respect he didn't feel. Oh, how he wished he were still taking orders from the late Cardinal Ricci.

"No. Nothing ... yes, something. Call the press office. Tell them to put out for immediate release a statement saying that a dead pope's letter cannot stand. Their usual mumbo jumbo."

The cardinal pivoted and packed off in a huff, reentering his private domain to pout and plot. But, before he made it past the threshold and into the safety of his lavish terrain, he heard the phones, all ringing at once.

CHAPTER NINETEEN

Domus Sanctae Marthae, Vatican City

TO ESCAPE THE AVALANCHE OF PHONE CALLS ABOUT POPE Augustine's now published encyclical, Cardinal Lavoti chose Casa Santa Marta. The apartment building next to St. Peter's Basilica provided accommodation for the comings and goings of clergy from all over the world. He knew the dining room would be largely unoccupied in mid-afternoon. He hoped to console himself with a steaming cup of tea laced with a shot of his favorite whisky, which he carried in a small flask in his vestment pocket.

The dining room had three hangers-on after lunch, only one he recognized. Cardinal Lavoti nodded toward Cardinal Justin Parina, Prefect of the Vatican Library. Little did he know that the man seated beside Justin was the very one whose head Lavoti had threatened to put a bullet through just hours ago. He took a seat one table away, noting the pair was comfortable together, probably old friends. Then he could not help overhearing.

"How did you hear about this, this scroll?" the younger man asked.

"Oh, from Yigael himself. Our interests are mutual in ways. And we're friends," Cardinal Parina responded.

"So, you're watching him as he watches those coins float around Paris?"

"We're keeping an eye out."

"In all this time there has never been a hint of such early writings. It's astounding," the younger man said.

A flicker of a smile crossed Cardinal Parina's face. "The next thing you know the Q Gospel will turn up."

Cardinal Lavoti paled. He considered the Q Gospel a dangerous threat to his Church. Even though Q remained undiscovered, the books of Matthew and Luke hinted at its existence, which was a constant worry to the conservative wing.

Q, meaning *source* in German, was drawing increased attention these days. It marked a return to what some thought were the true teachings of Yeshua. Q dealt not at all with Yeshua as a Messiah, or a redeemer who atoned for man's sins by his crucifixion or as the son of God who rose from the dead, all of which were the very foundation of Church doctrine. Rather, it espoused full acceptance of one's fellow man and embraced his adages about how to live a good, full, and meaningful life

"This old scroll could add authenticity to Q," Cardinal Parina said, "if it exists and if anyone finds it. If there is anyone who can, it would be Yigael."

"Oh, yes, no doubt there."

Lavoti got up. He couldn't help himself. "Justin, you mind if I join you?"

"Ah, of course not." Cardinal Parina gestured to the empty chair.

"I apologize for intruding, but I heard you referencing Q, and my curiosity got the better of me. Actually, its mention got my hackles up." Warming to his subject, Cardinal Lavoti's voice grew intense. "That diabolical gospel could bring down the Church. It negates all that our Church stands for. Why, is there news of it?"

"No, not really. Just some activity about an old scroll that *could,* repeat *could,* put in doubt that Yeshua was a Messiah."

Lavoti remained cool, but he could have fallen off his chair at such news.

"Do you know Father Francesco Ricci?" Cardinal Parina asked, turning toward his luncheon date.

"Oh, yes, so sorry. Ricci ... are you related to Cardinal Antonio Ricci?"

"Why, yes, Antonio was my uncle."

"The finest of men," Lavoti sang out. "My deep condolences," he lamented. "I have heard of you. Yes. Out there in Ostia. Where that unfortunate Julia business took place. Ah, yes. Troubling, all of it. What will we do?"

"Well, I do believe, it's done." Father Ricci was so amused by Lavoti's rapturous depictions and swift mood changes, he found it hard to stifle a snicker.

Cardinal Parina changed the subject. "Carlo, what say you about the headline in *La Carta* this morning, after all those hopeful rumors that finally just faded away. Now this. It seems our blessed Pope Augustine, God rest his soul, really did intend to shake up the Church."

Lavoti's face clouded over. "He would have them seize the altar. But no. I've ordered the press office to put out an immediate release telling "all those women" that their battle will have to start over. At least we've put out those flames for a while." Cardinal Lavoti sighed. And then, he realized he was speaking to the liberal wing, at least Cardinal Parina stood for the liberals. He remembered the cardinal's support, if quiet, for the Julia side. "I do believe there's been mention of Augustine's, ah, dementia."

Ignoring Cardinal Lavoti, Cardinal Parina said, "Perhaps it's time to rethink some policies. I do believe Augustine understood that."

Seeing the conversation veering toward calamitous, Cardinal Lavoti lobbed a ball. "The Church—"

Father Ricci caught it. "—may still be the largest single church in the world, but we're scrutinized continually. More than ever, our parishioners are calling us rigid and archaic and they're questioning everything."

"Yes, and we used to be able to crush all of it," Cardinal Lavoti spluttered. "It's not so easy anymore."

"And lately, especially now, people are leaving in droves and joining new denominations or forming their own." Cardinal Parina sat back in his chair, satisfied that the rigidly devoted man hadn't owned the table.

"That one is particularly confounding. Because, of course, ours is the only true church. It is getting harder and harder to fight for that idea. But fight it, we must." Cardinal Lavoti reached for the flask in his pocket but thought better of the idea and returned his hand to the table. "Now, what about this old scroll?"

CARDINAL LAVOTI PASSED by Father Rinaldi in a frenzy of rage on his way into his inner sanctum. A *secret temple scroll.* "Ha!" *I will never let these so-called testimonies against Yeshua see the light of day.*

CHAPTER TWENTY

Sepphoris AD *30*

THE NEXT DAYS AND WEEKS FELL INTO AN ENDLESS RHYTHM. THE young scribe would awaken to the aroma of nourishment, ingest spoonfuls of broth, and fall back to sleep. His father took on the task of helping him urinate and defecate into a pan, which he kept for the physician to examine. In the afternoons, he'd awaken to a bath, his mother changing his dressings, and he'd remind himself to blush. Later, she'd spoon her teas and syrups into his mouth, and he'd fall back into a state of sleep or unconsciousness again, until the light of a new day assaulted his sore, swollen eyes, a punishment he welcomed inasmuch as it declared he was still alive.

The morning finally came when he felt fully conscious. He still ached everywhere, but the urge to stretch his eyes wide, to look about, overcame him. Drawing in breath was another story. It felt like the dagger from the belt of the Roman soldier was stabbing into his back with every attempt. However, for the first time, it was clear that he would live.

It must have been clear to his mother, too, seeing that on

this morning she had sent his sister in with breakfast. This time it was a bowl of porridge rather than a cupful of seasoned broth.

His sister sat beside him.

He tried to sit up.

She placed her small, pale hand on his chest and nudged him back onto the mattress. "*Ema* says not yet. She needs to wrap you in plaster cloth, and then you can move about. The physician says it is time."

The young scribe lay back and allowed her to spoon the warm, sweet porridge into his mouth.

"What time is it?"

"Why? Are you late for work?"

"I mean, what day is it?"

"Oh," she said. "It is seven weeks since you found your way home."

The young scribe did not "find his way home," but he did not have the energy to battle with her over semantics. When he finished eating, he looked about the room. On the floor by his tunic were his old sandals.

"*Ema* had them cleaned. She restored them," his sister said, following his gaze. "You are thinking about wandering off again?"

She could be smart, that was for sure. He gave her the best scowl he could muster.

Then she stood and did a little dance, he guessed, to entertain him, and then she went out to help their mother. His lovely little sister. Her hair was as rusty as his, long and growing in spectacular, bouncy ringlets.

The smart shoes that Raphael had fashioned had not held up, after all. What was the lesson? He could hear his father asking him, "Think about the lesson, son, so you don't make the same mistake twice."

That afternoon the physician visited and, with careful

fingers, reset what bones had started healing out of place. With the aid of his mother, he applied plastered bandages, wrapping him up like one of the fabled mummies of Egypt. He could at least sit upright and finally relieve himself without his father having to hold a bedpan.

"*Abba*," the young scribe said as his father entered, "We must thank Ori."

"Whatever do you mean?"

"He protected me in the cave, and he clothed me. I may have died if not for him."

His father stared at him for the longest time before saying, "It must have been someone who looked like Ori." With that, he left.

"Oh?" the scribe wondered aloud. *He answered to the name Ori.*

Another week passed, and each day the young scribe improved. He had lost nearly half a *talent* during his convalescence and had not had much fat to spare at the start. His entire family and all the neighbors had made it their business to stuff him full. They fed him on a steady diet of lamb and beans and breads and sweet, honeyed treats. The attention was nice, and he was returning to himself physically. Yet his mind seemed to be appearing as a different self.

Though he hid it from his parents, he often woke at night on the verge of screaming, his skin clammy and bed linens soaked. He would dream of the sack of Sepphoris, of families burned in the great inferno, of soldiers everywhere. He would dream of his mother and sister raped and of his father tortured.

During the day, he did his best to put on a good face, but mostly he spent hours alone in his room, brooding and unraveling the unexplained details of the events since his return from Temple. Finally, he saw it.

His masters had sent him out to find evidence against a simple Galilean rabbi. He could pretend they had only been curious, but he couldn't lie to himself any longer. Even if he could keep his new notions from his father, he could no longer deny their existence, for they rose in his sleep like mist off the Sea of Galilee at daybreak. The high priests feared Rome. They feared change. They feared a new messiah. They feared what it would mean for them, and they felt trapped.

His father and mother had raised him to believe in authority, to trust his elders, to revere the priests. Yet, these priests, those whose authority he had trusted, bent their knee to the Romans. They set Roman soldiers against their own people. His people. Him. He had known this in his heart all along. Yet he had chosen to be blind until the spiked boot of Rome crushed his own thick skull.

His new sandals of calfskin with the secret compartment had not caused him trouble. It was tracking Yeshua that nearly cost him his life. The young scribe was expendable.

This was the lesson.

Yeshua carried no sword. The sandals Yeshua wore had no nails on their soles, no spikes, nothing to turn his feet into a lethal weapon. And his words, they were not new. The young scribe had learned everything Yeshua uttered thus far in Temple. His deeds? Healing the dying with a look or a touch. Okay, that was something. But the young scribe himself had been dying these last few weeks, and he became healed without any magic tricks from Yeshua. One can apply reason to most anything. Or coincidence.

The young scribe was sick at heart, lying awake in bed when his sister crept into his room and, with a warning glance, whispered, "Shh ... come quickly. Mother and Father are arguing, and it concerns you. Come!"

Ema and *Abba* never quarreled. He followed his sister to their father's *tablinum*.

"I'll not have it. I tell you, I will not! How could you send him away when I so nearly lost him?" His mother never cried, not aloud like this. "Husband, hear me now."

"Do you want him to be safe? Then he must leave for a while."

"You are an important man, husband. How is it that two ruffian foot soldiers nearly kill my son, yet he is the one exiled?"

"The soldiers have been punished. They have been whipped, stripped of rank, and we have been paid a year of their wages. He is not being exiled."

"Then, why?" she wailed.

"Because they have been whipped and stripped of rank, and they have had their wages garnished! Their comrades will be on the lookout. He needs to go, at least until this dies down. Do you want him to get killed the next time?"

"He was freed because of Antipas learning of his testimonies against Yeshua. He will be protected," his mother insisted, clenching her hands."

The written testimony against Yeshua is what freed me?

"Don't you see? He is trapped between these two worlds with no way out."

The young scribe felt sick.

"We keep him here. You aid him with these stories, and you arrange for transport of the scrolls. We secure a bride. Life goes on for the best."

"It is too late for that. Of his own wish, he will not stay here."

"Why not? No one has bothered us throughout his recovery."

"Look into his eyes the next time you apply your ointment to the wound on his forehead."

"What do you mean?"

"Like one teaches a weaver to braid or a fisherman to gut, he confessed of his disobedience and the details of his beating. It was a simple story, a string of facts. But you should have seen him speak of Yeshua."

The young scribe watched as his father's frame collapsed inward. He had never seen him so drained.

"What of it?"

"We cannot jail him here. That much I know."

"You are speaking in rhymes."

"He asked me to thank Ori for helping him in prison."

"Ori the builder?"

"Yes."

"Who was accused of raping Rabbi Uri's daughter?"

"Yes."

"Why, he was hanged in the courtyard three years back!"

"Exactly."

His mother worked to grasp what her husband was saying and then broke down in helpless sobs.

"We cannot jail him here, but we can postpone the inevitable. Maybe, who knows, after six months or a year, Yeshua will be in a faraway land, and our boy will come home."

Though his parents had made the decision without the young scribe's knowledge, he was glad for it. He could not imagine surviving another beating. The young scribe stepped into the room and wrapped his arms around his mother, who had collapsed in a chair.

"*Ema*, please, it will be all right." He tilted her chin up. "I will do as *Abba* instructs. It will be no different from when I was in Jerusalem. In time, I will return, perhaps with my bride and children to raise."

Her sobbing quieted.

"I am going to have fifteen of them. You will need to add rooms to our home!"

With this, she laughed through her tears and stroked his cheek.

The young scribe regarded his beaten father. "So, *Abba,* where am I off to?" He tried to make light of it.

"I was thinking Beth Shean. We have family there." Looking at his mother, his father added, "He'll be safe there, my love. We can visit him in *Tishrei* for *Sukkot.*"

<hr>

THEY WOULD WORK out the details over the next week. The young scribe would finish his testimonies to Jerusalem and dismiss Yeshua as a country rabbi not worth their time and attention. His mother would buy provisions, and he would be well equipped. The money garnished from the soldiers' wages would mean he could live for a while without worrying about working.

Lying awake had become standard, and that is where he found himself the following evening. Needing a change of scenery, he ventured up the ladder to the roof.

As the night wind ruffled his hair, he gathered his shawl around his shoulders. He closed his eyes and recited the *Birkat Hagomel* blessing, feeling grateful to have recovered. He missed sleeping among the stars.

Then, his thoughts turned to the sparkling Sea of Galilee. His mind's eye torpedoed in on the details of his recurring vision. He was traveling north by boat. All around him the water so still. His fingers created tiny ripples as they tickled the tranquil sea. His face tilted upward, welcoming the western wind. The North Star pointed her silver finger to his destination. At that moment, in that state, the young scribe saw his future, which he knew in his heart would take him to Yeshua.

CHAPTER TWENTY-ONE

Sepphoris AD *31*

THE YOUNG SCRIBE DID NOT WANT TO ADMIT IT BUT EVEN NOW, ten months after his beating, when he contemplated traveling the open roads, fear overcame him. He could hear the thump of the Romans' boots. He could smell the stench of their sweaty wool uniforms. He could feel the nails in their boots piercing into his forehead all the time, while he was eating, as he lay down to sleep, even as he rewrote in his scroll. Soon he would be traveling again.

The young scribe put down his writing instrument and pushed himself into a sitting position. He stretched his arms skyward. The sun burned directly above, showing the day was half over. He walked to the edge of the roof. His sister and his mother were in the side yard, shearing one of their three lambs. The pheasants housed in the coop that lined the outside fence squawked. Bread was baking in the stone oven nestled against the outer edge of the house, its smell a comfort.

His mother had washed a supply of tunics for his journey to *Beth Shean* and hung them to dry in the courtyard. He gathered those, even though his sister normally performed this duty. As he folded them, his father entered and presented him with an elaborately decorated leather satchel.

"It was your grandfather's."

"I do not think I have ever seen it before."

His father brushed his hand across the faded design. "Your grandmother gave it to him."

"It is beautiful, Father."

"Yes, it is. I was just a boy then."

"Who painted the design?"

"Why, your grandmother did, of course. She loved working with dyes. She would buy them in the city and go to the Temple to paint. She sketched this design outside the Court of the Women. I believe she used only a stone and her fingertips as tools. Her fingers were always purple, her favorite color."

The young scribe touched the satchel, running his finger along the faded, pink outline around the sun. He felt so honored to have it.

"This was the last gift she ever gave him, before he .... I thought you could use it to carry your scrolls, as your other satchel is no more."

The young scribe opened the flap. Inside, he saw a shiny, copper pen. This type of writing utensil was costly. He couldn't get the "thank you" past the lump in his throat.

His father said, "You're welcome, son. Think of us as you scribe your stories."

At this moment, it hurt to think about the journey. Fear that this could be the last night he'd spend at home with his family crept in, and he felt his heartbeat quicken. As he studied the pen, he became aware of the wind rustling through the trees and nearby goats bleating softly.

His sister came in. "*Ema* says it's time to wash for dinner."

. . .

LATE THAT NIGHT, the young scribe awakened with a start. His heart was racing again. He had not felt this alive since before he was beaten. The feeling of clarity and tranquility did not last, however. Thoughts about his future rushed in, colliding one on top the other, paddling against the current, against what the high priests had taught him, against his father's words of wisdom.

To the people of Jerusalem, Galilee was another world entirely. The elders trained him, worked with him, and taught him how to act. But no one prepared him for this mission. By sheer force of will, from a place deep within, the young scribe came to an original conclusion.

He could not go hide at a relative's house like a common black lizard blending in on the leaf of a cypress. He must continue as a spy and create a concise, authentic profile of Yeshua. He would base this testimony in truth, his truth as he saw it. Yet, under no circumstances would he convey the purpose of his mission to anyone. Not his father, not his family, neither the people of Galilee, nor the disciples of Yeshua. And not Yeshua himself.

He rose from bed, put on a fresh tunic, secured his old sandals to his feet, and slung his calfskin travel bag over his back. It housed a second pair of sandals, changes of clothes, a rolled-up sleeping mat, and a cloak to put over his head. Over his shoulder, he carried a bundle holding three goatskin cases full of water, and a parcel of fruit and bread. Nestled underneath his tunic was the decorated bag that held his scroll and writing implements. He wrapped the shawl around his shoulder and then he looked around the room, studying the shape of things in the shadows, securing a place for this life in his memory.

With that, like a golden jackal stalking a hare in the desert at midnight, the young scribe fled quick and quiet out the main oak door and headed east toward the glasslike Sea of Galilee. The wet season was ending. He hoped the usually mild month of *Lyyar* would favor him.

CHAPTER TWENTY-TWO

Campo Marzio, Rome
Present Day

THE IDEA CAME AS YIGAEL SAT IN HIS SIMPLE, SPARE APARTMENT with his adored tabby on his lap. *This will have to be in person.* Booking a next-day flight, he dropped off Abra with Mrs. Berlinsky, his cat sitter, set out for Tel Aviv, and climbed aboard an *Alitalia* Airbus for Rome.

After landing, he headed for his former Mossad office in the artsy San Lorenzo district. Yigael loved this spot, away from touristy Rome, so much so that, after he'd turned in his Mossad tags, he'd kept it. It made sense. After all, so much of his scientific work brought him to the Eternal City.

While organizing paperwork, Yigael smiled at the thought of her. He picked up his phone and tapped on the familiar number.

The voice on the other end said, "Well, hello. And where on Planet Earth are you this time?"

"Practically on your doorstep."

"You're in Rome?"

"I am. Dinner tonight?"

"I'd say no to anyone but you, Yigael."

"I'm flattered. *Babette*? Nine?" He knew she loved the unpretentious little eatery tucked away in a piazza not far from the Spanish Steps.

"See you there."

As Yigael took a seat, he ordered a Negroni and a champagne cocktail and said they'd take the specials. He had arrived ten minutes early. As Valentina approached, she did not disappoint. Even in her sullen state, having lost everything she'd worked so hard to achieve, she was stunning, a force.

Yigael rose and the two exchanged welcoming kisses.

"There you are, old friend," she said.

"Valentina, always beautiful." He studied her figure-hugging, plum-colored, V-neck dress, and then fixed his eyes on her feet. "Still wearing sensible shoes, I see."

Valentina looked down at her mile high, strappy stilettos and laughed. "I had to dust them off. These days, well, as you know, I'm not venturing out much."

They took seats on the wrought iron chairs.

"So," they said together.

"Good to see you, Yigael."

"Luca?" he asked.

"Still talking marriage," she said. "More seriously."

"So, I'm not out of the running yet." Yigael was jesting but only partly. He couldn't deny his attraction to the scholarly beauty whose independent air was a turn-on for the most discerning of the opposite sex.

Valentina knew his attraction. She also knew the depth of his grief following the heartbreaking deaths of his wife and young son in Jerusalem at the hands of terrorists. Valentina felt sure he would never fully recover.

She smiled up at the server delivering drinks. *"Grazi."* Then, she held her cocktail up. "And, to you, for remembering, *grazi."*

"Di niente."

"I can't think about marriage, Yigael. Even though I should probably jump at the chance, given Valeri and all. Maybe I'm just stubborn, but I have to get back on track on my own, somehow."

Yigael and Valentina's relationship began years back when they co-authored an article for *Archaeology Life* magazine that launched a war between straight-and-narrow and out-of-the-box scientists. Then, with Erika rolled into the mix, the trio collaborated on the mysterious Damascus Document. Since then, they'd dug, cleaned, conferred, and consulted in lab settings all over Europe and Israel. They'd laughed, dined, and confided in each other on a regular basis outside their work settings.

A discreet overhead light shone on Valentina's glossy, auburn bob.

Yigael studied her briefly. He had missed her. "Your future might not be as bleak as you imagine, Valentina."

"Don't forget Erika. We're both, um, bleakness personified."

"How could I ever forget Erika?" His eyes shot skyward. "I'm serious, Valentina."

"You have something up your, uh, sleeve, then?"

"You ever hear of the *Secret Temple Scroll*?"

"Sounds like something out of Indiana Jones."

"That's a *no*?"

"Yes. No."

"Well, settle in, my dear. Until recently, its existence has been little more than rumor, but now, we have some evidence."

"Wait, is this the scroll that allegedly contains testimonies from villagers in Galilee who knew Yeshua? Supposedly, he spoke against the Temple and the priests."

"The one."

DIANE CUMMINGS & JOHN I. RIGOLI

"Er and I translated some scrolls for a couple of rabbis a few years back. They referred to that scroll. I didn't pay much attention, to the rabbis or the scroll."

"Well, hear me out. Second Temple coins have been turning up—"

"Yeah, they're all over Israel. Like sand. I think I've got three in my bag. For luck," she said dryly.

"Not Israel. In an unusual locale—"

"Well, where?"

"Holy God. Can I get out one sentence before you jump in? Paris."

Valentina smiled at his outburst. "Paris. That is unusual. Okay."

"Philippe and Anna-Marie tracked the coins and Jacques verified them. We're assuming, well, more than that. They have to be part of the Temple treasure."

"Yeah, I get it. Find the coins, find the treasure. But the scroll?"

"With the treasure. All kinds of reasons we think so, but there's more. While all this running around after the coins is going on, the words *Secret Temple Scroll* pop up on a computer screen at IAA."

"What?"

"I know. Two thousand years? And it flashes before me the same time as the coins."

"In Israel."

"Where else would the Israeli Antiquities Authority be?"

"Don't get smart with me. I mean, finding something like this in the land of Jews would bring big questions about authenticity. How was it found?"

"Yes, a girl, well, a grad student was matching up fragments on the computer for her boss and came across it. Sam Gold. You know him?"

A server interrupted them with panko-crusted sea bass for Valentina and ribeye, rare, for Yigael.

"*Grazi.*"

"*Grazi.* Sam? Of course, I know him. Did he know about the scroll?"

"Nope."

"Did you see the originals?"

"Of course. They're under Plexiglas there. Judging by the papyrus, they seem to be mid-first century. They look good, so far, good enough for us to go ahead with the search."

"Too bad you don't have context. Is there anything readable around the words?"

"A reference to Herod."

Valentina looked off in the distance. "Huh. If it is real, a writing about Yeshua at the time he lived ..." As her voice trailed off, her eyes returned to Yigael's, wide with interest for the first time in months. "There's nothing else written even close to Yeshua's years."

"And we've got to hope that it rode along with the treasure to where we tracked the coins."

"Which is where?"

"Jacques and the crew have traced them to a site in France."

"Yigael, speed it up."

"Saint-Denis. The basilica there."

Valentina's eyebrows shot up. "What? You going through channels?"

"Some."

"Right. Permission from Israel but not the Church."

Yigael's stemmed smile told all.

"Searching a basilica and then stealing from it if you get right down to it? Well, good luck to you, Yigael. I hope you find it."

Yigael chuckled. "We can't do this without you, Valentina."

CHAPTER TWENTY-THREE

Piazza del Popolo, Rome

"ME?"

"That's right," Yigael said.

"What could I possibly offer to this quest of yours? Not that I'd want to. Lord, another clash with the Vatican?"

"You finished with your objections?"

"Almost. The Holy Office has ruined me. And Erika. And you want me to go back for more?"

"What more could there be?" he asked.

"Nothing."

"My point. There's nothing more to lose." Yigael leaned back in his chair, relaxed, and studied his friend as the server dropped off a second bottle of wine.

"What do you want, Yigael? I'm barely getting out of bed these days."

"I want you to sell Valeri."

"Oh, do you?"

"To the Church."

"Ah."

"As I recall, you and Erika have considered selling. You've told me so."

"You're a little late."

"Late?" Then he noticed Valentina tightening her lips and filling her glass. "What, Val?" He rarely used her nickname, only in their innermost exchanges.

"The Church already owns it. Rather Carlo Lavoti owns it, with his endless resources."

"You sold it to the Church, after all?"

"No, my friend. The bank pounced on us, locked us out. The next thing we learned was that Cardinal Carlo Lavoti bought it. He must have had it all set up."

"And you didn't think to mention it until now?"

"It all just happened. I was waiting for the moment."

"I'm sorry, Val." He sat in thought for a minute.

"Excuse me, Yigael, I need to, um, freshen up." She picked up her clutch and headed to *il gabinetto*.

"What if I told you I could get you back inside your lab?"

At that, Valentina spun on a stiletto and marched back to her seat.

"Look, I admit you had me there for a second. But thinking about it ... this might save us a lot of trouble."

"I'm glad it saves *someone* the trouble."

Just then, a distant voice called out, "Yigael."

Yigael looked over. "You didn't," he said to Valentina, then rose.

Erika strode toward him, her short, blonde curls, blown by the wind, sticking out in all directions. With outstretched arms, and before he could foist her off—Yigael hated public play-acting—she squeezed him tight and planted noisy smooches on both cheeks. "I should be irked I wasn't invited, but I know your proclivity for brunettes."

Yigael ordered more wine and some small plates for nibbling and brought Erika up to date.

"I'm riveted, Val. Salivating at the thought of reading what's on that scroll."

"He's not asking us to read it," Valentina said.

"Yes, I am. But that comes later. Ladies, I have funding from Israel for nearly all stages of the search. I need you, and I can pay you during this, er, interim period. And I would assume you wouldn't say no to a little, ah, support?"

The outspoken one said, "I wouldn't."

The more practical of the duo added, "I'm not able to refuse. However, it is most embarrassing."

"Oh, Val, get over it." Crushed and outraged when the bank took over, Erika just wanted to move past it. "Well, Yigael, what now?" She brimmed with eagerness.

Yigael explained that the first part of his plan would go on without them.

"Glad to hear that," Valentina responded. "Even if Lavoti did offend us by refusing to buy from us and then snapping it up from the bank, I don't think I could steal from my Church."

Yigael looked at Erika whose mouth was partially open. "Yes, we know you could, Er." He went on to describe the second phase and Valentina's part in it.

"And what am I supposed to do?" Erika asked.

"My dear, you will hold the space, as you hipsters say."

"I am not a hipster."

"I'll need you to be on standby, ready to move in any direction."

"So, who is this guy agreeing to let you use his land, the godfather?" Valentina half-joked.

"And that's why I love you." Despite Valentina's beauty, Yigael's real crush was on her brain.

"A mobster?" Erika said. "You've given me the collywobbles, Yigael."

"Look, this guy started out in the Soviet Union," Yigael said. "Took over the family business trading illegally logged timber on the black market. Added forgery and auto theft to his repertoire. He's been all over. Lived in Israel for a while building a drug business, and now he's a player here."

"Where?" they asked in unison.

"Countryside. Estate around—lucky us—Ercolano. You'd never know he wasn't Italian. Changed his name, bought up Italia Foods, and sells olive oil and cheese to make himself look respectable."

"Italia Foods. You mean Giordano Gallo? I've seen him on TV."

"Likes to be called Dano."

"Olive oil's pretty good." Erika dropped her chin and sneaked a smirk

"Skinny, wiry guy. Fine, three-piece suits. Flashes a lot of gold."

"And you're connected how?" Valentina asked. "Never mind."

Yigael shrugged.

"Lovely," Valentina said. "And what's to keep him from keeping the scroll? Selling it?"

"Bonnie's in jail."

"Bonnie."

"His third wife. He adores her and wants her out."

"Soulmate in exchange for a top-secret scroll sounds fair to me," Erika said.

"Unless he gets caught in the meantime and goes to jail. Then, Bonnie's out and he's in," Valentina commented.

"Okay, okay," Erika said, "I'm fascinated with the cops and robbers show, and I do admire a man wanting to see his lovely wife out of jail."

Valentina snorted a laugh, to Yigael's amazement. "But seriously, Yigael," she said, recovering, "what's really in it for us and Valeri?"

"Income, revenge, retribution ... how about restoring your reputation?"

He'd swayed neither woman by that.

"At the helm of a discovery that will change history."

"Been there, done that," Valentina said.

"A new beginning. I promise," Yigael said.

"You sound like my ex-girlfriend," Erika said.

"*Cameriere*, more wine!" Yigael buckled in for what he guessed would be a four-bottle debate about how he planned to get them back inside their lab.

It wouldn't be perfect. But it would be a start.

CHAPTER TWENTY-FOUR

@michaellevinlacarta: Just when you think you know your Church, she surprises you. www.https://LaCarta.-com/michaellevin-thevaticanbuysvaleri. #vaticanbreakingnews

The Vatican Picks up World-Renowned Valeri
By Michael Levin

Just when you think you know the Church—its bylaws have been around since the dawn of time—she surprises the world, this time by scooping up the research lab of the women it recently black-listed from both the Christianity and archaeology world playgrounds. Eminent archaeologists, Valentina Vella and Erika Simone, lost the once-top *Valeri Laboratorio de Conservazione* to creditors after scientists from around the world pulled their contracts following the Bishop Julia scandal. Truth proves stranger than fiction as official word is out that the Vatican snapped up Valeri at once after foreclosure.

As Vatican followers raised their brows, suspicious of motivation—some spoke of retribution, some spoke even of larceny —Cardinal Carlo Lavoti came to the Church's defense, denying all allegations of misdeeds. "Buying Valeri in no way addresses the sins of the archaeologists. The Church always acts benevolently toward all of mankind. We are the model by which one billion citizens seek to follow. At the same time, we need to heal the wounds close to home and hope that the two scientists will repent for their sins as a step in the right direction for forgiveness by the Church." When asked, Cardinal Lavoti declined to justify the need for this exalted laboratory.

While the sale price has not yet been made public, the deal with the "devil," as some might say, was done swiftly, and rumor has it the lab was greatly undervalued. Quite a deal for the Church. Too bad for the two scientists who, had they been able to sell it, would have placed themselves in good stead over their debt.

Vella and Simone have been contacted but decline to comment.

CHAPTER TWENTY-FIVE

Magdala AD *31*

Travel had been slow. The young scribe did not want to risk tripping on the Roman guard, so he'd avoided the roads. Roman soldiers did not care about the shorelines so much. These were just fishers fishing, generally no monkey business.

Magdala was a small fishing village along the Galilean Sea, a short distance south of Capernaum. By the time the young scribe circled the tiny town and arrived at the cusp of the sea, the sun was slipping away. He walked north along the sea's edge. Some workers were trading their day's work for olives and fruit. Others gutted their catches, their fingers digging deeply into the silver flesh. Small fires burned just off the shore as people were quick to cook fresh fish.

The young scribe sat down at the water's edge, took off his sandals, and dipped his feet in. The cool water was so clear and soothing as it gathered around his swollen feet. He could not wait until true nighttime when these men disappeared into their homes. He longed to be here alone, to discard his soiled clothes and bathe in the sea. Leaning against his hands, the young scribe threw his face back to meet the coming night. He was not afraid of the sea at night, so when it was time, he discarded his outer garments and charged in. The first thrust of the waves felt shockingly cold, but good. He splashed his face and surprised himself by laughing aloud. He swam farther out, twirling, submerging, and stretching his limbs, which suddenly felt ageless in the cushion of water.

With no desire to put his soiled clothes back on his damp body, he dug into his pack for a fresh tunic. He would arrive in Capernaum the following day, and it was important for him to meet Yeshua in clean clothing.

Having dressed, the young scribe retreated to the top of a low hill surrounded by trees and brush. Looking down from his chosen spot, he could see the moon and stars glittering off the water. He found a smooth rock, sat down, and pulled out of his satchel bread and figs that a merchant insisted he take as he passed through Cana. He hadn't felt so free or so happy since he was a little boy.

Exhausted and a little worse for wear after his journey, the young scribe unrolled his sleeping mat and settled under the cover of a blanket he had remembered to pack. He wanted to try and rest before the sun rose over the horizon. He stretched out and shivered. Still a chill at this time of year. He looked at the vast expanse of sky above. Around him, creatures stirred. Knowing the best way to be invisible, he remained motionless. Eventually, the stillness of his body lulled him into a deep, restful sleep.

It seemed he had just closed his eyes when he was startled awake by the buzz of men and boys laughing and chattering in the half-light. He sat up and watched as they lined up along the shoreline. Two youngsters stripped to the waist and jumped in, swimming out a bit and diving under the water to loosen the weights that kept the nets to the sea floor. They popped up again, spitting water, holding the edges of the netting. The larger men joined them, wading out, grabbing hold of the net. Together, they hauled it to shore. The young scribe packed away his bedding and set off in their direction.

On spotting him, the men yelled their greetings, welcoming him as just another weary day laborer.

Then, he opened his mouth. "Sirs, could you tell me where I am?"

This brought a hardy round of laughter.

"Oh, listen to the little lordling! 'Sirs, would you be so kind to tell me where I am'?" the largest fisherman in the crew echoed.

"Peter, leave off! You're frightening the whelp!" a gruff, older man added.

More fits of laughter trailed.

A different man, with the gait of a leader, approached him. "I'm Andrew." With that, he threw his arm around the young scribe. "Ignore them, boy. These ruffians have no manners at all. You are in Gennesaret. You have already met my brother, Peter. That other big one over there is John, and that pipsqueak is James, our fisher partners."

One by one, they gave him the kiss of peace. He was no longer ill of ease. "I am a scribe," he said.

"A scribe?" James asked.

"Yes."

"You don't look like you're much used to workin'," Peter quipped. "But if you'll help us finish getting the nets in, we'll feed you a good breakfast."

The young scribe's childhood dream of being a fisherman lay before him.

He stripped off his shawl and tunic and waded into the water dressed only in his *'ezor*, like the rest.

Before he knew it, the sun was halfway to midday. They all assembled on the beach and started a small fire to cook their lunch. John began to fuss over the young scribe as his own mother would, rubbing his bleeding palms with salve, spreading cold, wet mud on his crimson shoulders.

Peter handed him a slab of thin rock with a fish perched atop, one he had pulled from the fire. The young scribe had been having so much fun that he had forgotten about his hollow belly. He tore into the fish as if he had not eaten in days.

Andrew set off to the shoreline again to check the nets and wind them up. Washing, cleaning, and mending nets seemed to take more time than fishing. Peter ordered the young scribe to stay on the beach and nurse his raw hands while the rest set off to help finish sorting the fish and stowing the gear. Full and happy, he lay down and slept in the warm sun, a steady breeze cooling his charred skin.

He awakened as the men returned from their tasks. They passed around a waterskin, and the young scribe drank thirstily.

"We thank you for your help, boy. We're about to push off for home," Peter said. "If you tell us where you're headed, I'm sure we can point you on your way."

"How far are we from Capernaum?"

"Ah, well then. We are heading that way. You can ride along if you don't mind the stink of the fish!"

They packed him in on top of a pile of nets. John dunked a piece of cloth in the water, wrapping the young scribe's head and shoulders against the noonday sun. They did not allow him to row.

"You're our guest. You've done enough for today. Besides, you'd probably steer us aground," Peter joked. Well, perhaps he was joking.

"You have family there?"

"Not exactly. I am looking for a man named Yeshua from

Nazareth. I met him more than six months ago and hoped he might still be in the area. Do you know him?"

This drew another round of raucous laugher.

James smiled. "See, I told you he was one of us." Then, addressing Peter, he said, "He told us to fish for men, and we caught one our first day out!"

CHAPTER TWENTY-SIX

Capernaum AD *31*

THE SCENE ON THE DOCKS WAS CHAOTIC AS OTHER BOATS simultaneously pulled into the tiny harbor, unloading their daily catch. Men and women alike scurried about, helping with the barrels of fish, hoisting them onto scales, weighing them, and writing chits. Women lined the tables, gutting the fish, throwing the entrails to the hungry gulls, and tossing the cleaned flesh into wooden boxes filled with salt.

The young scribe had never seen anything like this. In fact, he'd never given a thought to how fish got from the water to his table.

The men and women on the dock treated Peter and James with polite deference.

Noting the young scribe's gaping mouth, James said, "Welcome to our little fish factory, boy. We employ a good 100 men and women here." He turned to Peter. "Could you check today's tally and see what we'll owe to the publicans tomorrow? They'll be demanding their cut." James made a growling sound.

Peter said, "Leave Andrew and John here. There's work to

be done." Then, he put an arm about the young scribe's shoulder. "James, we need to treat our new guest to a fitting meal!" Peter's face hinted at a smile.

"I couldn't agree more, Peter. C'mon, boy, I will show you the sights. Then we'll meet the others for dinner." James led the young scribe away from the fish factory and into the town.

Capernaum was smaller than Sepphoris, but not as poor as some of the towns through which he had trekked. The main street housed stately buildings, including a fine synagogue, as well as a bathhouse, which was where they seemed to be heading.

"First, we need to wash up a bit, boy. It's not good for a man of business to go about stinking of fish." James lowered his voice. "The poorer a man seems, the more they will try and take."

That was a lesson the young scribe had never heard. However, he felt as if he had long known it in his heart and seen it with his eyes.

They entered the baths and an attendant greeted James warmly. They said their obligatory prayers and the attendant took their dirtied clothing off for cleaning. The young scribe took out a fresh tunic from his rucksack.

James said, "Let me have a look." He gave the clean tunic the once-over. "This will do. It's better than what you showed up in."

"Well, I was traveling," the young scribe shot back.

"It's just that it would be well for you to dress as a man of your station."

The young scribe looked at him, surprised.

"Come now, boy. If we caught on the moment you opened your mouth, do you think you're going to fool anyone else?"

He took in a deep breath, deciding whether to tell James he was hiding from the Romans. Nevertheless, as they sank into the hot water, the urge to be free of his private burdens became all consuming. Then he saw James steal a glance at the scars on his chest and stomach.

When he finished his tale, the fisherman simply nodded. "You aren't the only one needing to avoid the Romans, boy. But you are with us now. No one is going to lay a finger on you."

After their baths, the young scribe felt better than he had in weeks. He followed James about on his errands, entering one of the colonnaded buildings they passed along the way. James was given a rather hostile respect as he negotiated with one officious little man or another.

"Publicans!" he spat under his breath every so often.

Once James finished his arrangements, they headed off to where the young scribe was to be a guest for the night. After the arduous work of the day, he was starving, particularly for the meal he helped catch.

They arrived at the home of Peter and Andrew right around sunset. It was a fine slate home, not the fishing shack the young scribe had imagined. James entered first to a round of greetings. At least a dozen people were sitting in the inner courtyard, men and women both.

"Yeshua, look at what we hauled in today!" James rejoiced, shaking the young scribe's shoulders.

Yeshua turned, eyes sparkling. "Good to see you back, Young Scribe."

CHAPTER TWENTY-SEVEN

Capernaum AD *31*

YESHUA APPEARED HAPPY BUT NOT SURPRISED TO SEE HIM. THE young scribe found it unsettling. As a woman approached with a cushion to recline upon, Yeshua motioned for him to take a seat.

With everyone settled, Yeshua began speaking on a fine point of the Torah, which drew in listeners. They packed the room, crowding the doorways.

The young scribe gazed around the room, feeling uneasy. Didn't Yeshua know these were not discussions for women? Of course, women were able to listen in at the synagogue and join in prayer. Of course, they could grasp the simpler parables and understand their duties under the laws and traditions. But to sit and study the law alongside men?

As he was trying to make sense of this peculiarity, a woman interrupted Yeshua.

The young scribe gasped.

All eyes turned to him, bemused.

The young scribe surprised himself by standing and objecting, "Rabbi, why did you not silence this woman? She has no right to speak."

"I would not be so smug, Young Scribe."

"Yes, Rabbi, but I am a man! She is but a—"

Yeshua's laughter stopped him cold. "Young Scribe, where is it written that our Father loves his male children and does not love his female ones?"

Ah, but the young scribe was prepared by all the years he had spent at Temple. "He does love women. He has given them to our keeping. Women are weak."

At this, the women laughed.

The young scribe blushed but persisted. "In the garden that the Lord gave for this world, he made one commandment: to eat not of the tree. Yet Eve disobeyed. And we were all consigned to plow the earth forevermore."

One of the women cackled. "It took the adversary to tempt Eve. It only took Eve to tempt Adam. They both disobeyed!"

Yeshua was smiling now, seemingly enjoying himself. "Young Scribe, do you think our Father makes mistakes?"

"No, of course not."

"Good. So, when He told both Adam and Eve not to eat from the Tree of Knowledge, do you think He did not know He would be disobeyed?"

The young scribe had no answer. But they all knew this was why women were subordinate, why women had such pain in bringing forth life.

"To choose wisdom, to choose knowledge, Young Scribe. It is not something one must take lightly. We can think of Eve as foolish or brave or both. But she chose—at the risk of angering the Creator—wisdom." He turned to the woman who had cackled. "And the serpent did not tempt her, Anah. He simply told her the truth. Young Scribe, these women are your sisters. They are wise, they are beloved. If you stay here, you shall grow to love them as I do."

In truth, he always knew his mother had more wisdom than his father did, though she was quiet in showing it. The young scribe was wholly confused.

To his relief, Yeshua said, "It is enough for today."

At this, people jumped to their feet, all speaking at once.

Andrew came in and took a seat next to the young scribe, wrapping an arm around his shoulder. "Welcome, brother." He kissed him on both cheeks and ruffled his hair. "*Ema!*" he called out.

A small woman peeked around a doorway.

Andrew jumped to his feet.

"Young Scribe, Peter's mother-in-law."

The young scribe greeted her, thanking her for the hospitality.

"He'll be joining us for supper, and to sleep."

Yeshua appeared at the young scribe's shoulder. "And could you bring the best wine, *Ema*? We have cause to celebrate. One of the lost sheep has been found."

Andrew laughed. "Is he a sheep or a fish? I can't keep up!"

The meal was splendid, the choices nearly limitless, with roasted fish, pounded fish, fish in vinegar, fish in cream. Thankfully, they also offered dates, nuts, figs, and greens. The wine was as sublime as any his mother had served at her finest table.

Despite the warm welcoming, the young scribe felt like an outsider. Women and men did not feast together unless blood or marriage bonded them, and never did they in public. Even at weddings and funerals, men and women had their own dining rooms. He also had the weight of his family weighing on him. What must they be thinking and feeling, waking up to discover he'd vanished?

It had been a long day. He had eaten too much and drunk even more. Warm, sated, and exhausted from being in overdrive, his head began to loll against his chest, and the room went silent.

Then, a sudden buzz of voices roused him.

He stretched his eyes open as a woman entered the room. The sight of her caught his breath. She was the most beautiful woman he had ever seen. He stared at her long, elegant fingers as she undid the clasp of her cloak, each beringed with silver jewels. As she removed it, silky, black tresses cascaded down her back like a waterfall. Her sapphire shawl was rich, almost shimmery, woven from the finest wool, no doubt. Her fine eyebrows framed deep, green eyes, and she possessed the lushest of lashes. They looked like butterfly wings fluttering as she blinked.

She greeted everyone as she moved into the room. As she reached Yeshua, she fell to her knees, took his hand, and raised it to her lips.

Yeshua beamed and pulled her into an embrace. "Mary."

CHAPTER TWENTY-EIGHT

Capernaum AD *31*

SEVERAL NIGHTS LATER, AT THEIR CAMPGROUND HIGH ON A HILL above Capernaum, Yeshua, his chosen twelve, and his disciples were enjoying a night out. It was a lovely place, surrounded by lush, sweet-smelling barley and tendering a spectacular view of the lowlands.

Lying back, supported by his elbows, the young scribe squinted at someone approaching.

"I am James."

"Another James? I recognize you from my first night at Peter's. Please, sit down."

"Yes, the other is the fisher. I am James, Yeshua's younger brother."

It never occurred to the young scribe that Yeshua had other siblings.

James seemed to have a particular interest in the young scribe, and he was wasting no time getting to his point. "I hear you have studied in Jerusalem."

"I have."

"A scribe, I hear."

"That too."

"How fortunate for us," James said. "These people are hungry for a scribe to record the words of Yeshua."

This was not the first time he had heard this suggestion. In truth, his training as a scribe would be far more useful than his abilities as an apprentice fisherman.

Yeshua ambled over. "I think our young scribe needs to see what real life is like and continue working on the sea." He smiled, verbalizing the desire in the young scribe's heart. "I think he's spent enough time indoors training in the Temple to last through eternity."

At that, they all chuckled.

"Let him work on the boats. It will toughen him up for the days ahead."

As DAYS TURNED into weeks that passed into months, with vigorous work, nourishing food, and fresh air, the young scribe's health fully returned. He began to look less like a boy and more like a man. His shoulders had broadened, his thighs had become thick and strong, and he had regained his sense of balance. His hair, no longer clipped short in the Roman way, had become a cascade of thick, rusty ringlets about his neck. It was reminiscent of his sister's often-disheveled locks, and he would chuckle thinking about what she would have to say about that. He doubted that even his mother would recognize him now.

His life took on a steady rhythm, and he was happier than he could ever have imagined. He spent mornings working, evenings learning, discussing scripture, and praying.

Yeshua taught at the synagogue every Sabbath. In Capernaum, even the Pharisees, the most conservative Jews who observed traditional law strictly, came to hear Yeshua teach.

They praised him as one with authority. However, the priests in Jerusalem were raising their voices and denouncing his every word.

For the first time since he had been a student, the young scribe's scrolls lay rolled in his satchel, clean of ink. He could not put his finger on why he hadn't written. Perhaps it was simply that nothing in Capernaum would interest the high priests. To the young scribe, Yeshua displayed only goodness. Some days, he would be working in a local woodshop, planing lumber, and building chests and tables that were in demand in some of the finest houses. Other mornings, Yeshua would come out on the water. The young scribe swore that when he was present, they caught twice the fish in half the time.

The young scribe had started sending letters to his family, no longer fearful his father would come after him. And they sent back letters, pleased that he was working with Peter, whose family was well respected throughout the Galilee.

One morning, when the four fishers, the young scribe, and Yeshua had gone out to sea and filled their boats with barrels of fish, Yeshua stopped them, holding a hand up. "Peter. We need to go back. We should hurry." With this, Yeshua began tipping the barrels out, freeing the day's catch. "Andrew, hoist the sail. Now, please."

"Yeshua, there's no wind. It's like glass out here. It'll be faster to row."

Yeshua gave Andrew a withering stare, and he hoisted the sail.

Yeshua went to the prow, holding up his hands in silent prayer. By the time they had unfurled the sails, the wind was up, and it sped the boat across the sea as if it were a bird in flight.

As the six of them pulled up to the docks, James' steward was there to greet them.

"Peter, Andrew, you need to be home. Come."

They jumped out of the boat, handing the ropes over to the men on the dock.

When they arrived home, they found the house in disarray and the women tearing about between rooms, gathering cloths and carrying basins of water.

Peter's wife ran to greet them, her face red and wet with tears. "It's *Ema*, she is on fire. I think she's been waiting for you to say goodbye."

A physician hurried into the atrium, face cracked with defeat. "James is with her. Peter, Andrew, I'm sorry, but there is nothing more I can do."

Without a word, Yeshua walked toward *Ema*'s sleeping chamber. Peter and Andrew followed. The young scribe might have stayed back, out of respect, but he could not help himself. *Ema* had been so good to him, treating him as one of her own.

As they filed in, Yeshua strode to where *Ema* lay, her body convulsing from the fever, a fire so hot the young scribe could feel it from where he stood outside the doorway. Her women-folk were trying to cool her head with wet rags, but it was clear their efforts were pointless.

Yeshua sat at the edge of the bed and placed his hand on *Ema*'s head. Her body stilled. Then, Yeshua took her hand in his, and she sat up. Just like that.

She seemed surprised to see everyone. "Boys, what are you doing here? Is the workday done already? You must be hungry. Let me see what Cook has prepared for dinner."

The young scribe had never seen such a thing.

That evening, after prayer, he thought about Ori the builder. Perhaps it was not so odd, to believe he had been helped by a spirit. And, outside the gates of the jail, he had heard that soft, unfamiliar voice. A woman's voice. Had this ethereal soul quenched his thirst? Later, his father swore he had not given him water and neither had his uncle. He told his son that they chucked him onto the cart and sped off. This had him stumped, for he could feel the wet rag across his lips, still.

For the first time since his journey began, he opened his satchel and unrolled a scroll.

Capernaum—*Chamishi 15 Sivan*

I cannot explain what happened in Ema's bedroom. She appeared near death, her whole body on fire. I have never seen a human face so distorted with anguish, pain. He did nothing to her. No henbane or mandrake. Yeshua appears to heal through intuition. Somehow, he can tell what each supplicant needs in a matter of seconds, before they even speak. For, with the touch of his hand, she was healed before our eyes.

CHAPTER TWENTY-NINE

IN THE WEEK SINCE THE GROUP FIRST MET IN THE MUSEUM basement, Josh had phoned Susan twice asking her to dinner. So far, she had rebuffed him. Now, they were face-to-face in Professor Herschel Banks's office. He had rushed in with Dr. Gold and Yigael Dorian, who had a dossier, with not much in it, tucked under his arm. Susan and Josh nodded their greetings. They all took seats in front of Herschel's desk, under the amber ceiling bulb that seemed to dim the place rather than light it.

Herschel filled his audience in on the route of the treasure over centuries and pinpointed Paris as its location.

"Paris? Quite a huge search area, Herschel. How do you boil it down?" Dr. Gold asked.

"Yigael worked his magic. He followed the trade of Second Temple coins to an old priest who was hawking them."

"I don't follow."

"I'm with Dr. Gold," Susan said.

Josh took over. "Okay. The treasure is last in the hands of

Dagobert I. He builds the cathedral in St Denis. He dies, gets buried there. Safe to assume the treasure is there. But we don't really know. Maybe he stored it somewhere else. We need a little more, a clue. Okay? So Yigael hears about Second Temple coins turning up here ... in Paris. We know that the coins are part of the treasure. So, if we can find the source of the coins, we find the treasure. And you know the rest. Father Fullier hawks the coins. He just happens to work at Saint-Denis."

"The treasure has to be in the cathedral," Yigael said. "We can only hope our scroll is part of it. In any case, we're going to find out."

Eager to move forward, Herschel said, "If we find our scroll, we anticipate quite an impact on the worldwide community, and we must prepare for it."

Yigael jumped in. "We're forming a sub-committee under the IAA: The *Secret Temple Scroll*—or *STS*—Commission."

"Members will be kept apprised of all developments," Yigael said. "In this way, we can keep the integrity of the project intact." Yigael was no fool. He would head the commission and keep the scroll in his absolute control. "Sam, we're asking you to join Herschel and me on the commission." He turned to Susan. "We'll need you to manage public relations, so you'll have to stick close by."

Susan was speechless.

Dr. Gold was happy to accept a place on Yigael's new *STS* Commission, but he figured his participation would probably be a long way off and told everyone they knew where to find him. With that and a "come on, Susan," he was off.

Yigael nodded as a way of officially wrapping up the meeting. He scooped up his work and headed for the door with the same energy he had on entering. Josh followed him.

. . .

"Coffee, at least?" Josh pleaded, as Susan leaned against her car, rifling through her massive shoulder bag for her keys.

Edgy and wanting answers, Susan ignored his invite but found the keys, opened her car door, tossed her belongings inside, and then shut the door and faced him. "Will you tell me what's going on here? How does Yigael Dorian know about my public relations background? And why would I be interested in doing PR for his pet project. You're railroading me. You didn't give me a chance to say yes or no. I mean, he just dominates, like, not the kind of person you mess with."

"That's Yigael."

"So, I'm PR?"

"Susan, the circle of people who know about the scroll is small. Since your background is in archaeology and, fortunately for us, public relations, we need you. You've been cleared."

"Cleared?"

"Yes."

"What do you mean 'cleared'? Who cleared me?"

"Don't worry about it, just a routine check. Done all the time."

"Wait just a minute." Susan's glare startled Josh into silence. "You'd better give me some hard answers. What is going on here?"

"Yigael used Mossad to look into your background. Whoever he works with ... it's the same."

"I'm not everyone. I'm me, and you're telling me that Yigael had me investigated by Mossad."

"Yes."

"Mossad?" she asked again.

"Yes."

"Yigael is Mossad?" Then, she hesitated. "And ... you?"

"The boss and I no longer work for Mossad, but he can get anything he wants done."

Joshua Isaac Reznik was the great-grandson of immigrants, to Israel from Poland. When he was a kid, he found a hero in his great-uncle, Jakub, who had entertained him with stories of his days in the war as a spy for the British. Josh followed his uncle, majoring in international relations and then venturing into the world of espionage. After training, Mossad assigned him to work under the renowned Yigael Dorian.

"So, when he left, you left too? To work for him?"

"Did."

Susan screwed up her lips. "I can't see why anyone would do that."

Josh stared at her, ruminative.

"And you can just forget about me having anything to do with Yigael Dorian and his little game," Susan said with force. "You can tell your Yigael the answer is no."

"You know, Susan," Josh said with the hint of a smile, "you need to start saying yes."

⁓

YIGAEL AND HERSCHEL, with Josh as errand boy, hatched their plan. They would send their team to Saint-Denis in the guise of studying the basilica—graduate students studying the architecture of the cathedral, their professor along to guide them. Yigael had papers drawn to present to the church administrator showing him to be dean at *L'École Nationale Supérieure d'Architecture de Lyon* and in charge of the study group. He'd seized names from a directory of former students and retired professors.

"Josh, I have Fullier's file, but I also want data on the cathedral administrator, any other priests assigned there, and staff. I want to know who's responsible for monitoring each section of the church. It's an enormous structure."

"Yep."

137

For Yigael, the best results derived from operatives already working in the target country. They were likely to have the best cover since they knew the language, were up on local slang, and savvy about the way of life. They blended in. These assets could take them where forged ID papers might not. With all that considered, Jacques, Philippe, and Anna-Marie would stay on. Carol Conners, a green-eyed American beauty queen who worked full-time for the agency, her cover a dot-org, would join them.

Yigael wanted two women on the team. "They're never questioned by curious onlookers, not like men," he would always say.

With their plan sewn up, Herschel stepped back, to return to his classroom. Now, Yigael would see it through.

CHAPTER THIRTY

Saint-Denis, France

AUDREY LAURENT, THE ADMINISTRATOR AT SAINT-DENIS Basilica, called a staff meeting on a dreary Paris Friday afternoon to announce that a team, a professor and three graduate students, would arrive on the upcoming Saturday from the architectural college in Lyon to examine their great cathedral. She informed those present that this would not be the usual one-day overview visit. They needed access to major facets of the basilica and the necropolis, which included the royal tombs, the crypt, and the chevet.

"Father Fullier, I'd like you to welcome the team, make them comfortable, and show them around." Mme. Laurent's smile revealed a dimple on the left side of her cheek.

Father Fullier flushed at the request.

Mme. Laurent chose Father Fullier because Yigael had directed her to do so, and she felt so intimidated by the man that she dared not object.

Father Fullier nodded in acceptance, to the surprise of the

administrator who expected a fuss from the old priest. He grumbled about any change in his schedule.

Lyon, France

YIGAEL HELPED JACQUES, Philippe, Anna-Marie, and Carol load their gear into a rented Land Rover. He handed Jacques a cylindrical leather carrying case of the type generally used by architects. This one was empty.

Two weeks prior, they had all arrived in Lyon by rail, checked into a hotel, and spent the time learning about the basilica. Yigael had briefed them on religious architecture from the Roman, Baroque, and Gothic eras. They studied renderings of the massive cathedral, scrutinized CVs of the entire staff, and learned daily operations.

On this early Saturday morning, the sun was bright, the morning clear, and spirits high. Yigael watched his team pile into the vehicle. He waved them off and then jogged toward his rental.

The distance to Saint-Denis through lush French landscape was about 400 kilometers.

With Anna-Marie taking the first turn at the wheel, the four headed north.

"Our primary job is locating and retrieving this scroll before anyone is onto us, and Fullier knows where the treasure is." The professor looked out the window. "So, watch him but don't be obvious. We need to be seen as studying not snooping."

They all knew this much already. After all, they were well trained. Carol, in the back seat, rolled her eyes.

"Carol," Jacques said. "As an American, you may not realize that if INTERPOL or Europol gets wind of the heist, it could mean prison time. We're dipping our toes into an international criminal operation that's tied to money laundering, fraud, organized crime. And during a global crackdown."

"I get it. We're not lobbing a brick through a coffee shop window to steal a Keith Haring replica. Roger that."

"Good," Jacques said irked. "As long as you 'get it.'"

The undercover operation was about to begin.

CHAPTER THIRTY-ONE

As they approached the basilica after the five-hour drive from Lyon, it was like stepping back into the Middle Ages, so veiled under layers of black soot was the church façade.

Emerging from their SUV in mid-afternoon, the group stretched, took a quick look around, and entered the rectory lobby, where a gray-haired secretary sat behind a low-set counter.

Jacques introduced himself as Professor Fabron and asked for Father Fullier.

The secretary rang for the priest, and he appeared a scant five minutes later.

Father Fullier singled out Jacques and extended his hand. "I am happy to meet you, Professor Fabron."

"And we are happy to be here. These are my students: Paschal, Elise, and Katherine." He gestured toward the trio. "They are all studying in Lyon. Paschal is my PA," he added.

Father Fullier, effusive in his greeting, pumped Philippe's

hand, and then grasped each girl by the shoulders and planted perfunctory kisses on each cheek.

"Come with me." He motioned for them to follow. "Let's get you situated." Father Fullier led the team to the old Benedictine monastery attached to the side of the basilica. He assigned each member to a spotlessly clean, spartan room. Along each room's outer ancient stone wall was one small, deep-set window that opened from the center inward. The rooms were identical, containing a single bed, a small table and chair, chest of drawers, and a steam heater. Bathrooms stood along a narrow corridor. Father Fullier invited the team to settle in, unpack, and freshen up, and then join him in the dining room.

Later, after moving their gear from the Land Rover to their rooms and unpacking, the team assembled in a dining room furnished with small, round tables and folding chairs. At the end, opposite the entrance door, stood a cafeteria-style serving counter with stacked trays and plates and flatware in round canisters. The room was minimally occupied: a priest read a newspaper at one table and an older woman in trousers and a work shirt sipped tea at another.

Although it was only five o'clock, an early dinner was being provided for the hungry arrivals. If the aroma emanating from the kitchen and tickling their taste buds was a sign, they were in for a delicious feast. A young woman standing behind the counter was ready to ladle food onto empty plates. They lined up, dishes in hand, and were served a hearty *cassoulet* of veal with white beans and dried sausages, along with thick, chewy bread and slabs of butter. As they sat down, the young woman placed carafes of water and red wine in the center of the table. Then, she surprised the four by giving Father Fullier a peck on the cheek and pulling up a chair herself.

"This is my great-niece, Gabby. Well, Gabriella, is her God-given name." Father Fullier gave a smile intended just for her but offered no further explanation.

As Anna-Marie and Carol made small talk, Philippe fixed a neutral gaze on Gabriella, studying her. The girl was wearing a burgundy-colored, pin cord, double-breasted lapel dress with a trimmed-in-white, notched collar. A white, knee-length apron covered her dress. Philippe nodded politely, noting that, despite her dated, conservative attire, "the niece" was quite appealing.

"I think it would be helpful if I were to provide some background on our basilica before you begin your study." Father Fullier raised an inquiring eyebrow toward Jacques.

"Indeed," Jacques replied. "We are eager to hear all about this beautiful structure."

"As you are probably aware by this time," Father Fullier began, "this cathedral is a place of worship but it's also a historical monument. For centuries, the original abbey spotlighted the history of the Franks, the Germanic tribes. Then, sometime between the sixth and eighth centuries, a Merovingian ruler named the abbey church a basilica, and the city was built around it."

Father Fullier explained that the church stood over a Gallo-Roman cemetery, where Saint-Denis was buried. "Colorful story, that," he remarked. "Saint-Denis was martyred around the mid-second century. He was the first bishop of Paris and, according to writings on his tomb, he was beheaded not far from here, in Montmartre, during a persecution of Christians. It is said, astonishingly enough, that he picked up his head, washed it off, and carried it eight kilometers to this very spot, before collapsing. A shrine was built right here where he fell. The shrine was replaced by the basilica and, ever since the tenth century, it's been the burial site for France's kings, queens, and nobles. Marie Antoinette, for one, is buried here. You'll see that our abbey church contains some fine examples of cadaver tombs."

"I understand that King Dagobert was the first king buried here."

"Ah, yes, Professor Fabron, that is true."

"Where precisely is his tomb?" Philippe asked.

"I'll show you tomorrow, Pascal."

Philippe couldn't read the old priest's expression, but he knew Dagobert's tomb must lay close to Father Fullier's coin collection.

"Abbot Suger began building here in 1136," Father Fullier continued, "and, by the end of the thirteenth century, the structure was completed. The basilica is Romanesque in style."

"With Gothic characteristics," Anna-Marie said. "Pardon the interruption, Father, the transitional elements make it so fascinating, don't you think?"

"I do, Mademoiselle Elise," Father Fullier said, beaming.

"You know a lot about the place, Father," Philippe commented.

"Quite a bit, and here's a bizarre little fact for you. During the French Revolution in the late 1700s, a substantial number of the tombs were pried open, the bodies removed and dumped into two large pits nearby. When the mass graves were opened some decades later, it was impossible to tell, well, who was who, you might say, from the pile of bones. The remains were thus placed in an ossuary in the crypt. Two marble plates in front of the ossuary bear the names of each monarch."

Anna-Marie looked at Carol grim-faced.

It took her a second, but then Carol returned the expression, remembering to play the role of a young student studying architecture, not a Mossad undercover spy on a mission to heist an ancient artifact.

Father Fullier smiled. "Most people consider this basilica quite comparable to Westminster Abbey, which, I suppose, is the reason you're here. And, yes, there is much to see and appreciate.

"Ah, one final note: As we begin our tour in the morning, please be sure to notice the gorgeous, rose window in the façade of Saint-Denis and the crenellated parapet on top. The stained-glass windows have all been restored to their original beauty."

Father Fullier rose from his chair. "I must go. Saturday evening Mass ... in a few minutes. He stepped away from the table, and then turned back. "Breakfast is between seven and eight. I'll meet you after morning Mass and we can begin our tour. Sleep well."

Just as Father Fullier left, without a word, Gabriella rose and retreated to the kitchen. She emerged moments later with two platters, one of *fromages français,* the other with an array of *petites patisseries.* The team dug into their desserts with enthusiasm. Philippe stole another glance at Gabriella. Soon, the four, sated by a scrumptious meal and fatigued from their long journey, got up and returned to their rooms for a good night's sleep.

MINDFUL of their mission and the need to get on well with their guide, the team was up early the next morning. They gathered for breakfast before eight and attended Mass at nine in the Merovingian Chapel, one of the small side chapels and Father Fullier's domain.

Father Fullier, surprised to see his charges in attendance, announced from the pulpit, "We have some visitors today." He looked in their direction. "We offer you our hospitality and hope your stay here is a happy and memorable one."

After Mass, the team, accompanied by Father Fullier, returned to the rectory dining hall, where Gabriella had prepared coffee and homemade pastries. Philippe, especially, ogled the plates of brioches filled with chopped, candied oranges, almond-filled croissants, and French apple turnovers. Philippe's weakness for French pastry was legendary among his Mossad cohorts.

With treats consumed, Father Fullier took the team back into the church for a general overview. "This is an old building. When you're not with me, please be careful not to damage it."

Three hours later, Father Fullier ended the first leg of his tour at a permanent model of the abbey and market town as they were in the year 1600. "I've arranged a private tour for you on Tuesday. Our docent will show you everything you want to see."

"Like the necropolis, Father?" Anna-Marie asked. "Which, we didn't have time for today."

"Yes, dear, and such," Father Fullier said. "But, if you could stay clear of my area," Father Fuller pointed to the Merovingian Chapel, "I have some things going on there, renovation and whatnot," he added vaguely. "Thank you."

No one had seen any indication of renovations during Mass, but okay.

EARLY MONDAY MORNING, Philippe was first to set out. Time to roam freely appealed to him. Going rogue was right up his alley. He took a note pad and camera to the church to begin exploring the very nooks and crannies Father Fullier had warned him to stay away from. He noted that King Dagobert's tomb lay near the Merovingian Chapel. An hour later, he decided enough was enough for one morning and headed for the staircase that would take him to his room. Looking up from his notebook, he spotted Gabriella disappearing around a corner.

CHAPTER THIRTY-TWO

Saint-Denis

MOMENTS LATER, A SCREAM PIERCED THE SILENCE, FOLLOWED BY a clatter of metal.

Halfway up the slender monastery stairs, Philippe turned, barreled down, and burst through the kitchen door to find the cookery floor flooded with water, a tall trashcan upended, and a distraught and wet Gabriella standing amid it all, looking horrified.

Water in two pots on the large stove bubbled ominously.

"Are you hurt?" Philippe asked.

"No, no. Oh, no, just look at this!"

Water was gushing out from a broken pipe under the sink.

"Calm down," Philippe said. "Where's the shut-off valve?"

Gabriella looked up at Philippe, dumbstruck.

"Big help," Philippe muttered. He bent down, rooted around, and found it hidden behind a bucket inside the sink cupboard. As he twisted, the rusty, old fitting broke off.

Philippe followed the direction of the pipe and saw where it exited through an exterior wall. He pushed open a side door to the alley, found the pipe in question and, very carefully, to avoid breaking another fragile, ancient valve, shut off the water to the rectory with a delicate touch.

Returning to the kitchen, he found Gabriella trying to soak up the water with an old mop. It was a fruitless effort.

"At least you won't have to clean the floor tonight."

"Very funny."

"Look, seriously," Philippe advised, "you'll have to call a plumbing service and have this water sucked up. There's nothing else to do."

Then came a roar from upstairs, "Blast and damnation!"

The two looked skyward, then headed toward the door to the hallway and peered up to the second-floor landing.

"What's wrong now, Uncle Claude?"

"This toilet won't flush, that's what's wrong. Bloody hell!"

"Uncle, your language!"

"All the saints and angels," Father Fullier mumbled before slamming his bathroom door.

Philippe and Gabriella burst into fits of laughter and returned to the kitchen only to find the two pots previously filled with boiling water empty and singed.

Gabriella threw up her hands.

"Pizza tonight, I assume," Philippe said.

"Uncle Claude hates pizza." She grinned.

"What do you say I help with this mess while you call the plumber?"

The day had somehow felt victorious for Philippe, despite being up to his ankles in water.

It was a disheartening day for Jacques and Anna-Marie, who had plodded through the cathedral pretending to be interested in every turret, transept, flying buttress, pillar, nave, gargoyle, and stained-glass window the ginormous place had to offer.

That evening, with the pipes repaired, the floor dry, and the pizza consumed—by all but a sullen Father Fullier—everyone left the table.

Philippe, though, under the observant eye of Jacques, rendezvoused from his quarters back to the kitchen where Gabriella was cleaning up.

Unsurprised to see her visitor, Gabriella smiled. *"S'asseoir."* Sit.

"Well, you're in a better mood," Philippe said taking one of the straight-back chairs. "How long have you worked here in the church?" he asked, as he watched her lustrous, golden hair change color in the lighting as she moved about the kitchen.

"Since I was sixteen and out of school."

"Why here?" Philippe asked.

"Long, sad story," she said with a put-on, exaggerated sigh. "I'm kidding, not really. My story isn't so different from many others."

Gabriella's father had abandoned his family and moved to Toulouse. "My mother ran a small cake shop out of our flat to make ends meet until she fell ill and could no longer do it." She looked down at her hands. "I took over then, worked and took care of my mother until she died."

"Tough. I'm sorry."

"Thank heaven for my uncle. He came to the rescue, so to speak. He moved me to Saint-Denis and here I am. And you?"

"Not much to tell, really," Philippe said. "My parents are gone and I'm studying a lot. Can you ever get away from this place, say, for dinner out?"

"I could, yes. But not on weekdays."

"Friday?"

"We could go to *Au Petit Breton*. It is the best. A night on the town. Yes."

"Paschal, a word?" Jacques said, poking his head into the kitchen.

The two exited the rectory and found a concrete bench alongside its east wall. Darkness shrouded the pair, except for a mist of light coming from a dimly lit lamppost standing at the street corner.

"I see your kitchen duties have kept you busy."

"She may know something."

"Did it occur to you to clear that with me?" Jacques asked coolly.

"It did, actually. And I would have. That kitchen mess threw things off."

"Well, she does seem close to her uncle."

"I asked her to dinner but she's not free till Friday."

"Any personal interest there, Philippe?"

"We've got a job to do," he said evenly.

You sure?

"My personal life is a mess. Why would I add to it?"

"Okay, then." Though hardly reassured, Jacques stood, rounded the corner, and went back inside the rectory.

Philippe lingered, thinking.

TUESDAY WAS TURNING out to be more of the same, wandering about the basilica, taking copious notes that were predestined for recycling bins. It wasn't even lunchtime and they'd visited and revisited everywhere possible. The team wondered what kind of enthusiasm they could possibly conjure up for the docent who was about to present a discourse on the features of the place. The least they could hope for would be a clue to the whereabouts of the lost, ancient treasure.

Gabriella must be scouring the soot off the building, Philippe concluded as he stepped away from the docent's oration. The kitchen had been absent of her lovely presence all morning.

By late afternoon on Tuesday, having had his fill on the history of flying buttresses, Philippe ducked out like a college freshman on the Friday before winter break. Returning to his room to clear his head, he found Gabriella placing a white rose on his pillow.

"Oh, I—I did not know you were coming back so soon. I was just freshening up all the rooms."

"Did everyone get a rose?" Philippe teased.

She stared down at her shoes. "Our gardens are so beautiful. Someone ought to be appreciating them."

Philippe did not have to walk far into the tiny room to wrap his arms around her and kiss her gently.

On separating, she asked, "Is the basilica measuring up against other buildings you've studied?"

"If you're asking if you're the most interesting structure in it, the answer is yes."

Gabriella blushed. "Well, from all I've been told, the basilica's uniqueness is not so much its architecture as the fact that all the kings and queens are buried here." She paused. "There is one thing, though ...."

"Yes?"

Gabriella studied Philippe for a moment before venturing, "I can show you something that no one else knows anything about. I don't know how important it will be."

"Okay. I'm game. You've got me curious."

"Then meet me in the sacristy at midnight."

"Midnight? Very mysterious."

"It is, in a way."

"Okay, then. I'll be there, Gabriella."

"Gabby."

"Okay."

"And, please, don't tell anyone."

"*Bien sûr*, Gabby."

After dinner, Philippe returned to his room, counting the minutes till midnight.

CHAPTER THIRTY-THREE

Gush Halav AD *32*

"WE ARE LEAVING DAY AFTER TOMORROW TO TRAVEL NORTH TO Tyre," James said to the young scribe as they untangled a net from a coral rock the next morning. "We'll stop at a few villages and then stay in Gush Halav first. You're coming, yes?"

The young scribe knew that Gush Halav was tucked next to Mount Meron, the tallest mountain, and that would be a sight to see. He had never journeyed farther north than this and was curious about what lay beyond his small scope of experience.

"Yeshua says we must travel without provisions, as we must trust in God to provide," he added.

"Sounds good," the young scribe said, falsely. *Traveling without supplies? No, that does not sound good.* For the first time since he had arrived in Capernaum, his mood turned sour. He realized that his happy days out on the water working with the four fishermen, whom he considered friends, whom he loved, was ending.

For the rest of the fishing day, all he could think about was catching Yeshua committing blasphemy so that he could end this journey, return to Sepphoris, and send his report to the Temple. Then he could get on with his life and settle down. *I think it is time to get married. Sometimes, late at night, I hear the sounds from a couple, and I cannot stop myself from listening. It is a sin, I know, but it is a world, an experience, I do not know. I am twenty-two and feel I can wait only a little longer.*

AT THE END of a week hiking through rough mountainous terrain deprived of marked paths, the young scribe grew resentful of Yeshua for putting them all through this arduous slog. He had jumped over or circled around so many snakes, he'd lost count. Once, a wild boar threatened their campsite. If it hadn't been for Thaddeus, a large, muscular man who'd joined the group only recently and who took down the beast, what might have happened was all too obvious.

The young scribe's spirits improved at the first sight of civilization. As they entered the gates at Gush Halav, he concluded someone must have alerted the town that Yeshua was coming, for an enthusiastic crowd had gathered, clapping and hollering. A young girl gave him a crown made of intertwined blossoms and stems of dried berries. Villagers handed him bouquet after bouquet of flowers. Families stood in the doorways of their flat-roofed homes, cheering and waving. The women rushed them and thrust jugs filled with cool nectar into their hands.

By late afternoon, the young scribe's jubilant mood had faded. So, craving the comfort of home, he caught himself again hoping that Yeshua would defame the Temple or speak against its laws, thereby committing a criminal act in the eyes of the Sadducees, and thus ending the young scribe's task.

He walked into the Temple late to hear Yeshua speaking to the crowd of the sin of killing. He watched as the townspeople stirred. Yeshua's words elicited sneers from some, sullen silence from others, and laughter from a rather dirty group of men with wild hair and torn clothes, who sat in the back.

Yeshua raised his hands. "I know it sounds silly ...."

"Silly? Not kill?" One of the wild-haired men, obviously a Zealot, yelled. "Have you any idea how the Assyrians here treat us? They pay less for our wool and charge us twice for wood."

The man beside him added, "You live in the South, where the Jews outnumber all others."

"Yes, I come from the South," Yeshua said, "where the Romans walk freely about Sepphoris. Their hostility is bitterly disguised, but we live with it each day."

The first Zealot pumped his fist into the air. "We must hunt the Romans! Beat them at their own carnival. Who are they to call this land theirs?"

Yeshua pointed to the man. "Thou shall not kill." His voice cut across the crowd. He was angrier than the young scribe had ever seen him. "You go after a Roman man with weapons and hate and you are no better than he is. The Romans want us to fight, so they can remind us of their strength and military mastery. They know fighting better than anyone does. It is the commandment by which they live. We must beat them with the commandment by which *we* live."

The crowd was quiet now. The Zealot's black eyes cut through to Yeshua.

Yeshua met his stare.

"A Roman with killing on his mind will not step back if I start reciting Mosaic Law," the Zealot replied. "He would probably spit in my face and then tear my arms off for pleasure."

"It is not an easy task, to spread love and humanity to cultures other than our own. In some situations, you will be faced with one whose heart has been bagged by hatred and evil." Yeshua rolled back his sleeves, his forehead damp with sweat. "From this person with a stone heart, you must turn away. To fight is simply to give in to what he wants."

"You think they would learn some kind of lesson from a group of shabby strangers who refuse to fight?" the Zealot snarled. "I came here today to see a man, a man of action." With that, the Zealots swiftly rose and left, growling about *justice* and *action*.

Yeshua took a deep breath and continued to speak.

By the time he had finished his oration, a feeling of peace washed over the young scribe, and he was pleased that Yeshua had not uttered any blasphemy against the Temple. That feeling of serenity had become standard after Yeshua's talks. He'd felt it before when, as a child, his father told him stories. The young scribe again began to doubt that Yeshua was any kind of threat, as the temple priests had led him to believe. He still appeared peace loving and nonviolent, a man who simply wanted to live according to a more enlightened understanding of the laws.

Of course, this still could be a front, a way to strengthen the bonds between him and his people. When a group had bonded as tightly as this one, it could become powerful, especially as it grew in numbers. They could become quite capable of causing havoc in Jerusalem and beyond. Was the young scribe witnessing the beginning of what one day would be referred to as an uprising?

Back at the campsite, the young scribe took a scroll from his bag and began to unroll it, unaware that a light-of-foot, young woman had danced up behind him.

She tapped him on the shoulder.

The young scribe half-turned his head, full attention on his scroll. "Yes?"

"You read and write. I remember." Her chin grazed his shoulder, as she bent over him to peek at the scroll.

The young scribe spun around, irritated. "Watch what you're doing." Then, a moment passed as he took in her blue eyes and quirky one-sided smile. "We've met before."

"Yes, in the grove. About two years ago?"

"Rebecca."

"Yes, you remembered."

"So, you found your preacher."

"Oh, yes, I have." Then, with wide eyes and great enthusi-asm, she said, "Do show me your instruments." She locked her fingers together behind her back and bent over, peering into his bag.

The young scribe pulled his pen from his bag. Unsure of what she might do next, he held on tight.

She pressed her finger lightly against the point. "It is like a needle." She giggled. "Oh, and now I will have a black finger, like so many of your kind. She giggled again. "Who are you? Or I should have said, what's your name?"

He fumbled with his belt. "Uh, they call me 'Young Scribe.'"

"That's not a name. That's a vocation."

"It's a profession."

"Why are you so snappish?"

The young scribe rubbed his hands over his face. "Okay, let's start again. I am happy to show you my, um, tools, my writing tools."

Rebecca clapped her hands, took a bouncy step, and sat down.

The young scribe chuckled. Then, keeping his appreciative eye on that remarkable upturned lip, he removed his inkwell from its canvas pouch. "The ink has to be kept close to my body in an upright position and sealed with wax or else it will leak."

"It's lovely indeed!" she proclaimed. "What is this ink?"

"Lampblack and gum. You learn how to mix the correct amounts of each with water to create ink. It just takes practice."

A man passed by them then and said, "Show and tell? Is that another item for the treasury?"

"Judas, this is the young scribe that Yeshua talked about back at Peter's. These are his tools."

"Oh, pardon me. I thought that perhaps they were new valuables to add to our funds. A scribe, no less, a man of high breeding. Well, well. Yes, I remember now. Yeshua said he hoped you were joining us," he muttered, walking away.

"Don't mind him. Judas Iscariot is the keeper of the treasury," Rebecca said. "Often, when new people join us, they give us some of their belongings. We use them to buy food and supplies so Yeshua can continue his teaching."

The young scribe was surprised. He did not realize preaching could be so profitable.

"Will you eat with me tonight?"

The young scribe could see that Rebecca's startling blue eyes danced as well as her feet. "Yes, of course."

"I have something to ask you."

CHAPTER THIRTY-FOUR

Tyre AD *32*

AFTER ANOTHER FOOT JOURNEY ALONG DUSTY, WINDING ROADS, they entered the gates of Tyre. The exuberance of the villagers upon their arrival, the light in the children's faces, the cheers, tears, and the glorious smell of flowers lining the gates created a joy that one could only describe as contagious. The young scribe could not recall a finer day.

They found themselves in a huge coastal marketplace. Walking along the harbor entrance, they saw the Romans' great grain freighters with their square sails. Two posts out in the water functioned as the gateway to the port for traveling ships. Strong, scantily dressed men unloaded goods from the ships. On this day, the stevedores were discharging a large Roman ship carrying wine in long, heavy, clay jars, each with a sharply pointed base. Yeshua stopped and watched while they carried the *amphorae* one-by-one to the land workers who stuck the acicular tips into the sand.

People of various ethnicities mixed with Romans to fill the busy streets of the marketplace. Clothing shops displayed Tyre's celebrated, purple-dyed garments. One entire street housed tailors creating clothing from endless yards of fine fabric. As they walked past, the sight of fluffy, white cotton, a fabric made in India that was hanging from ropes, awed the young scribe.

The town boasted restaurants with private dining rooms as well as counters that faced the street, and snack shops offering tempting, hot, fast foods. The young scribe savored the aroma of smoked meat and cooked vegetables.

The scents in the marketplace, of frankincense and myrrh, made the young scribe homesick for Jerusalem, where balm mixed with oil made for a popular perfume. He longed for more money to purchase a few things for himself: a dish of artichoke hearts, a mantle made of fine, purple silk, a tunic made of the soft, white cotton he'd just viewed. He dreamed again of the comfort of his own home, of writing at his own desk. He was warming to the notion of a bride.

Yeshua walked through the throng of trading and selling with the relaxed grace of a learned man. People turned to look at him, impressed by his height, his beauty. He returned their curious glances with smiles and greetings. The young scribe could see people taken by this man whom many called *master*.

TYRE—*SHILISHI 8 Tammuz*

At first, only a few came to hear Yeshua's stories and teachings. Now, a great many come each day. They present him with sick babies, half crippled men, and women with bodies so bent their torsos look like tree branches. They stand in line, happy to greet the new miracle man with the magic hands. Naturally, Yeshua cannot cure everyone but, so strong is their belief in him, no one is angered. Thus far, he has saved a baby, an old woman, a coughing child. Saved them, for he recognized their needs instantly and instructed Mary to their aid. So, these people turn away, with a certain understanding, believing his God must have a plan for who can be saved and who cannot. And they return, for they think, at a later day, God's plan may change.

THE YOUNG SCRIBE watched as Yeshua became a beloved man in Tyre. By the time the third Sabbath arrived, Assyrians and Jews, normally foes, sat together to hear him speak. Nobody knew quite what magic had made it so, but here they were, smiling and nodding to each other. They brought Yeshua gifts, but he refused them. He accepted only food, and often asked the disciples to give it to the poor.

During their stay, new people joined Yeshua's new sect. The young scribe logged more names than usual each day. He did not know how many would leave their town when Yeshua decided to move on, but he could not help feeling excited by the influx of fresh faces. As Yeshua had said, even the smallest change is significant.

WORD HAD SPREAD of the Zealot's continuing cries for an uprising. Unfortunately, Yeshua's response to the angry radical had not traveled with him. The Romans responded, however, with increased presence around Yeshua, which frightened the young scribe. Whenever the Romans stopped by their campground, by their bearing, they reminded the followers of their threat. Yeshua paid them no mind, but the young scribe's heart drummed whenever he saw them.

. . .

ON THE EVE of their fifth Sabbath, Yeshua decided his work was finished. He announced they would be moving on. Judas would travel into town to purchase food supplies and more water jugs. It seemed Yeshua had softened his "God will provide" stance to allow for the purchase of food. For that, the young scribe was grateful.

THE YOUNG SCRIBE and Rebecca retired to their favorite stretch of dried grass for her reading lesson after that, the last she would have in Tyre. Rebecca had begged him to teach her to read. After much arguing, and a nudge from Yeshua, he relented. He used the scroll he wrote on each day to show her the characters and what they denoted.

"Find 'Capernaum,'" he said.

He could feel her breath on the back of his neck as she leaned down to look at the scroll.

"You are learning fast, dear Rebecca. It is a good thing we have recently gained so many new members or else I fear you would be finished before we reach Sidon. And then, what would we do?"

She fished a heavy strand of hair from her lips. Her thick hair always seemed to sneak out of her head covering and find its way into her mouth. "Then I suppose we would have to teach me how to write."

He shook his head and smiled, for he had no response to such a mad idea. Then, he pointed to the scroll. "Find 'Andrew.'"

She leaned over the material, eyes traveling across the ink-stained characters. She whispered to herself while scanning through the names until her hand rested beside *Andrew*. She smiled proudly.

"You are too quick with this." The young scribe pointed to the next name.

She struggled a bit, her voice shy.

He studied her, awed by her flushed cheeks, sweet lips, and the stray strands of her wispy, black hair. Her long, thin fingers crawled down the calfskin as she read off the names. Her skin was as vibrant and radiant as a child's. For the first time, he noticed how long her neck was. He imagined himself pressing his lips there and taking in her scent.

"Hey, you are not listening. Am I boring you?"

"You are not boring." He tapped her nose, then immediately felt horrified for doing so.

"How old are you?"

"Just turned twenty-two."

"I am seventeen, you know, older than most girls when they are brides. My parents matched me with eight boys from Cana, but I refused them. The last one was Joseph. He was the best, honest and all, but I did not want him. Nevertheless, I could not protest. If I refused him, my parents would have forced me to marry someone else. And that person could have been a sight worse than Joseph."

"What did you do?"

"I ran away. It was lucky for me that Yeshua came through town. I went down to the river to hear him speak and decided right then that I was leaving with him. I cannot say that my motive was pure."

This sounds familiar, the scribe thought.

"Anyway, my father never would have let me go, so I had to figure out the best time to get away."

"How did you do it?"

"The fortunes were with me. Yeshua and his group were leaving before dawn, so I could get to the campsite without anyone noticing. The moon was a sliver, thankfully, and I just sneaked out of the house and ran. A couple of torches were my beacon. So, here I am, a follower of Yeshua. I could never go back. At first, I was afraid *Abba* would come after me, but I do not worry about that anymore. When you came, I was surprised you did not know me."

"You've changed over two years. I guess if I had seen your eyes ... well, they are quite unforgettable. But my mind was elsewhere, I have to say."

She shrugged. "I am surprised you are not married. I suppose that is the choice of pursuing an education. You can wait. I could not wait, but I wanted to. I think you are lucky."

"I feel I am ready to marry now."

She studied him for a moment, her chin resting on her hand. "You probably are." She started to laugh. "But for the wrong reasons. Oh, look at you blush!" She patted his hand. "You should not be ashamed."

"We should not talk about this. You embarrass me."

"Why should we not talk of this? So silly how we all keep quiet about it." With her lopsided smile in place, she pressed her finger to his lips. "You should not be embarrassed." She rose, her bemused eyes fixed on his. Then, she scampered away.

CHAPTER THIRTY-FIVE

Tyre AD 32

DESPITE ALL HIS MISGIVINGS, QUESTIONS, AND DOUBTS, tomorrow would likely prove to be a remarkably interesting day, for Yeshua was to recognize the young scribe as a follower.

Chamishi 9 Tammuz

Yeshua is kind and honest, a man of higher morals and skills. He is a man the Sadducees should seek out, not fear. Yet it is not my place to instruct the Sadducees. I realize he could be a good man who simply hopes to create a new Kingdom of God, or a dangerous man who seeks to overthrow the Sadducees and create a revolt against the Romans in Jerusalem.

It is with these trepidations that I step toward this ritual today with a stone in my heart. I must admit that I am not pleased to forsake my background and education by vowing allegiance to Yeshua.

On the other hand, he is a Jew. His beliefs are rooted in Jewish law and tradition, even if he teaches a unique way. Therefore, by taking his vows, I am not completely turning away from my own spiritual leaders. Yet, they would not be pleased if they knew what I was about to do today. If I do not allow the hand of Yeshua to baptize me, the disciples, even the chosen twelve, will see me as the impostor I feel I am.

Shishi 10 Tammuz

Have I changed? I do feel strangely different, as if my head is clearer and my eyes see better. He spoke so gently and yet with such conviction. Suddenly, it was not hard to believe him. I almost thought the sky had opened above me. Then I realized it was a natural phenomenon, just a mix of chilly water and warm sun in my eyes.

After the baptism, I began to understand the message Yeshua has repeated more than once: "The Romans and the Jewish order will one day disappear, but the people will survive." The Jewish order will end?

Though Yeshua tells us about an uprising, the big question is when will all of this take place? Does he believe the Jewish order will dissipate slowly or does he expect a quick, catastrophic event, a rebellion? Again, he implied the imminent end of the Roman Empire. Does he think the two societies will cancel each other out?

What is perhaps more important is what he leads these people to believe. Is he telling them, through quiet but relent-

167

less words, that he is their only salvation? Is he influencing them to believe that their old way of life will vanish? So far, his discourse at my baptism is the first time I have heard these puzzling words.

I hope to see Yeshua alone again, so I can simply ask him. Now that I have allowed him to baptize me, I think he trusts me more.

Everyone is ready to move on. I best get to my feet.

As the young scribe closed his scroll, he felt Yeshua look over his shoulder. He put down his pen, turned, and held his gaze.

Yeshua sat beside him on the stone bench. "There isn't much time."

"I am ready."

"No, not that."

Yeshua gave a wave to the followers, all assembled, ready to go. Then, he turned back to the young scribe. "I know that you're weary. But you are so close. Do not deny your heart further, for, as you can see, it is already betraying your mind. And it is with our hearts that we forge through this life, doing God's work."

Then Yeshua put his hand on the young scribe's cheek.

Though he understood not what Yeshua was saying, the young scribe's eyes misted at his warm, soothing touch.

"Thank you, Scribe, my champion, for writing my words."

He should have been the one thanking Yeshua, for he did not deserve his praises. But the lump in his throat prevented him from speaking. He was a man who had his pride, after all.

As Yeshua joined the others, he bowed his head in thought, and that is when he saw it.

His allegiance to Yeshua was literally written all over his scroll. His heart had succumbed though his mind was not yet ready.

The scribe—no longer *Young Scribe,* he noted—stared at his scroll, in awe of Yeshua's power.

Yeshua is right. This is where I am supposed to be.

CHAPTER THIRTY-SIX

Saint-Denis
Present Day

AT 11:55 PM ON THE NOSE, PHILIPPE EXITED HIS QUARTERS AND found his way in the half-lit hallway through to the sacristy, where Gabriella awaited him.

"Follow me and be quiet," she said.

She led him through a doorway into the church. In the shadows of a dark corner, she motioned him to stop while she looked around.

Philippe studied Gabriella, puzzled.

She indicated with a look for him to be patient.

In moments, Father Fullier appeared carrying a small flashlight. He crept toward the altar under which the martyr Dagobert was buried. A flutter interrupted the stillness, as a dark shadow swooped down from overhead. "Damned pigeons," he muttered, "crapping up the place." His next move was no surprise to Gabriella. He bent down behind the altar and pushed a center marble stone, which opened as a hidden door and crawled through. The door shut behind him.

Gabriella whispered to Philippe. "Always in the middle of the night. My uncle comes down here once a month, on the first Tuesday, and leaves with his box of secrets. Then, early Wednesday morning, he drives to *Village-sur-Colline* to visit his best friend, Father Allard. They grew up together there. He won't be back until Thursday evening. He doesn't know I know about this."

A minute later, a grinding sound warned them the door was reopening. Philippe and Gabriella shrank back, holding still. Father Fullier emerged carrying a small box. He closed the hidden door behind him and left the sanctuary.

In that moment, Philippe knew where all those fenced coins were coming from. He tried to hold his exhilaration in check. "I would love to go down there."

"Ah, I don't know," Gabriella said. "Maybe it's not a good idea."

"Why not? I'm studying the cathedral, all of it."

"It's my uncle's secret, though."

"We won't disturb anything. We'll just look."

Gabby cocked her head. "What are you, anyway, some kind of spy?"

"You got me." As Philippe gazed into Gabriella's gray-blue eyes to distract from the deceit, a distant squeak of the floorboards caused them both to look up sharply. "What's that?"

"I don't know."

"Shh." They backed farther into the shadows.

They watched as two priests entered from the street into a side door and beelined toward the altar.

Something was off. Philippe felt it.

They started pawing everything all around the area in search of ... something.

Then one of them smashed the display case with an elbow,

causing a muted sound of shattering glass to tinkle throughout the church.

"What are you doing?" the other so-called priest asked.

Philippe heard the question uttered in Italian. He wondered the same thing.

Then, the man who shattered the case, reached in, grabbed a chalice, and flung it onto the floor.

That's when Philippe charged from the shadows, leaped over one pew and then another into the center aisle, and raced toward the altar.

Philippe had neither fear nor doubt about his ability to take these two down. He had overseen much more than this for Mossad.

On seeing him, the thieves sprinted for the side door from which they'd entered. The one who'd done the vandalizing was gone in a flash, but his counterpart was slower at the draw, and Philippe grabbed a fistful of cassock and yanked him back.

And it was on.

Gabriella, frozen in place, watched from the wings as Philippe spun the guy around and knocked him to his knees with a left jab, right crossover combo. She knew real fighting when she saw it. She and Uncle Claude secretly enjoyed a good, televised match from time to time.

The thief got up and lunged at Philippe, tackling him. They hit the floor and rolled around, tearing at each other.

That's all it took for Gabriella to burst out of her hiding place and rush forward. Once she got her wits about her, she shouted, "J'appelle la police!"

That distracted Philippe and the thief enough that they broke free of each other.

Philippe yelled, "Gabby, *Pas de police.*"

The thief, amazed at the sight of someone else in the midst of things, muttered, "I didn't sign up for all this." Then, realizing he was free, he heaved himself toward the open side door and barreled through it.

PHILIPPE WAS on his feet heading toward Gabriella. Police interference would disrupt everything, and the team would have to abort their mission. This could not happen. "Gabby, please, let's sit down for a moment and regroup."

"Oh, *mon Dieu*, you're bleeding."

Philippe wiped his nose on his sleeve. "I'll be fine. It's nothing."

"We need to call. Time is of the essence here, Paschal."

"It would be, ordinarily," Philippe responded, sitting. "But not now."

"No? Why not?"

"They're not coming back. Sit down, let's talk about this."

"Fine. I'm waiting," she said, crossing her arms and refusing to sit beside him. "And, please, can you explain that Tyson Fury move? A bit out of character for a student studying churches."

Philippe thought. Which way to go? To reveal a Mossad plan was to betray the team, something he had never done. And it could land him in legal trouble. Yigael would lose his mind, and temper, if his mission went up in smoke.

"The thieves have been scared off and won't return tonight," he began. "If we notify the police, first of all, your uncle will be alerted that you were in the church spying on him."

"Hmm." Gabriella bit the corner of her lip.

"And what difference will it make if the police come now or tomorrow?" Someone will discover the broken glass and the chalice at some point, and they'll report it then. And we—you —don't have to be a part of it."

"What's the second thing?"

"What?"

"You said 'first of all,' implying you have a second thing."

"Right." *What would Yigael do?* Philippe didn't have much choice. "Gabby, sit, please."

She sat.

"What I'm doing here is not all fun and games, even though it might seem like it. All flirting aside—I'm serious—we are searching for an ancient Jewish scroll that has been lost for 2,000 years. This scroll could rewrite religious history, and we believe it's in this cathedral. We've traced it from first-century Jerusalem to, well, here." Philippe hoped his solemn expression would convince Gabby to cooperate.

"And who are you?"

"Well, you're right. I'm a spy. We all are. My name is Philippe Gaston."

"And you think this thing you're after is down there?" she said, pointing to where Father Fullier disappeared through the hidden door.

"We do."

"Well, then, let's go."

Philippe couldn't believe it, but Gabriella had been surprising him since the moment they'd met. He followed her to the altar, then fumbled around on the underside of the marble, looking for the spot that would open the small door.

Gabriella reached down and pressed dead center on the release. The door swung open.

They stooped down and crawled through a short passageway that led to a staircase, which ended at a heavy, wood door. The ancient hinges moaned as Philippe pried it open. He dug his mobile phone from his pocket and pressed the flashlight icon. The light revealed a space about ten by ten with a low arched ceiling.

A vault, Philippe thought. Opulent artifacts, obviously from an ancient world, crammed every possible space. His eyes swept over all the gold and silver transformed into holy vessels and instruments, sacred objects, menorahs, and more.

Gemstones, especially emeralds, embellished many of the priceless articles. *The treasure. Part of it anyway. No pure gold lampstand, no golden menorah.*

Philippe had no time to savor the riches. He turned his attention to shelves lining two walls crammed with old books, documents, and scrolls, some flat and piled high, others rolled and fitted in any which way. Many were dark, almost black, appearing to be unreadable. If he were to find the *STS*, would it tell them anything or would it be useless, destroyed by time and the elements? He noted that the vault was airtight, obviously built to preserve these spoils. Still, anxiety crossed his face. Rummaging through all these ancient texts could take days, time he didn't have.

"How long before this place comes to life?"

"Cleaners arrive at six."

"So, we've got a few hours."

"A few hours? I don't think so. You'd better hurry."

"Look, if you help, we could work faster and get out sooner."

"And just what would I be looking for?"

"Wish I knew. A scroll that looks different from the others. Maybe a seal on it."

She moved to one wall and began thumbing through the dusty, old documents. "*Dégueu*," she said looking at her dirty hands. Yuck.

"I know, what a mess, but it's dirt from roughly 2,000 years ago. Imagine that."

"Still dirt."

The two thumbed through scrolls for the better part of an hour. Gabriella separated out the scrolls she thought Philippe should look at.

"What are you doing?" Philippe asked, eyeing a group of rolled scrolls on the floor.

"Just possibilities."

"Why didn't you say?"

"Well, have a look. They all have seals."

"All of those have seals? You're joking."

"I'm saving my witty nature for when we are well and good out of here. *Mon Dieu.*"

Philippe sank to the floor and started fishing through Gabriella's stash.

She pulled one out of the stack. It looked in quite good condition. "Hey, I might have found something here. I'll shine the light on it."

Gabriella directed the phone's flashlight so Philippe could study it.

While most of the scrolls appeared to be sheepskin, this one was a more durable skin, and lighter in color, more yellow. The scroll was worn at the top edge. Worn-out cords that had encircled the seal had unraveled and hung loosely. However, a simple bowknot still tied the ends together. Excitement stirring, Philippe gently carried the scroll to an ancient bench at the side of the room and laid it down. An embossed gold seal depicted the Jewish Temple. Underneath, an inscription in Hebrew. The first few letters were barely discernible, but Philippe was able to make them out.

"Philippe, *allons!*" Let's go!

"Just a second, hold on."

Philippe unrolled part of the parchment, noting that if this was the *STS*, written so long ago in Yeshua's time, it was in remarkably good condition. Still, he worked slowly so as not to damage it. The first written section was tattered, partially eaten away. As he continued unrolling the parchment, letters appeared. Squinting to make them out, he saw that they matched the style, shape, and form of the Second Temple period. Once he began to unroll the next section, its condition improved. *Someone wanted this scroll to last.*

Watching him, Gabriella asked, "What do you think?"

"I've never seen anything like it, but I'd like to look a bit more, make sure there isn't something else."

"I don't think that's wise."

"Please, Gab, just for a bit. We're okay here for a while."

"Gab? Really? Gabby is as short as I go."

Half an hour later, Philippe was still reviewing it.

Gabriella was pacing. Then she stopped. "Okay, we're done here. Let's go. I mean it. Before something happens."

Philippe didn't object. He was convinced he had "it." At least he hoped so. Wasting no time but taking great care, Philippe rolled the scroll back up and retied it.

"What are you doing?"

"Taking it out."

"Oh no, you're not. You can't do that. *Niente da fare.*" No way.

"It will be safe with me, with us. I promise. Look, I couldn't have done this without you." He wrapped Gabriella in a bear hug. "Thank you," he whispered.

"Let's go," she said, and the two headed out the door, closing it behind them.

They scrambled up the narrow stairway, crawled under the altar, and out the secret marble doorway. Philippe switched off his flashlight, leaving them in a pitch-black sanctuary. They felt their way along the aisle, inching their way toward the side door. Then they nudged it open and fled into the night.

CHAPTER THIRTY-SEVEN

Saint-Denis

PHILIPPE RUSHED BACK TO HIS ROOM, SHOVED THE SCROLL UNDER his bed, and then barged into Jacques' quarters.

"What's going on?" he muttered. "The place on fire?"

"Wake up. We have to talk. Now. Right now."

"Okay, okay." Jacques switched on the small table lamp beside his bed and propped up on his elbow. "What?" He motioned his uninvited guest closer. "What in the world happened to you?"

"I've got the scroll. At least I think so."

"Did you wrestle it from a bear?"

"No, Gabriella found it, just handed it to me."

Philippe relayed the details of his late-night excursion, wrapping with, "And, when I saw Father Fullier come out of there with that box, I knew it had to be the old coins he was fencing, and that we were in the right place. I had to get down there right then. Sorry, I know you're 'clearance.' But because of the thieves, that meant the police, and ...?"

"Philippe, no worries."

After a beat, Philippe asked, "Where's the case?"

"Oh, right. Where's the scroll?"

"Under my bed."

"Ye gods!" Jacques leaped out of bed, jerked open the bottom dresser drawer, and pulled out the round, leather carrying case. Here. See to it. I'll call Yigael." Then, Jacques asked, "What's with the girl? We have to keep her quiet."

"Gabby won't say anything."

"Gabby?"

Philippe looked uncomfortable. "Had to." Without further explanation, he darted out.

Jacques grabbed his phone and called Yigael.

"What?" Yigael said on the first ring.

"You don't even sound groggy." Yigael didn't bother to reply, so Jacques continued. "We have a scroll. It may be *the* scroll. May be nothing. But it could not be left behind. Philippe found a hidden passageway, but was interrupted by thieves, which he ran out of the building."

"Good God, a burglary to boot. Details on that."

When he'd heard all he wanted, Yigael's mind turned to the mayhem local police could cause. "Okay, all of you, out."

"What?"

"Leave. Now. Follow the plan. You know the drill. I'll move Susan and Josh into position."

With the order in place, Jacques was dressed in a jiff and packed.

As their training had demanded, Philippe and Anna-Marie were packed and ready to go. They darted out of the old monastery in less than eight minutes by Jacques' count. Philippe hopped in shotgun, the scroll safely in his grip. Anna-Marie tossed both of their bags into the back seat and slid in.

Jacques fired up the Land Rover and flew down the road away from the church. Halfway to the crossing, Philippe said. "I think you'd better turn around."

"You think?" Jacques said with a smirk, still racing down the road.

"Carol."

"*Merde*," Anna-Marie said. "Why are we always losing Carol?

She jerked forward as Jacques swerved into a U and started back. Then, shooting her a look, he said, "Why didn't you get her up?"

"I thought Phils was getting her up," she replied.

"I've got the scroll!" Philippe barked.

Jacques stopped near their quarters.

Anna-Marie hopped out of the car and sprinted, quietly, thanks to her sneakers. She was fast for such a petite person.

Five long minutes later, she and Carol exploded from the building.

With Philippe now behind the wheel, the Land Rover sped over gravel and out of the churchyard. It was a wonder none of the lights went on and nobody caught them.

CHAPTER THIRTY-EIGHT

The Road to Sidon AD 32

THEY SET OFF IN HIGH SPIRITS, THEIR FAITH IN YESHUA unwavering after so many had come to hear him. Three new people joined the disciples on their hike to Sidon.

The land was pebbly but level, making the walk more comfortable than what they usually faced. A narrow creek paralleled the road. On the first night, they camped near a small waterfall, where the creek water draped over a stairway of rocks. The sound of the water, though soothing, kept the scribe awake. After a while, he gave up, filled his lamp with oil he had purchased in Tyre, and walked down to the lower creek. Seated at the edge, he slipped his feet into the water.

Though the ideal time to write, he couldn't pull his thoughts from Rebecca. How he longed to kiss her, and oh, how she seemed to detect it. He was a smart man of the Temple, and yet weak, unable to control his emotions. Wanting so to rid himself of this inner ordeal, he decided that from now on he must ignore her.

"Always the insomniac."

He looked up to see Rebecca standing next to him in the moonlight. Every instinct told him to say goodnight and disappear, but a strange weight seemed to pin him to the ground. "Insomniac? What is that?"

"It means you cannot sleep. I myself have trouble sleeping." She sat next to him and swung her feet into the creek. Briefly, their legs touched, and he flinched as though burned.

"At least it is nice here." She stretched her arms above her head.

The scribe slumped forward.

They sat in silence for a short while, listening to the water trickle over the rocks.

"Scribe?" Her voice was quiet, almost a whisper.

What would it be like to hold her right now, to slide his arms around her and feel her lips part beneath his? What would it be like to bury his face against her neck and feel her thick hair fall against him?

"Hey, you, there." She was louder this time. "Why do you treat me this way? Sometimes, you look at me as though you hate me. Other times, I try to speak to you, and you do not respond, even with a glance."

Her eyes shimmered in the moonlight, and the scribe looked away, afraid of her power over him. All around, he heard water moving, grass swaying in the wind, people snoring. The night sky was so clear. "You did not do anything. I just think ...." He folded and unfolded his fingers. "I need to speak to you less."

"I do not understand. If I did nothing, why do you not want to speak to me?"

He sighed and shook his head. "I am not ready to talk to you about this yet. Can we leave it at that? I miss my home, miss Jerusalem. I am not sorry I am here. Though, you have to admit

it has not been easy. I long for something familiar, that is all."
He tried not to notice how beautiful she looked without a cover
over her lush hair. "I think I shall go to bed now."

She nodded. "I will be awake for a while. I am sorry."

"You should not be. This is not about anything you did. I
need to spend time alone, writing and recalling what life was
like before. I cannot remember my father's work chair. I miss
the festivities surrounding the betrothal of my sister. I really
must go."

She opened her mouth to say something, then shrugged.
Her skirt lifted and he could see a hint of her bare calves
circling in the water.

"Goodnight," she said, her eyes fixed straight ahead.

He walked away thinking how stupid he must have
sounded. He paused briefly to look back at her. The outline of
her body, backlit by the light of the moon, was almost too much
to bear.

The next day was awkward. He did not speak to her, except
in passing. He was rude and insulting toward everyone else.
Suddenly it was too hot, the water tasted like clay, the vegetables lacked flavor. Even Yeshua's questioning eyes suggested he
could see something was going on. He was afraid Yeshua would
get him to admit something he did not want the man to know.

The followers were traveling slowly because their numbers
had increased. They walked along the Levantine coast, pausing
often to let traveling merchants pass by. It was a wonderful trip,
the high cliffs displaying a startling view of the Mediterranean.
Yeshua wanted the group to arrive in Sidon refreshed and eager
to meet new people. He did not want them to straggle in as they
did the last time, their clothing soiled and their bodies
desperate for water.

At dinner that night, the scribe watched as Rebecca sat next
to James, balancing a bowl on her lap.

John arrived and sat down next to the scribe. "So, you're in love with her."

"I don't want to talk about that. And I'm not."

"Of course, nothing can come of it. Her priority is Yeshua. Which is more than I can say for you."

"What do you mean?"

"I see you, Scribe, angry, distracted, losing sight of your purpose."

"She always wanted to read, but they do not teach women."

"Afraid it might cut into their cooking, sewing, or watering-the-garden time, I suppose. Anyway, you taught her, now find your focus." John took a mouthful of beans. "Sorry to eat while I talk to you, but I am frightfully hungry. But I think it is great, what you are doing."

"What do you think I am doing?"

"Writing all this down so others may read it someday. And then, everyone will remember your name, for not everyone will meet Yeshua in their lifetime. When children are born and they read the story of Yeshua, how he turned water into wine, how he healed countless sick people, you will have been the one to write it. How many other scribes can say as much?"

The scribe sighed. "I really do not think of it that way. I suppose you have a point. I never thought about what happens to these scrolls later."

He smiled. "Then why do you write them? I gave you the idea. You should be right proud of me to have suggested it."

The scribe laughed quietly.

"I finally see a smile, Scribe. It is about time."

He nodded and continued to eat.

"Very nice. You know, she cares for you as well."

The scribe stopped eating and appraised his friend. Realizing how naïve he was, he went back to his food. "We really cannot talk about this ...."

As if she could hear them, Rebecca turned her head just as the scribe twisted in her direction.

He pulled away from her gaze. "What do I do?"

John bit his lip. "You are asking me? How should I know?"

CHAPTER THIRTY-NINE

The Road to Sidon AD 32

THE SCRIBE COULD NOT RECALL HOW MANY DAYS HAD PASSED since they had left Capernaum. The sun rose and set. The days were hot. He had walked and walked. His legs were sore, and his ankles were bleeding again from the leather straps rubbing his skin raw. If he could travel barefoot, he would. *Oh, for Rafi and a new pair of sandals.*

They had been on the road since dawn. Finally, they came upon a narrow, sluggish stream overhung by trees and filled with grass. Nonetheless, they knelt and tried to strain the grass away before gulping large mouthfuls of dirty water from their cupped hands. *A humorous sight,* Scribe thought.

Thaddeus had brought along two of his friends. They were all skilled hunters, thankfully. Scribe thought that Thaddeus was the largest man he had ever seen. He also thought that without their efforts, the followers would starve. The three hunters set out for dinner, while the others rolled out their mats, and Scribe washed the dried blood from his ankles.

Yeshua often sought out Scribe for conversation, which, he

had to acknowledge, was always purposeful, never frivolous. That did not mean that Yeshua could not be humorous. Far from that. That aside, this time, the scribe wanted to speak to Yeshua, though he had not yet come up with a suitable way to approach him. He was thinking on just that, as he moved from the stream to sit in a small patch of shade at the edge of a copse.

"So, Scribe," Yeshua said, standing behind him, squinting against the sun. "You have questions?"

"I do." *How does he always know?* "It is something I cannot figure out, even as I have heard the story many times, about the wedding at Cana. I thought that perhaps you had brought the wine and let everyone think you had created the so-called miracle."

"Scribe, I do not know how to answer this question without it sounding false."

"Tell me something, anything, about that day," the scribe pleaded.

Yeshua sat, leaned back, and let out a tired, lengthy sigh. "My mother knew this young couple, had known Joseph since boyhood. He was named for my father, after all.

"I went to the wedding to meet the family. Peter, Andrew, John, and some others were with me that day. We came without wine, without food, without gifts. We were not the most desirable guests, I would say. Even so, Joseph's mother was so welcoming. But then, she despaired that she could not offer us wine because she had none. She placed a jug in front of me, which she said held only water. She thought the wedding was ruined and feared having no wine would be a bad omen for Joseph and his young bride.

"I felt terrible for her. I stood there for a long time, looking at that jug. I wished so much for it to hold wine. I never looked into it, mind you. I stood there with my hands on it and wished for wine. Eventually, Peter got thirsty, and so we opened it.

"It contained no water. It was wine, by far the richest, most satisfying wine I have ever tasted. The woman and her family claimed I had created a miracle. I have wished for far greater things and have not seen my wishes realized. For all I know, there was wine in that jug right from the very start. I will say this: that jug seemed bottomless, for the stream of wine was endless. It never ran out."

The story seemed unfinished, but the scribe believed him.

EVERY DAY, Scribe prayed that they would reach the next village by day's end. Sometimes they would, but then the respite would last about as long as a stray leaf in low grass. It began to feel as if the wind carried them along. Tyre was now but a mirage in his mind. The reception they had received echoed in his thoughts. He used it to help keep pace when he walked. And his memories, he used those too.

He remembered Gamaliel, his favorite instructor, smiling when he caught him running his finger through the dust of his worktable in the student quarters, creating the Hebrew character for house. He pictured the fine spires of the Temple, appearing to bend behind waves of heat. *Will I ever see those places again?* The scribe visualized his home, his father in his chair reading, his mother baking bread.

And Rebecca .... Sometimes, he rose early so he could watch her sleepy face come alive in the first light of morning. See her kind eyes open and her lopsided smile greet the day. He had stopped teaching her to read Jewish script for the longing of her, afraid desire might overtake him.

Mercifully, his mind stopped spinning as they reached another campsite and found flat land to lay out their mats and listen to Yeshua.

Nearing Sidon—*Rishon 12 Av*

*To look at Yeshua by firelight is to see one unlike any other.
He is a marvel, a man of grace with a face from which you
cannot look away. He is like the greatest artwork, stunning
in his ability to seem perfectly still, and then a statue come to
life. A glow seems to come from within him, as though a ray
of light begins in his feet and surges up through his body. I
think that when early scribes imagined heavenly beings, they
must have envisioned someone like Yeshua.*

*I think Yeshua is a man of God who opposes only cruelty,
dishonesty, and hatred. He does not seek to overthrow
civilian rulers or even the Sanhedrin by twisting the minds of
his followers. I believe he is proclaiming a new world order,
in which people of good regard everyone as sisters and
brothers.*

*So, once again, I am confused. When I hear him speak other
than the Law, do I follow my heart, knowing this man is
perhaps what the world needs most at this time? Or do I
determine to write to the priests of such?*

*The voices from Jerusalem seem far away from me tonight,
that much I know. I am pleased to be here and eager for more
of his word.*

The following day, they reached Sidon. Like Tyre, it was one
large center for trade. Goods traveled north to Antioch in
Assyria, then to Rome and other parts of the Empire, while
cloth came from India, China, Asia Minor, and Gaul where the
local shops weaved it into clothing. Garments were Sidon's

main export, followed by grain, olive oil, plums, and balm. It also received fancy foods like wine from Italy, carrots, and pickled meats from Gaul. Sidon was a beautiful Phoenician city with strong Roman influences and a spectacular view of the Mediterranean.

An invitation had gone out for Yeshua, the chosen twelve, and Mary to stay with a host family while the rest would camp in a village to the north of Sidon. Yeshua invited Scribe to stay at the house. Ordinarily, the scribe preferred to sleep outside with the others, but not this time. He wanted distance between Rebecca and himself.

The days passed in a blur. Scribe watched stone-faced as Yeshua tended to the townspeople, caring for everything from snakebites to stomach trouble. Melancholy over Rebecca stirred in him like water bubbling over a pot. He refused to speak to her but always knew where she was.

That night, nestled down in his straw mat, asleep as were the others, he was awakened by the tickle of a large, black bug crawling up his leg. He sat up to flick it off, then eased back down against the hard slab of mud floor. Pulling his tunic to his chin, he heard someone whisper.

"Scribe, come."

Scribe recognized the voice. He slid off his mat and followed Yeshua into the courtyard. They took seats on a stone bench.

"She is quite a lovely woman. And highly intelligent."

So, he knows.

"Scribe, I understand your feelings. Believe me, I do."

"You want to talk to me about Rebecca?"

"It's either that or watch you mope about, which is quite unpleasant. You can be a miserable, old wretch, you know that?" His dazzling smile gave way to a curdled chuckle.

"It is just so hard to be with her here and not be with her."

"Well, you cannot ask her to leave. She has a right to be

here, just as you do, as I do for that matter. I wonder if she will ever return to her husband."

"Her ... *what?* What do you mean?"

"Yes." Yeshua slapped him on the back. "Oh, didn't you know? Yes, she is married."

"But she never said." He gulped. "She never ...."

"Did she never say? Or did you not hear?"

"I feel she has betrayed me, dishonored me."

"Rebecca did not want to marry. She made this clear to her parents, and Joseph's parents. That was why his mother felt the loss of wine to be a sign the marriage would not last."

"That was Rebecca's wedding?"

"Yes."

"Joseph is as fine a man as any. However, Rebecca wanted a life of the mind, of study, of knowledge."

"So, I am right not to speak to her."

"I do not see that as a solution. She is leading a life like that of any man who studies the Torah. It is unfortunate this life is not available to her and so many like her."

"Still, I think I should stay away from her."

"I think you shall be over this soon enough. I think that no one can drag you away from your commitment to God."

Scribe bristled at Yeshua's opinion, but he kept quiet.

Yeshua clapped Scribe's thigh with the back of his hand, rose, and moved back inside.

Scribe stayed out. *I do not see Rebecca coming between me and my commitment to God. I do not have the commitment to God shared by Yeshua, John, and probably a good many others. I am weary of this traveling, although it is quite pleasant here in Sidon. I am tired of walking through the streets and listening to Yeshua talk to people who do not care about the Kingdom of God. These people are busy trading, exchanging coins, buying and selling. I dream of the comfort of a home, my own home, writing at my own desk, and the smells of my wife's cooking perfuming the house.*

As he lingered outside on the balmy night, his attention shifted to all he had neglected after Rebecca came into his life. He looked up at the stars, not quite believing he had ignored them for so long. What would his teachers say about that? They had trained him in the science of astronomy and expected him carry out his duty to read the stars and carry the news of impending holidays to Jewish citizens.

Earlier that night, before going inside to sleep, Scribe overheard villagers, who lived near their campground, discuss the onset of the date harvest at the end of the month of *Av*. The time was passing so quickly. He had left home early in the month of *Lyyar*, the first month of the dry season, and now, a year had passed since he had seen his family. The hottest month of the summer, *Elul*, was fast approaching. At the end of *Elul*, the rainy season would begin.

There was talk among followers of traveling backward toward Gush Halav, Capernaum, and finally Nazareth. Yeshua considered resting at home in the height of the rainy season before embarking on trips next spring. Scribe thought it a fine idea, but it unnerved the disciples who had left home under questionable circumstances and now knew no home other than the campgrounds they shared. It was only talk, but Scribe hoped Yeshua would decide favorably.

CHAPTER FORTY

Sidon AD 32
Chamishi 9 Av

Yeshua keeps quieter here, carefully choosing those with whom he speaks. He is not oblivious to the Roman threat. Mostly, he reaches the hearts of others through his Sabbath services. I have noticed steady growth in the number of those who attend. By opening his mind to the troubles of so many, he allows little time for himself.

FROM A SMALL, ROCKY RIDGE A DISTANCE WEST OF THE HARBOR entrance, Scribe found the perfect place to cool off and watch the stevedores unload. The ridge was just off the road from the northern village into Sidon. He had come across it one day, quite by accident, as he looked for a hidden place to relieve himself. Now, here he was. It was a tranquil place with the soft smell of the sea at his cheeks.

Mesmerized by the view, he barely noticed when Yeshua scaled around the ridge. Holding onto scraggly branches, he inched his way toward the scribe.

"Well, hello. Strange, I knew this place was so alluring someone else would find it."

Scribe smiled politely. He was not in the mood for company.

"It is some distance from the path," Yeshua said, sliding down next to Scribe.

"I suspect we are not the only ones who know of this." Scribe pointed to the stevedores. "Certainly, those men can see us over here and may come here to rest after work."

Yeshua shook his head. "I think not. They work until sundown. This is not the sort of ledge one might want to visit at nightfall."

Yeshua and Scribe looked down. Below them were wet crescents of rock, regularly pounded by the sea. Even though they were not unduly high up, to fall upon these rocks would be deadly.

Scribe noticed the waves swelling, smashing the rocks with more urgency. "When the waves hit like that, it is a sign that a boat is approaching."

"Or leaving," Yeshua said.

"No. When a ship leaves, the waves pull away from the rocks. It is almost lonely, to see the rocks with nothing around them."

"Are you leaving?" A large ship began to pull into the harbor. The ship's sails puckered and breathed as it moved.

"What a strange thing to say, Yeshua. I fear I do not understand."

"Do you miss Jerusalem, your life with the Temple as an employee of the Sadducees?"

The ship was inching closer, its sails now wider, heavier.

"I miss Jerusalem. I do like being in a city with so much activity, the scents, the open restaurants, my fine clothing, especially my private room. I simply miss the structure of my old life."

Yeshua gestured to the waves slamming against the rocks as the ship approached them. "They sound angry."

Scribe nodded. "I wonder if they are, you know, being invaded like this. Perhaps the sea does not like the Romans any more than we do."

"Do you wish to return to Jerusalem?"

Scribe looked at the waves for a long time. "I always thought I would work there, marry there, and eventually live in quite a grand style. A few slaves, some luxurious, silk pillows, and fine food. A cool place to write. Plenty of water. Musicians, should I choose to pay them."

Yeshua did not answer.

The ship waited for a smaller ship to pull out before it could position itself along the dock.

"I do not think I could have slaves now, Yeshua. My father always did have poor Jewish slaves. I never thought much of it. It was the way things were."

Yeshua sighed. "Slavery is part of the structure of our culture. I do not expect it to disappear any time soon. We are all practically slaves under the Romans, except for those few in Jerusalem, those few higher-ups you longed to join."

"I am different now. That is who I was, who I wanted to be. I cannot be that now."

The smaller ship pulled away. The water stretched and thinned over the rocks and was eventually sucked into the vortex of the sea.

"I see what you mean about the waves," Yeshua said. "You have spent some time here."

"You have changed me. I no longer want wealth, not if it comes at a poor slave's expense. I wish for a simpler life. I think I am sick for home. For my family, for the roof I slept on. The certainty I met each day. Everything is uncertain now, though not without its entertainment."

"I expect we shall travel to a few more towns as we make

our way back toward southern Galilee. Then all are welcome to return to their homes for a bit. I plan to. I miss my family, though I am not received well in Nazareth."

"Why is that?"

The large ship, probably a grain freighter, was now docking. The stevedores stood by to unload its cargo.

"I do not know, exactly. I think the people in town cared very much for my father and were angered I did not choose to continue his business. I was quite a good stonecutter, you know, carpentry too. It was disrespectful to my father not to take his role. He was truly a great man, in a rather quiet way. My brother has honored him by continuing his carpentry." Yeshua relaxed and leaned against the rock ledge.

"I had something else I had to do. I did not choose this. I have no plan, as you can see. I only know I must keep going. I must go on and show a new world is before us."

"I do not know why I am drawn here either. I only know I must be here, with you."

Yeshua patted Scribe's hand. "I am glad I have not lost you, Scribe."

As the stevedores began to unload huge sacks, heavy with grain, Scribe forced a smile.

―――――――

IT HAPPENED SIMPLY ENOUGH AND, in one moment, the antagonism between Scribe and Rebecca vanished.

After supper that evening, Yeshua and the others went into town, leaving Scribe to stay outside and camp for the night. As he fired up his lantern, Rebecca's face popped out of the darkness.

"Oh. You did not go with the others?"

Seeing no need to respond to the obvious, she sat down and curled her legs under her shawl.

Sitting beside her, watching the stars dissolve into being, Scribe could not ask for more.

They talked long into the night.

"I was a mischievous kid. And, here I am, running off without my husband, to travel like a group of criminals fearing capture."

"You seem to have left out some, er, details about leaving your home that day," Scribe said coyly. "Do you want to fill me in?"

She wiggled around to face him. "I might as well. You see, it was after the celebration of my marriage vows when everyone had danced and drunk too much. In the case of my new husband, he was flopped over our marriage bed, dead to the world all night. So, just before dawn, I left. That's it." She folded her arms into the shawl. "I do miss my family."

"I miss my family as well."

"So you said. Is that why you have been so beastly?"

Ignoring her, he said, "Oh, look at the stars, Rebecca, the sky is changing above us. We have but one more month of summer left."

As with anything, she was an avid pupil, eager to learn about the stars. He introduced her to the constellations and showed how their shapes revealed what time of year it was.

"It's so amazing to think of all those gods worshipped by the mighty Greeks, and now the Romans. How could they keep track of it all? I have difficulty remembering all that is important in the Torah." Rebecca touched the design on the scribe's satchel, the design his grandmother made.

Scribe could not imagine a happier night, how it felt to be near her, to listen to her, to see her chest heave as she took a breath. He did not know he could become this enchanted by a woman. He realized now how powerful it was, how useless it was to will it away. Instead, he knew he must learn to live with it. By any standard, he saw that it was far easier to be with her than away from her.

With that, a pair of thick, meaty hands came down hard on Rebecca's shoulders.

CHAPTER FORTY-ONE

Paris
Present Day

JUST SHY OF 2:30 AM ON WEDNESDAY, THE TEAM OF FOUR arrived at *Paris-Gare-de-Lyon* and split up. Jacques and Philippe headed into the station. Anna-Marie and Carol hopped up front to return the Land Rover to the rental agency and then head to their respective flats.

AT 3:00 AM, the high-speed night train rocketed out of Paris with Jacques and Philippe on board. They had purchased second-class *couchette* cabins in hopes of catching some sleep. Jacques called Yigael to inform him they would arrive in Turin in a little more than five hours.

ABOUT THE SAME time in Jerusalem, from the passenger seat of Josh's Jeep, Susan sent her neighbor a text reminding her to check on Black Boni and Simba, her kittens, in her absence. Then she stared at her screen, suspended in time, waiting on a confirmation.

On hearing the *ping* and seeing her look of satisfaction, Josh headed out of her complex for Tel Aviv, where they would board a jet for Turin.

AROUND 4:00 AM, in the quiet of the night, in a typical Paris neighborhood, as Carol opened the passenger door of Anna-Marie's gris Peugeot 308 Gti to head up to her flat, she said, "I think it's weird he tossed the chalice."

"*Pardon*?" Anna-Marie asked, the comment jarring her out of autopilot.

"Philippe said thieves broke into the display case and tossed a chalice onto the floor."

"*Oui*. And?"

"They clearly weren't after the chalice if you catch my drift. They tossed it. They left it." On that note, she hopped out with a "*bonsoir!*" slammed the door, and left Anna-Marie alone with her thoughts.

AT 8:00 AM, Josh and Susan landed in Turin and de-boarded. Two local Mossad agents met them and handed over train tickets and a shopping bag, which contained two hats.

FORTY MINUTES LATER, Jacques and Philippe, who had the leather cylinder tucked snugly under an arm, stepped off the train in search of two "tourists," one in a red baseball cap, the other in a floppy, straw-colored sunbonnet. Easy to spot, just a train car away.

Nobody in the busy Italian railway station paid a bit of

attention as the four grouped together for what appeared to be a chance encounter. Philippe released the container into their care without notice. Susan slid it with care into her tote and fastened the top with a kiss lock. Then she frowned at the two tall men. *They were carrying this thing around for all the world to see.* She was about to speak her mind but thought better of it. After all, she was new to this sort of high-stakes, interactive, microfiche-free lifestyle.

As Jacques and Philippe left to catch a return trip to Paris, Jacques phoned Yigael to tell him the handoff was a success. Meanwhile, Josh and Susan headed for Platform 332B to catch the train that would take them from Turin to Rome.

Once the pair found seats in their compartment and secured the scroll between them, they relaxed for the first time in hours. As the train rumbled to life and accelerated out of the station, Josh said, "We should stay there after."

"What?" Susan asked.

"Stay in Rome, see some sites, go to dinner, grab a hotel if the mood strikes."

Susan gave him a strange look.

"You said you haven't done any traveling. And your cats are fine."

"How would you know?"

"They're cats."

Susan scrutinized Josh, then, and with an edge, asked, "Do you have any pets, Josh?"

Josh shrugged, better not to respond, he figured. On the inside, however, he had a gleam of hope. She had not said "no."

After taking awkward silence to new heights, the four-hour trip came to a halt in Rome. The mission was to get the scroll to "one of the world's top archaeologists" by noon, who, they were told, would be waiting in Yigael's Rome office. They were over an hour ahead of schedule.

Josh hailed a cab.

Just as they made their way into the San Lorenzo district and rounded a corner onto Yigael's street, Josh spotted the man himself staring down from his second-floor suite. Then he spotted two of Yigael's guys standing outside: Abba and Nicolo. He made eye contact but didn't even nod, as he didn't want to make Susan more uneasy than she already was.

When Josh and Susan reached his office, the door opened as if by magic.

"Let me have it," was Yigael's greeting.

"Seriously?" Josh said. "Not even a hello? I think we've been in three countries since this morning."

"Two," Yigael shot back.

A natural smile, serving as a hello, sprang from under the brim of Susan's straw hat. She directed it at the tall, striking, thirty-something woman dressed in a fitted, black suit who stood behind Yigael like a female James Bond.

Valentina nodded a hello back.

Susan scanned her own attire—a white blouse, jeans, and loafers—and her smile dissolved into thin air. Why hadn't she thought this secret agent thing through more thoroughly?

Yigael would not have missed being the first to see what could turn out to be the *Secret Temple Scroll* if his life depended on it. He had left his apartment for Tel Aviv in high spirits, catching the earliest flight, first class, to Rome.

He stuck out his hand.

Josh handed him the cylinder. "Hello, Valentina."

"Hi, Josh."

"Come in. A coffee?" Yigael asked.

Josh proceeded to step into the office when Susan hooked a hand around his wrist and blurted, "Thanks, but we have, um, we're running late."

Josh froze. *Whoa. I didn't expect that.*

The reality of it all setting in, Susan was not comfortable

with the idea of coffee and small talk at this juncture in her new career.

Josh took a half-step back.

"Okay then, see you in Jerusalem." Their departure did not disappoint Yigael. Nothing personal but he had a scroll to see about.

CHAPTER FORTY-TWO

Quartiere San Lorenzo, Rome

VALENTINA AND YIGAEL LEANED OVER THE TABLE, STARING AT THE leather case. Yigael had waited his whole career for this moment. He could hardly believe it was real. In fact, he hadn't expected it to be happening this soon, but he'd learned that it was best not to question the ways of the world, for she hardly ever answered.

Valentina imagined that the contents of this scroll could be the puffer she and Erika needed to revive their careers. She prayed by night and hoped by day that a miracle would reveal itself. Could this be it?

The suspense was proving intolerable. Yigael had just opened his mouth to urge Valentina to open it when the door flew open.

"Well, it isn't going to open itself," Erika said. "What are you two waiting for?"

"Very funny, blondie."

"Sorry, I'm late. I know this is the biggest of deals. I guess, well, I didn't think you'd retrieve it so quickly, and so easily."

Erika turned to Yigael to explain. "I had to hop a last-minute flight out of Munich to get here. Visiting my brother."

Yigael was no less knowledgeable than the women were when it came to interpreting early writings. In this case, though, he wanted reassurance, without bias, that this document was what he believed it to be. Before their fall from grace, governments and religious institutions all over the world had sought out Valentina and Erika for their abilities as translators and interpreters. Few others had their uncanny abilities to assign individual lines, loops, strokes, and spaces to specific scribal hands. Valentina, especially, could identify a writer from just a few characters.

Yigael regarded Valentina and stepped back, giving her room to breathe.

She sat and stared down at the long, round, honey-colored tube. "Classy case," she remarked, noting the hand stitching and adjustable shoulder strap.

"Only the best."

As Valentina snapped open the lid and carefully removed its contents, electricity shot through her body, bringing her back to life. This was what she lived for and, oh, how she'd missed it these last months. She noted the leather ties and recognized the seal. "Whatever might be inside, this is a rare find." She traced a finger over the seal. "Second Temple priests used this seal for their letters."

"Let me have a look." Erika moved behind Valentina for a better angle. "Yeah, they designed it at the start of the first century and used it up until the Temple was destroyed."

Valentina untied the cord and unrolled the first scroll segment. "This is in remarkably good condition. Not often we get one that's ready to read." Once past the outer section, she unfurled the next sections with ease. "Well, it's long enough. Looks like it may be more than ten feet."

"Look at that surface," Erika commented, "really thick,

thicker than most of this period. That's calfskin. Different. We usually find sheepskin."

"The writing is on the grain side, and it looks like the script is the rustic, semiformal type of the Herodian era. Second Temple, for sure." Valentina perused the scroll. "Hmm."

"What?" Yigael asked.

"I recognize this hand," Valentina replied.

"I bet you say that to all the scrolls."

Erika chuckled. "She kind of does."

"I'm serious. I can't think who but it's familiar."

Erika leaned in, hovering right over Valentina. "Let's have a read." She started, "... *on this sacr temple ... roll reign of Her ... and under the direction and authority of Caiapha ... high priest on this year of the Emp ... Tiberius these testimonials are brought forth from ... witness in the ... Galilee ....*"

"Holy God," Yigael yelped. "The script actually refers to witnesses? This is more than even I can believe."

"I think you've got something here, Yigael." Valentina kept her eyes on the scroll.

"*We've* got something," he reminded her. "But first things first. Now, roll 'er up."

"What?"

"We have to bury it."

"So soon?"

"Yes, my dear. Grab your things."

"Now?"

"Yep. Let's get going."

Valentina hesitated.

Yigael gave her *the look.* "You have a train to catch and a dig to crash."

"Well, I have plenty of time. The action doesn't start for a few days yet."

"No, you don't have plenty of time. You need to get there now, make yourself comfortable, and become part of the team.

I want you knee-deep in bones when Dano announces his find next week. That way nobody will question why you're there. And when he hands you the scroll, it will be quite natural."

"Yep, okay," she said, rising.

"I'm waiting on Herschel. He's collecting some items to bury with the scroll. Bones, a few artifacts, especially a holder for the *STS* ... and it has to look old. He's gonna fly them over. We've got plenty of time."

Valentina took one last look at the apparent *STS* and growled at Yigael. Then, she pecked him on the cheek.

He placed a small, black, nondescript phone in the palm of her hand.

She gave him a look. *Really?*

He pecked her other cheek, whispering, "Precautionary."

She slipped it into her suit pocket, picked up her weekender and her enormous red tote, and left.

Yigael secured the door behind her.

"I don't have a train to catch." Erika slid into Valentina's seat to get closer to the scroll.

A moment passed.

"So, Philippe Gaston," Erika mused as she studied the scroll, "seduced the priest's niece."

"Yep." Yigael sat down in his high-back, leather chair.

"And she gave up a two-thousand-year-old, top-secret document. That's interesting."

Her offhanded comment drained the color from Yigael's face.

"You know," Erika went on, "I can't tell a good-looking guy from a pizza but, 'Great job, Philippe!' You need to promote that one, Yigael."

Yigael jumped out of his chair, jerked this way and that, then headed toward the window and grabbed the sill. "My God. How could I not have seen it?"

Erika lifted her chin. "Yigael, what is it? What's wrong?" She got no answer. "Yigael, are you okay? Are you having a heart attack? Talk to me."

Yigael whirled around. "Gabriella was in on it."

"Huh? What on earth do you mean?"

"It was the other way around."

"The other way around?"

"*She* 'handed' *Philippe* the scroll."

"She ... *handed* ... Philippe ... the scroll ...." Wrapping her head around Yigael's words, she shrieked, "Gabriella led him to the scroll?"

"Yes, exactly."

"You mean Philippe didn't seduce her?"

"That's a bit beside the point." Yigael groaned.

"Yigael, breathe." Erika rushed to his side and stroked his back. "Breathe, sweetie."

Yigael took a breath and calmed himself.

Erika turned his chair and got him into it.

The picture was forming. "Yes, yes. Let me think. And Fullier, the priest, led all of us to the basilica," Yigael added, puzzling it together. "The coins were breadcrumbs."

This was huge, beyond huge. Revelatory.

"How would he even know about the scroll? It's not exactly common knowledge. As you say, only a handful of rabbis have ever talked about it."

"Well, that's not completely true."

They thought about that for a minute.

"Two ways to look at it," Yigael said. "One: Maybe Father Fullier doesn't know anything about the scroll. For him, it's about the treasure."

"But what's with all the smoke and mirrors?"

"Anyone's guess. Maybe to keep the treasure out of the hands of the Vatican," Yigael theorized.

"But why? I mean, he works for the Vatican. He's a cog in their wheel. Why wouldn't he just notify them?"

"He may believe the Vatican wouldn't give it back to Israel. I don't know."

"Well, I don't get that part. And two?"

"That treasure has been in the basement for eons. Maybe that's given Father Fullier a chance to look over everything down there. Maybe he's read the *STS* and knows it needs to be discovered but, for some reason, he doesn't want to involve himself."

"Right." Erika snapped her fingers. "Hey, what about those thieves who tossed the chalice?"

He thought for a moment. "They were looking for the treasure, too, maybe even looking for the STS. They followed the trail of the coins just as we had. And this was no coincidence." Yigael never believed in coincidences.

"You don't believe they were in cahoots with the Vatican, do you?"

"I think they were instructed by the Vatican, but I may be able to find out for sure." Yigael punched in a number and waited for the pickup. "Justin, you know anyone talking about the Jewish treasure lately, or more specifically, the Secret Temple Scroll? Past couple of weeks?" Yigael blew out a puff of air. "Yeah, you mean it? Okay, thanks. Be in touch."

"Cardinal Parina?" Erika asked.

Yigael nodded. "Lavoti. It'll be his men ... the church thieves."

"Carlo Lavoti! My god, will we never see the back of him? He buried poor Pope Augustine's encyclical, and then he stole Valeri from Val and me. No telling what else he's been involved with. How can I be surprised he's behind this?"

"Simmer down, Er, Gabriella's potentially in a lot of trouble here. We've got to—"

Just then, Yigael's secure line buzzed in his pocket. He grabbed it and started talking. "Jacques, trouble. You have to get back to Saint-Denis. Gabriella could be in danger. Get her out."

"Yes, we know. Anna-Marie phoned. Carol figured it out and tipped her off."

"Carol?" *You never know.*

"Yeah. We're ten minutes out. If the Vatican is in on this ...."

"It is, and the old priest will be in danger too. I'll handle that," Yigael said. "As soon as you grab Gabriella, head south. I'll organize a safe house. Be in touch." He hung up.

"Why's Gabriella in danger?" Erika asked.

"Thieves, one of them, saw her, heard Phils say her name. It won't take Lavoti much time to work all that out." Yigael's eyes dug into Erika. "You cannot say a word to Valentina about this."

Still reeling, Erika said, "You did not just ask that of me!" Then, with hands shaking, she slid the scroll into the leather cylinder.

"Yes, I just did. And I mean it." Yigael took the case from the desk.

"Is she in danger?"

"Sit tight, Erika." He thought for a moment. "Better yet, get over to Valentina's flat. Stay there. Overnight, if you haven't heard from me." Yigael kissed her cheek and saw her out the door. "I'll be in touch."

"What are you going to do?"

"Our timetable's changed, but the game's the same, with a few tweaks."

He picked up his phone again. "Dano, change of plans."

CHAPTER FORTY-THREE

Quartiere San Lorenzo

As soon as Erika left, Yigael invited Nicolo and Abba inside and handed them the leather case with the scroll inside. Anybody who tried to lift it from these two, well, they might as well bring an army.

"Get down to Naples. Go to the hotel. And wait."

They nodded and left.

His next call was to Josh. "Change of plans," he said before Josh could say hello. "I need you in the South of France. It's urgent. Father Fullier's in danger. He is either on his way or already in his hometown. *Village-sur-Colline.* He'll be visiting Gustavo Allard in the cottage next door to *L'Eglise sur Colline*, the village church. And that's *Father* Allard, by the way."

"Susan too?" Josh asked, fingers crossed. "Can't leave her on the side of the road."

After a beat, Yigael said, "Yeah, good. A couple works better if you get questioned."

"Okay."

"Hop a flight to Marseille. I'll have a car waiting at Arrivals. Call when you're on the road."

Forty-five minutes and a myriad of encrypted phone calls later, Yigael was ready to leave. In the original plan, where the Vatican wasn't onto the treasure and the old village priest and his simple, doe-eyed niece weren't masterminds, he was personally on site, preparing the scroll for burial. Now, he needed to disconnect from this stolen, ancient artifact. He would be dead if he showed up arguing with the Church over it. Golman would see to it.

Yigael tried to convince himself that the scroll's first journey, the trip out of Saint-Denis, was a success. At least there was that. Gabriella's lips were sealed. If she had been able to tell her uncle about the evening's events, he wasn't going to announce the scroll's disappearance. Based on Philippe's story, Lavoti's thieves didn't appear to know where the treasure was hidden. But they were warm. And, as the scroll wasn't in their possession, chances of them still hunting for it was high. Add to that, based on the fight he fessed up to, there was no mistaking Philippe for a sleepwalking altar boy. So, the Vatican was onto them. Of that, Yigael was certain.

He locked up, departed his office, and clicked the door open on his rental car. Fastening his seat belt, he sat for a moment, unsettled, itching for the scroll's descent into the ground before anyone else—the Roman Church or the Italian government— got their hands on it.

CHAPTER FORTY-FOUR

Sidon AD *32*

REBECCA SPUN AROUND AS SCRIBE LEAPT TO HIS FEET.

"Hey," he shouted. "Hands off her. What are you doing? Who are you?" The only light came from the lantern Scribe had lit earlier, so it was difficult to see, but he struck out with both hands and landed on a shoulder. As he pushed a man away, a second man, emerging from the shadows, raised a warning fist.

Rebecca sank. "No, don't," she said. "There is no need for a fight, for goodness' sake. She turned toward the scribe. "This is my uncle. That other one, who likes to fight, is my brother. It's quite clear what they intend."

It was clear to Scribe too. "Look here," he said, "Rebecca is fine, she is happy here. She's learning so many things. Why, she can read."

"That is no matter," her uncle said, not unkindly. "She'll have no need for reading. Rebecca, you cannot walk away from your marriage vows. You know that."

"Bec, the whole town is talking about you."

"Reason enough I should stay here."

"You cannot," her brother said.

Scribe felt powerless. He could do nothing to help her. Perhaps, if it had been earlier and they had seen the two arrive, they might have been able to hide. But that would simply have put off the inevitable. Her family, it seemed, wanted her back. Under Law, she had to go.

Rebecca realized the futility of arguing. "I will go with you," she said, "but you have broken my heart. I shall never smile again or live another happy day."

Rebecca's uncle, who had always held fondness for his niece, smiled softly to himself, knowing that no one could take the joy from her for long. Her light was too bright.

THE VISIT to Sidon was beginning to feel more like a holiday with the relaxed manner of Yeshua's lessons and the long afternoons the disciples spent on their own. The women frequently worked with the impoverished families in the villages north of Sidon, helping them learn to sew and bake bread to sell. Yeshua encouraged everyone to find helpful ways to spend their days.

Though he did his best not to show it, the days were agony for Scribe. He had felt a pain like no other when he watched Rebecca walk away from the camp. When he thought of her blue eyes and cockeyed smile, he felt himself rip apart.

John and Matthew must have noticed, for they suggested Scribe take them to the ridge overlooking the dock, which they had heard about but not seen.

On the way, Andrew marveled at the seascape. "This is the most beautiful place," he said, taking in the sandy shores around them. "Especially here, along the Mediterranean."

"I do quite fancy it here myself," Scribe said.

"I do not fancy seeing those arrogant Romans each day,"

John growled. "Marching about with their regal clothes and their hardware. Acting as if all the land is graced by that beastly gate."

"I must have learned to ignore them, spending all those years in Jerusalem. I certainly do not like them, but I do not see them as you do," Scribe said. "I see right through them."

"I wish I did not notice them," Matthew said. "I fear that one day someone will recognize me and ask why I no longer work for them. Then they will learn about Yeshua and the strength of his influence, and they will feel threatened. They will come after me for leaving and him for leading me away."

Their breathing became more uneven as they labored up the hill.

"Why do you fear this?" Scribe asked. "What have you to hide?"

John and Matthew exchanged glances. "Matthew collected the taxes in Capernaum before he decided to come with us." John wiped his damp forehead with the backside of his forearm. "Oh, it is so hot. On days like this, I wish I could shed each strand of my bloody hair."

Now Scribe understood. In Judea and Galilee, Jews despised tax collectors. Their inordinate sums virtually crippled all but the wealthiest. Their own kind regarded them as traitors.

"It is not a profession I took pride in," Matthew said. "Nor is it something I chose."

"I do understand," Scribe said, while thinking his own father got along quite well with the Romans. He accepted their money.

"I do enjoy all of you who have joined with Yeshua," Matthew said. "You do not judge me."

"It is the way of God," John said, "but it is easy to slip up. That is why Yeshua has come before us, so we do not forget."

When they reached the ridge, they scrunched together on

the rocky ledge, stripped down to their underclothing, and filled their palms with a particularly fragrant olive oil John had purchased in town.

"Yeshua would be disgusted by our waste today," John muttered as he slathered the oil over his chest. "I feel terrible, but not too much so." Laughing, he passed the bottle to Matthew.

"How did you meet Yeshua?" Scribe asked John.

John pressed his knees to his chest, his eyes falling closed. "We heard about John the Baptist, who was washing people in the river and telling them they will become closer to God. It sounded like a full load of donkey poop, but we went anyway— Andrew, James, and I—and the Baptist washed us. I can't say I was thrilled, though, when he asked us to confess our sins for all to hear. But we did it, and there in the wilderness, we came across Yeshua."

Matthew handed the oil back to John who gave it to Scribe.

Scribe began to lather his own body, feeling ungainly beside John's beauty.

"He was haggard and thin when we met him, not the man you see now. He had been alone and fasting."

Matthew leaned forward to meet Scribe's gaze. "For *forty* days."

"He could barely speak when he saw us," John went on. "He seemed more animal than human. He spoke to us of the temptations he had faced and of God's spirit living in the wilderness. He spoke with such conviction, this wild man.

"Well, there we were, face-to-face with this man who had survived all that time on his own, despite the threat of snakes and the other vermin that scatter through that wasteland in the high hills. God certainly had to be looking over him. We encountered him on our way back and he seemed a good deal saner. He talked about the Kingdom of Heaven here on earth, of God living in our hearts and minds, not only in the Temple as the Sadducees would have it. He was what I had been looking for."

Recorking the oil jug, Scribe said, "I am glad Yeshua did not ask me to confess my sins the day I was baptized."

"That is his way." John flicked his hand against a flying bug.

"I daresay," Matthew said, "if each man confessed his sins, most would make the women criminals."

"That's true," John said. "Mosaic Law tells us a woman offender in that situation should be stoned to death. Now this is curious to me. If we desire a woman and lie with her, is the woman alone a criminal? What about the man? Well, either way, it is silly to contemplate given Yeshua certainly does not advocate stoning anyone to death. Quite the opposite."

"That is the difference between him and all those priests running around in Jerusalem." Matthew grinned and shook his head. "Why, if they saw how we lived, with women among us, they would be stoning them from morning to night. And they would not care a whit about us men. But, after all, it is we, with our lusty hearts, who are at fault."

Scribe agreed. If he were to have acted on his feelings for Rebecca, her crime would be punishable by death, yet no punishment would come to him. He believed in Mosaic Law, but he could not imagine anyone stoning Rebecca. The thought was too terrible.

"Did you travel back north together?" he asked John.

"Yes, and there we introduced Yeshua to Andrew's brother Simon. Yeshua took one look at Simon and renamed him 'Peter,' meaning rock. Of course, with his skatty ways, Peter is anything but a rock. But he is very devoted to Yeshua and spreading the word."

John glanced through narrowed eyes at Scribe. "Do give me some more of that oil, fair Scribe. Please, do not tell Yeshua, though, and do not write it in your parchment!"

Scribe chuckled and handed the jug to John, who rubbed

more oil onto his chest and pulled his head cover far over his forehead to shade his eyes.

John studied the harbor, watching the activity around a medium-sized freighter. "How did you find this place?"

Scribe sighed and then told them the truth. All three men laughed heartily.

"Such a beautiful place for a lowly piss," John said, laughing even more.

CHAPTER FORTY-FIVE

Sidon AD *32*

"SCRIBE!" SOMEONE GRABBED THE NECKLINE OF HIS TUNIC AND yanked him awake. "Come. Now. We have to leave." Scribe sat up, attempting to adjust his eyes to the black of night.

"What's going on?" Scribe yawned.

"Scribe, on your feet. Get up. Or be killed."

Scribe hoisted himself up. "Thaddeus? Is that you?"

"Leave everything. We have to go." Thaddeus was frantic. "Come on. Now!"

The scribe could see shadows darting about. He could feel a collective panic.

"That Zealot, the one in the synagogue, the Romans have stoned him to death. They now seek Yeshua. They will certainly kill him and the rest of us!"

In darkness devoid of all starry light, they trekked east out of Sidon into heavily forested land, where they scaled rocky ledges all night. Scribe held his breath, never looking down but stepping as sure-footedly as he could, considering one slip would spell doom. Slippage was only one of the perils they faced. The threat posed by wildcats and boars loomed, as did the persistent danger of encountering Roman soldiers.

At daylight, they left the roadsides and dug into the wild brush.

Sundown saw them setting up camp where they felt safe. No one had eaten since dinner the previous night. Thaddeus and his two men took to hunting, while the rest built a fire and rolled out mats.

Yeshua announced their next stop as Caesarea Philippi.

WHEN THE SCRIBE lay down in the thick of the mountainous terrain after many nights in hiding, he grew desperate and paranoid. He imagined wandering off to write only to find himself left behind as the group pressed on. The scribe was a follower, but he was not a chosen one. Would they forget him? Could they? And suppose they were not well received in Caesarea Philippi. They would have to escape again without enough food or water to replenish their weary bodies and souls. His flailing heart overcame him.

The travel into Caesarea was slow, the road crowded with merchants and workers hauling supplies. They often had to step aside to let the others pass. In the end, the trip was trouble-free.

What a comfort entering the city. Caesarea lay in an extraordinarily beautiful setting, lush and full of life and unlike any place the scribe had ever experienced. After living in Jerusalem, he had not expected the Roman city to surprise him. Though built by a Roman governor, it was still a *Jewish* city, and Jewish culture was everywhere. Artwork, books, Jewish dress ... all looked familiar, a solace to the scribe.

The appearance of Caesarea, though, belonged entirely to

Rome, the beige-colored columns and the intricately carved street sculptures of Roman military leaders said a great deal about the Greek and Roman foundations of the city. Public fountains, toilets, bathhouses, and markets hummed with the steady activity of visitors from all over the world. Like Sidon, the city throbbed with the pulse of buying and trading. The scribe had never seen such an abundance of richly colored fabric, exotic scents, and styled house necessities. One potter's shop caught his eye, so shiny was his collection of brightly painted bowls, jugs, and cups. Scribe noticed a bowl painted so elaborately the colors shined like jewels. The potter's asking prices were far steeper than anything he had seen. Yet, the Romans, their dark skin damp with the aroma of luxurious oils, dropped coins faster than a child shed an unwanted mantle on a muggy day.

The question of lodging became an issue. Roadside inns, with their crowded halls of drunken, often dishonest and criminal tenants, were unsuitable, particularly for the women. There was no comfortable campground around the busy city. And, fearful of appearing suspicious to Romans, staying in the home of a kindly host willing to put up a group of travelers was unlikely. The lack of preparation angered the scribe. Here he was again, Yeshua the leader, dragging his loyal contingents into the Roman capital with no thought of where they should stay.

John and Peter left the rest sunning by a cool fountain while they searched for sleeping quarters. Scribe sat down on a stone bench and glanced at the sky, the flame of the sun shrinking to make way for the moon.

They did not linger in Caesarea Philippi. Yeshua seemed out of sorts and restated that he wanted to go home, a disappointment to the scribe, who had looked forward to days of steamy baths followed by jugs of wine and warm meat pies.

They stopped in Capernaum. Peter and Andrew reunited

with their family. Some went home. Others found friends with whom they could stay.

The thought of fresh clothes and his mother's cooking was more powerful than his fear of Roman soldiers, so he and Yeshua headed south, Yeshua to Nazareth, Scribe turning off for Sepphoris.

With his long hair, healthy beard, and broad shoulders, Scribe found no trouble making the journey home. His family scrambled and prepared a sumptuous meal to welcome him. Like old times, by nightfall, his father motioned him to the roof.

His father expressed worry for the scribe's safety among the Romans and seemed agitated that his son did not seem to take him seriously. Scribe did, but his fear of the Romans was now secondary to his desire to be at Yeshua's side.

Father and son argued and, once again, Scribe's father recounted the horrifying story of the widespread crucifixions that took place in Sepphoris, claiming his own father's life. Once more, Scribe defended Yeshua, which brought an angry outcry from his father and then brooding silence.

His father believed the rebel, as he now regarded Yeshua, would bring harm to families, friends, their villages, and throughout Galilee.

As they lay there staring at the dazzling stars, there was nothing more to say.

He had his spare tunic already packed. His mother was searching for it to wash, but he'd done that himself a few nights back. He felt guilty when he looked into her eyes. They were flooded with love and concern. Yet, as he lay his head to rest on this seventh day home, his thoughts turned elsewhere.

Sepphoris—Shabbat 14 Tishri

Today as my world here lies down to sleep, I shall disappear.
I am sure one day I will return. I hope my family can accept

my decision. They must have noticed that I am different now from the person they once knew. The son they nurtured on the path to Jerusalem has now chosen a new life. I love my parents still, just as I did when I was their son, the temple scribe. I hope they can love me still, as I am now. With Yeshua, my life has purpose. I have a reason to greet the day. I long to see him, to hear him speak, to see the bright greeting in his eyes as he whispers, "My champion." I hope I am still his champion. I hope I have added something to his life, for right now he is my champion, my strength. He and only he can tear me from the darkness I have found in the world. He alone can inspire me to use my talents. He is all the hope I know. I must get back to him to do my small part for the mission.

CHAPTER FORTY-SIX

Saint-Denis
Present Day

MONIQUE MORISSETTE WAS ALL SMILES AS SHE DASHED ABOUT regaling her tour group on the splendor of the magnificent cathedral. As she strode officiously toward the altar, students trailing, she stopped short on spotting the chalice by the side door and the shattered display case.

Monique gasped just as a young American in her group, uttered, "Dude, check it out!"

Another chimed in, "Holy sh—"

Monique raised her arms high. "That's enough! Back it up. Back it up ... and follow me." As she scuttled toward the administrative offices, she shrieked, "Madame Laurant. Madame Laurant." Her liveliest tour group yet trailed her like a litter of curious pups.

Minutes later, Inspector Henri Jacquot and a subordinate had summoned everyone present at the cathedral to the apse for questioning: the administrator Audrey Laurent; the cook and housekeeper Gabriella Fullier; a quivering docent

Monique Morissette and her litter, and two workmen who had been washing windows. If not for the disappearance of four members of a study team, Inspector Jacquot might have considered this a routine break-in, possibly by youth in search of assets to fence for drug money. Still, nothing was stolen, and no one present seemed to know anything. Gabriella remained silent, holding tight to an empty basket on her lap, as Inspector Jacquot considered possible motives out loud.

Eventually, with a sigh, he dismissed the group and told Madame Laurent he would follow up but thought it was likely a couple of young hooligans.

Outside, just off the garden adjacent to the monastery, perched on a branch of a black pine, Philippe watched as a small crowd, including two officers of the law and Gabriella, exited through the side door of the basilica.

With basket in arms, she headed for the garden to pick the day's selection of ripe vegetables.

She's a cagey one, he thought. *It's business as usual for her.* Philippe watched her pluck a green tomato from the vine. "That one needed another week," he whispered down.

Looking all around, Gabriella spotted Philippe up the tree, hiding behind a thicket of jade needles. It took her a second to recover and get into character before uttering, "Phil-Pascal! You came back! But what are you doing in the tree?"

"Cut the crap, Gabby. You need to get to the black Kodiaq SUV parked just past the farmer's market on *rue Deux.*"

Gabriella just stood there.

"Gabby, go, you're in danger. I'll explain in the car. Though I'm sure you already know!"

Without further comment, Gabriella fled the cathedral garden for the monastery, one sad, little, green tomato bouncing around in an otherwise empty basket.

Five minutes later, with an overnight bag slung over a shoulder, she stepped off the cobblestone walkway bordering the farmer's market and into the SUV that had Jacques at the wheel, Philippe riding shotgun.

"My uncle," she said buckling in as Jacques pulled out.

"We'll find him at Father Allard's?" Jacques asked, looking at her in the rearview mirror.

She nodded.

"An agent is headed there."

"*Merci*. And who are you? Your real name?" Gabriella asked, addressing the driver.

"Jacques Ignatius."

Philippe turned in his seat to face her. "You can start talking anytime."

Despite the seriousness of the situation, there was always something amusing about a man with a bruised ego. A half-smile formed on Gabriella's face.

On realizing that was all he was going to get—a clandestine smirk—Philippe uttered, *"Uncroyable!"* under his breath, and turned around in a huff. Unbelievable!

CHAPTER FORTY-SEVEN

Ercolano, Italy

VALENTINA BOARDED A TRAIN FOR THE TWO-AND-A-HALF-HOUR trip to Ercolano, where she would reconnect with a colleague and get herself invited as a guest archaeologist onto a dig in progress. Checking into her hotel and changing into casual wear, she walked the short distance to the ruins where, oblivious of the new developments that transpired after she left Yigael's office, she found Kara Maggi.

"A sight for sore eyes, even if you are a mess," Valentina teased as she approached Kara.

"Valentina? Hi!" Kara stood and brushed off her dusty dungarees. "Imagine seeing you here." Taking in Valentina's clean and pressed khaki trousers, crisp, fitted, powder-blue button down, and woven calfskin shoulder bag—signature Valentina—she said, "I suppose a hug will have to wait. What brings you seaside?"

"I'm meeting Luca for a getaway, but he got delayed. Business."

"Well, it's, um, great to see you."

No one knew what to say to her these days. Valentina no longer took the awkward tension personally. "You too."

"How are you?" Kara asked, but before Valentina could answer, she added, "I'm so sorry about everything. To lose Valeri. I know what your lab meant to you."

Not a naturally vulnerable person, Valentina nodded an acknowledgment of thanks.

"And Erika? How's she?"

"Good. Back in Rome. How's your dig going?"

"Best job I've ever had." Kara meant that as a *thank you,* as this was the only real job she'd ever had. But, with Valentina out of work, it felt more like an open-mouth-insert-foot moment.

"I didn't mean to interrupt."

"No problem."

"Are you free for dinner?"

"Tomorrow, I am. We could go to *Primo.* Hey, let's get out of the sun. Just over there." She pointed to a gray canvas-covered area a short distance away."

"Sure."

Kara Maggi had been the head archaeologist on the site of what was classified as an ancient shoreline for several months, excavating near the boat caves and the land that had been shoved into the sea and buried by Vesuvius. It was believed to be a site rich in artifacts, as it was nearby the Villa of the Papyri, where an entire library of artwork, papers, and letters had been uncovered.

Valentina had been offered the position of heading the team. However, she and Erika were already committed to Valeri, so she recommended Kara, who'd been six months out of her PhD program and without any job prospects in sight. This wasn't for lack of talent. Kara had a real mind for recognizing artifacts and cataloging them, but everyone else in the field saw her as a pretty face, since she'd paid her way through school with modeling jobs. The archaeological community had an appreciation for everything under the sun, but they just weren't into advertising it on billboards, of which Kara graced many, selling everything from undergarments to diamonds to spring water. Her exotic features and tall, slender frame got her everywhere with talent agents and nowhere with hoped-for future colleagues.

Kara led Valentina to the shady area that served as an onsite lab. The artifacts were tagged, all cleaned up. Except for one.

"These are all ready to be sent to Naples Museum," Kara said. "Let's sit."

Valentina surveyed the collection. A jar or cup with a decoration on the side. A long chunk of rope attached to an egg-shaped cut of leather, which reminded Valentina of a child's swing. "Look at this belt," she said. The buckle, belt plate, and strap end were perfectly preserved. "Quite a find." The belt was decorated with images of dolphins. "And this canister. They aren't rare, but they are not that common either. This one is really old, I'd say." She gestured to pick it up. "May I?"

"Yes, certainly. We found it over there." Kara pointed to the first in the row of caves. Valentina studied the object. "Hard to tell what it's made of with all this ash and soil still encrusted all around it."

She held it up and checked for identifiable markings but found none that rang familiar. "Huh? It's light," Valentina mused. "May I open it?"

"Absolutely."

Valentina felt her phone buzz inside her bag. She checked who was calling: Erika. She hit *Decline*.

Valentina began pulling at both ends of the object. A lid popped off one edge and landed on the ground. Kara picked it up.

Valentina peered inside the canister. "It's empty," she said with a shrug.

"Huh?" Kara said. "I thought we might find a scroll in there." Kara could barely believe Valentina was sitting here in front of her. "You said you were free? You could join the dig this week. It'd be an honor."

That was easy, Valentina thought. "Well, why not? Sounds great." Then her phone *pinged.*

It was a text from Erika written in Jewish Palestinian Aramaic, the dialect of the Galilee during the Second Temple period. Just a handful of people could read this ancient language, but only Valentina could decipher Erika's shorthand: *Vatican is closing in on scroll. Bury it now.*

Valentina's adrenaline hit the roof, but she kept her façade calm and steady. *Yigael's men haven't excavated the land yet, and Herschel's package of artifacts with the container hasn't arrived. Think.*

She stared at the container before her. "Look, I know this is not protocol, but can I 'borrow' this?"

"You want an empty canister? Right now?"

"Yes. To cross-reference these markings with a reference book I have. It's for another project. Nothing really, but you never know." *Good Lord, can't I do better than that?*

It would be hard for Kara to deny Valentina. She had been the only person to take the model-turned-archaeologist seriously. In addition, the best career advice Kara ever received had come from Valentina: *"We're not in search of artifacts alone. We are seekers of truth."*

"I'll go grab the sheet," Kara said, "and you can sign for it. I'll have the museum fast track the paperwork on Monday, and it'll be yours for the next two weeks."

"Thanks, Kara. I appreciate it."

"I'll be right back."

"I'll be right here."

No, she would not. No sooner had Kara turned her back than Valentina dodged out of the tent.

Back at the hotel, she checked out and exited, rolling her luggage behind. She took care to hold her satchel tight against her body, so she could feel the shape of the canister pressed between her elbow and rib cage. It was her only source of comfort at this point.

With no clear plan in mind beyond leaving the hotel, she hailed a taxi and hopped in. "Naples, *per favore*."

"*Si, signora*."

Valentina took out the burner phone Yigael had given her and called the only number programmed into it.

It rang and rang and rang.

CHAPTER FORTY-EIGHT

Village-sur-Colline

"DO YOU EVER DO ANYTHING OTHER THAN WORK?" JOSH ASKED Susan. He was at the wheel.

She was creating renderings in a notebook of alternate routes from Father Allard's home in the south of France to the safe house Yigael had arranged. "We can't exactly Google Maps a route if we're on the lamb," she snapped.

"Bite my head off, just making small talk."

Susan looked out the window. Josh had been right. She hadn't explored a single part of Europe since she'd been overseas. Glowing orange, the sun was starting to think about its descent below the horizon. The terrain was surreal, like a postcard. "When I was a little girl," she began, trying to relax, "our sixth-grade class took a field trip to the Smithsonian in Washington. When I stepped inside the Natural History Museum and saw those old writings in hieroglyphics and the Egyptian exhibit, I was hooked."

"Nice."

"What about you? How did you land in, ah, your line of work? And with the infamous Yigael Dorian?"

"Not so complicated, really." Josh related to Susan how he had followed his great uncle into the intelligence world. "It's not so surprising that Yigael tapped me to work for him because our backgrounds are so similar. He's not the most socially graceful person but we work well together. There's an ease about it."

"Nothing looks easy with Yigael Dorian from my perspective. What do you do for him?"

"I don't work undercover, not normally. I'm just a flack. I do his advance work. And try to keep him under control."

They both laughed.

"And you chose here because?" Josh asked, drawing out the word *because*.

"To steer clear of my sister's wedding, which is about a month out. I'm almost to the finish line."

"Coming halfway around the world to avoid a wedding." He laughed. "That makes perfect sense."

"Actually," Susan said, "I was thrilled to think about working in the Israel Museum, near the Knesset and the Supreme Court. Wow."

They drove in silence for a bit until she asked, flippantly, "Hey, what are we supposed to do when we find this Father Fullier, anyway? Interrogate him about the treasure, then kidnap him, and outrun the Vatican?"

"Pretty much."

At that, Susan's heart skipped a beat. She felt queasy and turned to look out the rear window to see if they were being tailed. Then, she studied Josh, searching for an indication he was joking or at least exaggerating.

He gave her a look. "Yes, you got the steps out of order but we're to kidnap Father Fullier if he won't come willingly, destroy all evidence of him having been at Father Allard's, including that rusty, red artifact he uses to get around, get him to the safe house, and question him there. All the while outrunning the Vatican cronies. That is the plan."

"Can you pull over?" Susan had the car door almost halfway open.

"What?"

"My *pasta alla Norma* from lunch wants out."

Josh pulled over, just not fast enough.

AN HOUR LATER, Josh slowed the car, pulling up to the home of Father Allard.

"Father Fullier's little, old car ... that's got to be it over there. Let's go," Susan said, unbuckling.

"Not so fast." Josh put his hand on her forearm.

An old, red car was indeed parked down the street. But that made no sense to Josh. There was no need to park so far away from one's destination in the countryside, particularly if one was up in age. He opened the glove box and grabbed a gun that Yigael had planted.

"What are you doing? Why is that in there?! Guns aren't even legal in France." Susan started panicking. "Call Yigael."

"Stay right here. I'll be back," Josh said, hopping out.

Susan watched, with an empty stomach, thankfully, as Josh scoped out the simple, cottage-style home beside the quaint countryside church. She watched as he knocked on the door and an old priest answered. Then, she watched as they exchanged what appeared to be niceties before Josh smiled, nodded, and headed back to the car. None of that, though seemingly pleasant, put her at ease.

Josh sat down and took a moment to collect his thoughts. Then he turned to Susan. "Don't panic."

"Call Yigael!"

"I said don't panic."

"Then tell me what not to panic about."

"Okay, Father Allard said that Father Fullier called and canceled the trip due to fatigue." Then, he added, "Feel free to panic now."

Susan dropped her head in her hands.

Was she crying? About to hyperventilate? Josh couldn't tell.

Susan was not on the verge of mental collapse. Quite the opposite. She needed a moment to gather herself and focus. She was no Mossad agent. In fact, she'd never even seen a gun up close until five minutes ago. But now, a man's life was at stake.

By the time Susan raised her head, she had concocted a plan of her own.

Josh was on the phone with Yigael. "Fullier never made it to Father Allard's. The church thieves likely have him."

"Or he could be hiding somewhere," Yigael added.

Josh was silent.

"Let's not discount anything due to age. The man led us to the scroll, remember?"

"Alright," Josh said.

"Jacques and Philippe have Gabriella, and they're a few hours out. You two stay put for now. Grab a hotel until further notice."

"Got it." Josh hung up. Oh, to explain that to Susan.

"I think we need to find a hotel, so I can get online," Susan said. "We can't be traipsing all over the South of France looking for people we've never met in places we've never been. This is the twenty-first century. Let's take advantage of it and find out everything we can about Father Fullier and take it from there."

What a relief. "Works for me," Josh said and drove a couple of blocks into the heart of the village.

.   .   .

235

YIGAEL YANKED on a light jacket and went for a walk. *Timing. It is not on our side now.* There was no reason for Yigael to think Valentina was in imminent danger. However, he had set up a concrete plan for her immediate future. A plan she would never stand for if she knew.

CHAPTER FORTY-NINE

Capernaum AD *32*

EACH DAY IT SEEMED AS IF THE SCRIBE'S PAST LIFE SLIPPED further from his mind. The boy who went to Jerusalem, who swore to live by the strict codes of the written and oral Law dictated by the Sadducees and Pharisees, that boy was no more. He came to understand that those who testified against Yeshua were either misinformed, under pressure, fearful, or needing money. And the priests: once he had believed their words about the rebel, but now he knew they were simply untrue. It was exciting, belonging to something so evolving.

By the time he reached the shores of the Sea of Galilee, Scribe had decided the scrolls, on which he had recorded events and impressions from his first days with Yeshua, must not go to the Sanhedrin, but be kept for posterity. Just as Yeshua gave the gift of life and hope to so many, asking for nothing in return, the scribe determined it was his duty to see that Yeshua's deeds were never forgotten.

Scribe could not perform healing. He did not incite hope

and promise with but one look. He did not possess Yeshua's tall, elegant stature or his prominent features. He could not lower his voice to make a point, for surely no one would show interest. However, he *could* scribe, and so he would continue without question. By the power of his pen, he could keep Yeshua alive in the hearts and minds of men and women long after his lifetime, for the skins on which he wrote would long outlast him.

Yeshua was the last to make his way back to Capernaum, and he seemed renewed. A grand celebration dinner marked his return, followed by dancing in the road on this mild *Tishri* night in front of Peter's home, with John playing the flute.

The scribe, drunk on sweet wine, joined hands with Yeshua in a circle dance, if one could call Scribe's efforts a dance. He broke the circle, leaping and galloping around with such fervor that everyone stopped to watch, whooping and hollering. Reveling in his light-headedness, he flung himself forward toward Yeshua, only narrowly escaping a collision. Yeshua hooted and pushed him off, sending Scribe flying away toward his next victim.

Scribe did not recall ever throwing his arms around so many people with such joy and deep affection. These people were his friends, his new family. They were like him. They believed as he believed, lived as he lived.

THE NEXT MORNING, Yeshua told Scribe of his mission. As he spoke, it was with dread that the scribe wrote down the terrible words that foreshadowed Yeshua's future. There was resignation in his voice and a weariness that contrasted with his urgency to have his words recorded with pen and ink.

"You are my leaders," Yeshua said to the somber faces lit by the flames of the fire at supper that evening. "You are the teachers and the givers of the way." He clasped the scribe's hand. "You are my champion. You are the one who records our story, so the word may survive long after our lives are over."

Hot tears hit Scribe's eyes, and the moment became more than he could bear. He was a scribe and had his education, but he could not match the blind devotion of John, the strong arm of Peter when he cast a line to sea, the skills of James with a hammer, or the hunting techniques of Thaddeus, and so this singling out humbled him.

As the scribe resumed his writing position the next morning, he was grateful that the act of looking down at his scroll could hide the expression on his face, especially after Yeshua spoke his first words of the day.

"We will proceed south to embrace those who know us not."

Scribe knew it was futile to try to stop him. Yeshua understood the risks posed by such a route—they would enter Jerusalem just as Passover was approaching—but he refused to yield.

Scribe continued to wonder why, if Yeshua thought he would die by Roman hands, he would not fight or let his followers fight for him? Death was not something to be welcomed, yet he seemed satisfied to walk right into it.

Yeshua's stance angered Scribe but never for long. Sometimes, when Yeshua walked, his hair billowing behind him like a cloud, Scribe studied him, and Yeshua would catch him out. He would smile, and the scribe knew no stronger love. His affection shone upon them like stars raining glitter. Scribe loved his laughter, the sheer joy he imparted, often in the quietest moments. It made him forget, for a time, the terror in his heart.

Capernaum—Sheni 4 Shevat

It is strange to think of one person being God, the Creator, and the Giver of Life. I have been with Yeshua enough to know he is indeed human. I have heard him snore, seen him squat beside us after large meals, and noticed the dark circles under his eyes when he is exhausted. He is a man, a bright, witty, beautiful, captivating man. And, though I do not believe Yeshua to be Mashiach, the Anointed One, I am not sure I will ever encounter such a one. I do know this: I have neither known, nor will I ever know, anyone else like Yeshua.

My fears about his imminent death have diminished somewhat, thus making it difficult to believe that this man of such stature and influence could die. But then, he must at a point, if he is human, which I believe him to be. Mostly.

What, really, is he?

Whenever I have convinced myself of his true nature, something happens to alter my perception. Is he a vessel through which God operates? I have often asked Yeshua these and related questions, and he always finds strange ways to keep from answering.

"My name is Yeshua," he said just this morning. "And I am a builder from Nazareth. As I have told you, I left that life behind when I set out to spread the Good News."

"But how did you know what to do, what to say?" I asked him. "Does the Lord speak to you? Do you follow his guidance daily?"

"Dear Scribe, of course you must know, the Lord speaks to all of us. To hear, one must only listen."

Well, I have been listening for the Lord for many days in succession and he certainly says nothing to me, even when I beg it of him. "So, Yeshua," I asked him, "if you are a man just as I am, why can only you hear the word of the Lord?"

This was but one of a thousand questions he has responded to with but a smile.

CHAPTER FIFTY

Gennesaret AD *33*

THE FIRST STOP ON THEIR NEW JOURNEY, AS DICTATED BY Thaddaeus, was Gennesaret. Scribe welcomed the opportunity to visit the village, having missed it on his journey to Capernaum. The town was situated just south of the strip of beach where he first encountered the four fishers and where he often taught Rebecca to read and write.

He could not help but visualize her, appearing, perhaps, from the stump of a nearby pine tree, her long hair spilling from her wrap. Just to see her again, to touch her one more time. To hear from her own lips. *I am content. Though I miss you, life is peaceful with my husband.* He looked at Yeshua, leading the group with John and Peter on each side. They were his comfort. He loved them.

They arrived in Gennesaret shortly after the midday meal. Word trickled out among the other neighboring towns, and crowds began to gather to see him. Gennesaret became more populous than Capernaum, as families, children, old rabbis surged into the village.

Yeshua and several of the chosen twelve were staying at the home of an old potter. As usual, Yeshua requested Scribe stay with him to document all that occurred. Since Yeshua rarely had time to rest and Scribe was expected to remain close by, the trip became exhausting for Scribe.

Before Gennesaret, when Yeshua had to greet new visitors, even when he was too tired, Scribe could always escape to a hillside or secluded grove. Now he found himself by Yeshua's side all the time with no time to himself. While Yeshua had the stamina, the patience, or whatever was required to deal with the onslaught of visitors, Scribe did not. He spent his time brooding, writing silently. At supper, he could not relax with the others, and his responses were often hostile and abrupt.

Many more villagers poured into Gennesaret upon learning that Yeshua was on his way to Jerusalem. Scribe could not keep up with the flood. He began hating the feel of cloth against his thigh. Other disciples, aware of his angst, became his servants, rushing to purchase more lamp gum ink for his pens and pressing cups of water into his hands before he could ask for it. At night, they heated a large pot of water to soak his damaged hands.

After the most recent service, Scribe could stand it no more. As followers lined up to greet Yeshua, he saw his opportunity and slipped away. He found a stream that filtered through a trestle of branches and rocks. Stripping to his undergarments, he stood beneath the rush of cool water. He screamed, shocked by its chill, his limbs shrinking against his torso. When he adjusted, he took in the beauty of his surroundings. Only a short distance from the town's western border in a thicket of pine, almond and carob trees, the stream threaded through rough grass and brush. The almond trees were in full bloom, their white leaves like stars of cotton. Seeing a petal fall, he reached out and enclosed the silken clove in his fist. Sweeter than the spices of Sidon, the fragrant blossoms perfumed the air. He heard movement and turned, alarmed. The pink nose of a reddish fox popped up from a bush not far from his feet.

"Hello," Scribe said happily. The fox dashed away, its fur damp. Scribe laughed heartily, then turned to face the water. It splattered his cheeks as he stretched his arms to receive it.

Lying beside a tree, Scribe stretched his legs and they curled into a tight ball. *I shall sleep a bit. Seems only fitting I should rest.*

Scribe was already drifting off, seeing strange faces and hearing music from another time. It was quiet, the sun shined seductively above him, and he was blissfully alone. He remembered his father extending his hand to a small child. The child jumped forward and fell. His father laughed and tucked the child under his arm.

Of course, the child was him, though it didn't seem possible now. A memory from someone else's lifetime.

"I see you Scribe, and I know you are tired," Yeshua said after the Sabbath, when they were preparing to sleep. The room was dark except for the glow of a single lantern.

"I am not so tired."

"I see you are not used to such, shall we call it business, around you. I want you to know how much I appreciate your patience." Yeshua gathered his mantle around his shoulders. "Thank you. We shall leave this town soon and when we do, I think the other villages will be more subdued."

Scribe nodded, afraid to say anything that would reveal how exasperated he was.

CHAPTER FIFTY-ONE

Jerusalem AD *33*

THEY LEFT GALILEE IN THE MIDDLE OF *ADAR,* CLOSE TO THE END of the wet season, and moved southward into the regions of Decapolis and then Perea. In village after village, they found more people who knew of Yeshua and were eager to welcome him into their lives. They left their homes and joined in the journey. Because they pushed to visit many villages with hopes of reaching a maximum number of potential converts, their journey was exhausting.

Finally, they reached Jericho. After a brief respite, camping along the river and bathing in its waters, the group set off on the final leg of their journey. The moon told Scribe they would arrive in the holy city days before Passover. He thought of the steep hillsides, the stone steps, the cold lines of the Grecian buildings he had left more than two years prior. At the time, he was anxious to prove himself to the temple authorities. Now, he would return a different man entirely.

As they neared the gates, jubilant talk and booming

laughter caught everyone up, especially the first timers to the great city.

"I hear it is the largest building in Jerusalem and you can see the whole city from the top stair," a young girl cried out.

"I hear it has a gold roof that sparkles like jewels in the sunlight," Andrew said.

The young girl turned to the scribe. "You lived in Jerusalem. Is it true? Does it have a golden roof?"

The scribe nodded.

She clapped her hands and jumped up and down.

Scribe laughed at her spontaneity—*was I ever like that?* —and then raised his eyes to the enormous crowd.

The joy was contagious, to everyone. As they approached the northern gate, the gold roof of the Temple shined so intensely, it caused one to squint. The massive building rose high, the stone impossibly white against the red-orange sand of Jerusalem. With its columns of smooth marble and gold-plated trim, the Temple was even more beautiful than Scribe had recalled.

The eastern wall of the city came into view. Herod's Temple grew larger and larger. The disciples cheered wildly.

Yeshua crossed the Golden Gate and rode into the city on the back of a mule. Falling into the shade as they passed through the great stone arch, the road in front of them was lined with faces from Gischala, Bethsaida, Nain, even Nazareth.

Scribe walked behind the mule, as did John, Peter, and the rest. The erect position of Yeshua's shoulders showed how elated he was by the reception. Men, women, and even children flanked the road waving fresh sprigs of palm.

Men fell to their knees, hands clasped over their hearts. Flat, brown hands pressed against the mule's coat as it passed.

A man screamed, "He will show the new world its leader for the light of God shines within him!"

Scribe watched as Yeshua bowed his head and thought he was probably embarrassed by such high praise.

They finally arrived in the reaches of the lower city. They found the market jammed with visitors and merchants toting animals. Yeshua stepped from the mule and the animal was led away.

Approaching the Temple, Yeshua's crowd mixed with the thousands of pilgrims there for Passover and all became boisterous, not at all reverent as one might anticipate in reaching such a holy place.

Scribe realized Yeshua would be unprepared for the scene he was about to encounter. To the scribe, what went on in the courts of the great Temple—with the moneychangers, the trade of sacrificial animals, and the stink of dying beasts mixed with the aroma of kabobs and perfumed oils—was normal. In fact, the aroma of lamb cooking on an open fire made his stomach rumble and caused him to wonder when he had last sat for a leisurely meal.

It would be different for Yeshua. And Scribe had not thought to warn him about the commotion ahead. He pushed through the pilgrims but failed to reach him in time. A glimpse of Yeshua's face told Scribe he was right to worry. It was near black with fury. That's when he knew they were heading straight into disaster.

Scribe watched as Yeshua, with blistering speed, bolted into the circus that was the market at midday. The mild, temperate man who taught love, acceptance, and restraint was nowhere to be seen.

The Court of the Gentiles was alive with trade activity. Lambs harnessed by new owners were led against the stone floor of the Court. Large birds squawked inside cages. The uniformed Levites moved through the crowd calling out, "Tyrian shekels!" the only coin accepted by the Temple. People lined up at tables to purchase animals for sacrifice. Levites used the surfaces of the tables to spread out their coins.

By ancient custom, a man would purchase an animal, a rich man a bull, a poor man a bird. The man would then pass through the Court of Women to the Court of Israelites, where the priest would slit the throat of the animal, its blood a symbol of the animal's offering to God. Lamb would be thrown over a large fire to be eaten during the Seder meal.

While the others moved about, thrilled by all the activity and the beauty of the Temple, Yeshua became still as he surveyed the crowd. Over the heads of the visitors, Scribe could see lines of Roman soldiers staring down at them from the rectangular stone brick of the Antonia Fortress. The scribe thought perhaps Yeshua was unnerved by their presence, but Yeshua's attention seemed to gear more toward the animal tables. The merchants stood patiently, lamb cages at their feet. The Levites stood in front, pouches trembling with coins.

CHAPTER FIFTY-TWO

Jerusalem AD *33*

THEN, LIKE A LION, YESHUA RUSHED AT THE TABLES TOPPED WITH coins, chinking as they changed hands. The scribe gasped when he flipped them upside down—one, two, three—with the strength of ten men. Then, in a thunderous voice, he condemned the mindless slaughter of animals, setting free all those still alive.

In no time, Yeshua pronounced a resounding rebuke on Israel. "You have turned the Temple into a marketplace. This is a place of worship. It is not intended for personal gain. It certainly is not intended for cruelty to animals! God shall cast wrath upon you! You shall pay for your sins. If not now, then on the day of your judgment!"

The mood quickly shifted. There was anger inside and on the temple steps, shock among visiting pilgrims, and disbelief on the faces of followers. Yeshua seemed in some other universe, not quite lucid.

Scribe, who knew the workings of the high clergy and the aristocracy of Jerusalem and the immediate danger they could face, called together the chosen twelve. "We need to get him out of the city. No debate. Let us go."

Working as a unit, they backed their way out of the temple grounds to the outskirts of the city.

For the first time, Scribe worried not only about Yeshua but about the safety of the scrolls. The priests could level a grave charge against Yeshua for his actions. In that case, Scribe could well be identified as a follower and ordered to hand over his scrolls as evidence. Would they twist his words to justify Yeshua's conviction? Could his writing cause Yeshua more harm? *I will hide them in the folds of my mantle. If anyone comes for me, I will burn them.*

Scribe knew the Sadducees well. They lived their days engrossed in rituals and examinations of the law. Scribe might try to explain, but they would never understand that he loved Yeshua more than anyone he had ever known.

They camped at the base of a hill and lit a fire of twigs and dried leaves. Yeshua's eyes looked watery and burning red. His words were monosyllabic. The scribe wondered if he sensed something horrifying on the horizon. He could not get out of his mind the sight of the soldiers lined up like executioners at the gates to the city. Worry about their leader interrupted his sleep throughout that night.

Scribe, Andrew, and John ventured back into the market-place the next morning, leaving the others behind with Yeshua. Scribe immediately saw members of the Sanhedrin together. He spotted his favorite teacher, Gamaliel the Elder, and approached him. With his appearance so changed, it took a while for Gamaliel to recognize his former student.

"All grown up, then," Gamaliel said, as the two exchanged warm greetings. Then, he issued a warning. "You had better report in. Caiaphas wishes to question you," he said. Gamaliel was a servant to the high priest.

"But I have left."

"If you do not comply with his demand, you risk arrest."

"I will talk to him, tell him the whole story. However, I will have only words of praise for Yeshua."

The warmth left Gamaliel's voice. "You were my student. I favored you over the others and I expected to see you back, working among us. How can you disappoint me this way?"

While the three were in the city, Thaddeus and Matthew scouted for a new campsite. They chose one at the base of a hill just outside of Jerusalem in Bethany. It lay adjacent to an olive grove known as Gethsemane.

It was the most beautiful place the scribe had seen since they had left Capernaum. They planned to stay there for the remainder of their trip. Scribe would have been happier if the Roman Legion had not stationed themselves directly above their campsite. But there they were, always watching.

Yeshua's mood at dinner that night was still grave. Scribe could hardly force himself to eat. He prayed they would travel north next, for this journey was not going well.

As the Passover Seder approached, Scribe felt they had lost the people's goodwill, and he longed to return to Capernaum, the village that always extended her hand to them. Jerusalem, by contrast, was far too ambitious for their little mission. The people who came there sought spectacles beyond their ability to orchestrate. Yeshua often said that change comes slowly, and, if they tried to move too fast, they would destroy what they had achieved thus far.

The scribe believed he was witnessing that fact before his very eyes.

Bethany—Shilishi 9 Nisan

I have always found the sacrifice of an animal to be most unpleasant. The last gasping and gurgling in the animal's open throat ... no, I cannot stomach it. In the commotion of the emotionally charged crowds pressing in from all sides, it is often even impossible to leave without blood on your sleeve. But this is how things have always been done. Certainly, I have never questioned it. Of course, Yeshua questions everything, and this is one of the reasons we follow him. Over time, he has stirred up dilemmas we have kept dormant, or ignored, within ourselves. I am just not sure that Passover is the proper time to question these rituals of sacrifice.

CHAPTER FIFTY-THREE

Naples
Present Day

NICOLO AND ABBA SAT IN THEIR SMALL MOTEL ROOM IN SILENCE. In their line of work, they were used to waiting, but it was after eight. It looked like their connection was a no show. Maybe it was time to worry. Maybe it was time to call Yigael.

A tap on the door and Nicolo grabbed his Glock 23 as Abba peeked around the edge of the curtain. He motioned for Nicolo to stand down and then opened the door to a frazzled Valentina.

"Do you know how many seedy hotels I searched to find you two?"

"No, *signora*. We do not," Nicolo said.

Valentina shook the feeling of anger and panic, entered, sat on the musty bed, refocused, and started again. "There's been a change of plans. I have a canister for the ...." As she looked around, Abba handed her the leather cylinder that contained the scroll.

We need to seal it in here, and then bury it. Now."

"*Sì*," Abba said.

Valentina noticed they were dressed in construction worker attire. Though surprised by their compliance—they seemed to be one step ahead of her—there was no time to evaluate anything. Off the map since morning, Yigael had forced Valentina to rely on her female intuition for the better part of the day. When that ran dry, she called Josh, who suggested seven likely locations for the two agents. Tired, edgy, hungry, sweaty, and out two hundred euros in cab fare, she retrieved the canister from her bag and slid the scroll out of the leather case. There it was again. In her possession for the second time that day.

Abba took the leather case from her and put the lid back on. Then, he stuck it in his duffle, to return to its owner.

The two operatives watched intently, as she inserted the scroll into the newly acquired canister and sealed it back up.

By the time she looked up to let them know she was all set, they had their jackets on and duffle bags in hand. "So, he won't call me back, but you guys are in-the-know and at-the-ready?" She couldn't help herself.

"We will take it from here, *signora*," Nicolo said.

"You'll 'take it from here' my tushy." Valentina rose from the bed, put the canister back in her woven satchel, and draped it over a shoulder. "Who's driving?" she snapped.

Abba and Nicolo gave each other a look and followed her out.

A minute later, in the parking section in front of this off-the-beaten-path and mostly vacant motel, the trio climbed into a nondescript, scuffed-up, pickup truck.

Hauling a backhoe on a trailer, they drove out of Naples heading back to where Valentina had, ironically, come from earlier that afternoon. Abba offered Valentina a bottled water and pouch with fresh almonds for the journey. For this, she was grateful.

CHAPTER FIFTY-FOUR

Siena, Tuscany

JACQUES, PHILIPPE, AND GABRIELLA HAD MADE GOOD TIME ON the 1,100-kilometer trek from Saint-Denis to the safe house in Siena, stopping only to refuel and arriving in under twelve hours, just before midnight. Though, between the anger and the sexual tension dampening the mood in the Kodiaq, the journey had been endless for Jacques.

The safe house was in the thick of things, right in the center of Tuscany during peak tourist time. Jacques knew Yigael had chosen this spot intentionally for that reason. Their comings and goings would be invisible among the throngs of visitors circulating through the medieval town's bustling streets day and night. And the residents would have no idea who they were. They'd blend in, appearing to be there on business. Mossad agents, posing as security guards for VIPs, would guard them and their lodging day and night. They would use the Campo, Siena's main square, as a lookout point. No one could enter Siena without first passing through the Campo on foot.

Jacques had connected with two agents on the lookout on their way in. He felt confident in the locale.

Once they settled inside the stucco walls of this turn-of-the-last-century, three-bedroom flat, Jacques got a call. He held the phone to his ear, then grumbled, "Yep," and hung up. "I'm heading out."

"Can you grab me a ...?" Philippe started to say, but Jacques was gone, leaving him brooding in the *salotto*.

Minutes later, Gabriella exited the bathroom. "I'm all set if you need *les toilettes*."

"I'm fine. I'm like a camel," Philippe commented.

"Have you heard from the others, about Uncle Claude?"

"No. Have *you* heard from Uncle Claude?"

She gave him a look, a definitive no. "I am going to lie down."

Before she even took a step toward a bedroom, Philippe was all over her. "What's your end game?"

"*Pardon?*"

"Your end game? Your master plan? Your scheme? What's your angle?"

"It is not my plan. Therefore, it is not for me to reveal. What is yours?"

"To get to the truth."

"I like that."

"You like that? What's that supposed to mean?"

"The truth. It is always better than the alternative. Do you not agree?"

"That's rich coming from you."

Gabriella threw up her hands and stormed off.

"Gabby!" he called.

The slamming of a door was her only response.

No sooner did Philippe exhale his irritation than the front door opened to Yigael, who was returning from his walk, followed by Jacques.

"Yigael, hello."

Yigael nodded.

"No one's heard from Uncle Claude, in case you're wondering."

"Then we wait," Yigael said, sitting down.

CHAPTER FIFTY-FIVE

Ercolano

ABBA SPOTTED THE DESOLATE CONSTRUCTION SITE BY ITS fluorescent-yellow flag, flapping from a marker stick. Yigael had instructed Nicolo and Abba to make realistic preparation of the land for the updated irrigation system. Easy enough, except now they had but hours, as opposed to days, to mark the property and dig enough trenches to make it look legitimate.

They set down lights, and then the agents leveled off one area for rough grading, setting stakes and string lines, denoting where the system would go.

They'd been hard at it for some time. Valentina watched from the pickup until she couldn't take it anymore. She emerged with the satchel containing the scroll in tow. "I can't just sit in there. The minutes, it feels like they're moving backward."

Abba nodded and handed her the spool of rope. She took direction from Nicolo, as Abba sprang onto a backhoe and started digging.

About an hour before daybreak, when they had done

enough to confuse the few onlookers that might pass by on a morning stroll, hot and hungry, they broke for more packaged "treats," eating in the truck.

Then, they began work of a different kind.

Valentina placed the canister in Nicolo's care as if it were a newborn, which made her laugh on the inside. They were burying it, after all. Then, she grabbed an extra shovel and started digging. Valentina was no stranger to a shovel.

She hadn't spent much time in the dirt as of late, but it wasn't because of recent circumstances. Running a laboratory didn't really afford her the time to venture back into introductory-level tasks of an archaeologist, such as getting dirty in the field. She missed that part. Burying what may turn out to be the world's most controversial artifact was high stress but exhilarating. She could feel bits of the fine, gravelly earth under her fingernails and smell the magnesium in the soil. Looking up, she nodded to Nicolo, who placed the canister into her outstretched hand, and then she dropped it into the earth. Standing up again, she dug into her trousers for the coins she wanted to add. After scattering them, she and Nicolo dropped to their knees and began to cover up the lot.

On completion of this segment of the mission, Valentina jammed the head of her shovel into the ground and wiped her brow. "Okay, if someone wants to take me to the nearest hotel, I can shower and get ready, go to the boat caves for a few hours, then come back here once the scroll is discovered."

Abba gave her the tiniest of nods, stepped away from the site, turned to face the imminent sunrise, and placed a call. "It's done," he reported to Yigael.

Valentina figured he was calling Yigael. She wanted to grab the phone and scream into it but knew better. It wasn't Yigael's fault the Vatican was on their tail. Still, why had he abandoned her for the last twelve hours?

"Any problems?" Yigael asked.

"Well, she's still here with us."

"What?"

"She insisted."

"Get her the hell out of there."

"Okay," Abba said.

"Be damned sure she is on that plane."

"Okay."

"And stay there until security arrives."

"Okay."

"No screw-ups. Please." Yigael hung up.

Abba turned and, with a nod, Nicolo escorted Valentina to the pickup, which, as far as she knew, was her ride to a much-needed shower and a tasty cappuccino.

CHAPTER FIFTY-SIX

Siena

YIGAEL POCKETED HIS BURNER PHONE AND WALKED FROM THE *terrazza* back into the *solatto*, where Jacques and Philippe, having not slept a wink in the past forty-eight hours, were waiting for answers.

He stopped. "It's buried."

At that, the men relaxed.

Gabriella emerged from the kitchen with *caffés* for everyone. Then her phone *pinged*. She sat, read the text, and set her phone screen side up on the table. "My uncle."

Philippe picked it up and read: "*Gabriella, I heard you went away for the weekend. Where to? We could meet up on my way home.*"

He placed a hand on her shoulder for comfort. "It's going to be okay, Gabby."

"Somebody catch me up," Yigael demanded. "May I?" he asked, with a hand thrust in Philippe's direction.

Gabriella nodded, and Philippe handed him the phone.

Yigael reread the text and scrolled up, looking at older

messages, mostly having to do with groceries. "You think this is a clear sign that someone has him?"

"I know it is. Because he called me Gabriella. He never calls me that. And the whole message is strange. He didn't write this."

"You need to tell us what you know," Yigael said. "If your uncle has been kidnapped, he is in danger."

"The Vatican. It is the Vatican behind this," she said.

"How so?"

"Uncle Claude found the treasure about a year back. It was around the time Julia Episcopa was discovered and everyone was talking about her. Well, a female bishop from a past century did not sound strange to my uncle, and he did not agree when the Church dismissed it. Still, he was prepared to go to the Vatican and tell them about the treasure. But when Pope Augustine died, he changed his mind. He had no facts, but he knows very well what the Church is capable of."

Yigael fixed his eyes on his shoes. Jacques and Philippe exchanged a quick look.

"In any case, it no longer felt right to reveal the treasure. We know it is big news. Uncle Claude was afraid that if he told the Church, we might not be safe. We might be in their way. And what would they do to us? We did not have careers they could ruin. We are not high-profile people. We are no one. If we disappeared, who would know?"

Yigael nodded. "I understand." He stretched out a hand. "Please, continue."

"Uncle Claude wanted to get it into the right hands. Yours," she said, cocking her head.

Jacques and Philippe peeked at Yigael.

"My fans stretch far and wide," he said, looking as clueless as they were.

"Oh, they do," Gabriella said. "My uncle is definitely a fan, Yigael. He crossed paths with your father when he was in the

French Resistance. They worked together in the underground, moving Nazi targets in France out to safer ground. Then, when all that was over, he went into the seminary, and your father wed your mother. They stayed in touch until your father passed away. My uncle followed your career in the Israeli Army and the Mossad and then as an archaeologist. 'Like father like son' he would say. He hoped to meet you one day."

Yigael was humbled, as he always was by stories about his father.

"He knew there'd be risks planting the coins. But he hoped to attract your attention before the Vatican got wind of them."

Yigael turned to Jacques and Philippe just as his phone rang. "Josh, we're not dealing with just any priest," he blurted.

"Tell me about it. Susan's pulled up everything but his favorite color over the last twelve hours. He received the Legend & Merit Award for his work in World War II, freeing hundreds of Jews from the Nazis. Did you know that? This guy could've been anyone, a general, a prime minister, a king, but he followed a religious calling."

"Right. That's the good news."

"And the bad?"

"He has been kidnapped. By the Vatican."

CHAPTER FIFTY-SEVEN

Parioli

AT HALF PAST EIGHT IN THE MORNING, A FUMING VALENTINA marched into her apartment, where Erika was waiting.

In the safety of her home, Valentina was finally free to vent.

Erika braced herself. "How was your flight?"

"How are we supposed to get chosen to translate the scrolls if I'm not there among the crowd to fight for it after it's dug up?"

So much for small talk. "I don't know, Val. I'm on an extremely limited need-to-know basis too."

"He won't even answer me! I keep calling and calling." She dug in her satchel and retrieved the burner phone, then she gave it a dirty look and threw it across the room. It hit the couch and bounced off, landing under the coffee table. "Have you talked to him at all?"

"No. I wasn't even supposed to talk to you. I'm sure he's terribly angry with me for not keeping my word."

"Not as angry as I am with him. I'm going to kill him!"

"Why don't you hop in the shower? Maybe it'll help you relax."

Valentina's blue button-down was gray with dirt and sweat. "A shower? When the scroll is supposed to be discovered any second now?"

Erika sat down on the sofa. "There are two things I know about Yigael. One, he'd never do anything to jeopardize an opportunity to discover a piece of history. Two, you know he'd never do anything to hurt you."

Valentina collapsed, dirty clothes and all, onto the other end of the sofa. Erika had a point. "Then, what's happening?"

Erika had no answer but knew it was more of a rhetorical question, anyway.

The phone buzzed. Valentina looked around.

Erika crouched down, grabbed the burner phone from under the coffee table, and handed it to her.

She pressed *Accept*.

"Valentina," Yigael said.

"Yigael, just tell me what's going on. And why haven't you been picking up?" She reminded herself to breathe. "No, never mind. What's going on with the scroll?"

There was a knock on the door.

"Now what?" they said in unison.

Erika opened it. "Yigael?"

He looked about as somber as they'd ever seen him.

"What are you doing here? Won't this look like a setup if you're not back home?" Valentina asked.

"They have Father Fullier."

"They as in 'they'?" Erika asked.

"Yes. And, though I have since learned that the man can handle himself, it doesn't change the fact he's in his mid-eighties."

"Oh, God." Valentina said. "Yigael, sit down. What do you mean handle himself?"

After Yigael shared Father Fullier's past, heavy silence ensued.

Then Erika said, "David v. Goliath. Why does David win in that story? It just gives everyone else false hope."

Their match against the Vatican was done before it had begun. They hadn't even gotten in a punch.

"I appreciate your initiative, everything you've done to get this scroll in the ground, Valentina," Yigael said, then turned to Erika, "You, too, blondie. In no small part, we made it this far because of both of you."

Wholly defeated, Valentina said, "Well, I'm going to shower."

"Valentina?" Yigael said as she walked past him.

Valentina studied him. "You know what you have to do now, Yigael." She left for the shower.

CHAPTER FIFTY-EIGHT

Village-sur-Colline

SUSAN'S LAPTOP WAS TAKING A BEATING IN THEIR ROOM AT *Chambres D'Hotes Les Fleurs.*

Josh was wearing down the carpet with his pacing. "Anything else? Anything?"

"Yes, blue."

"What?"

"His favorite color."

Josh made a face. "We're talking about an institution that offed the holiest man on earth without blinking."

"That's hearsay."

"Sure, okay. We have to find Father Fullier. Bottom line."

"Or Father Fullier has to find us," Susan said.

"What?"

"I've been thinking ... if we offer the Vatican a ransom in exchange for one old, French priest, they'll release him. We'll demand they tell us where he is."

"They couldn't care less about money. They want the scroll."

"Exactly." Though Susan hadn't really slept in over twenty-four hours, she perked right up and started typing like a maniac.

Josh crouched behind her at the desk and watched as she DM'd journalist Michael Levin on Twitter and told him about the scroll. "What are you doing?"

"We need a middleman to strike the deal."

"The deal? We need to talk to Yigael."

"You call Yigael. In the meantime, I'll secure a middleman."

Secure a middleman? "Susan, we didn't go through all this to hand the scroll to the Vatican on a silver platter!"

"You and Yigael and Professor Banks and Dr. Gold all said that it's about the truth! This scroll, if it's worth anything at all, is not a prize to be won. And a man's life is at stake."

A tiny bell went off, informing Susan she had a notification.

"Whoa," Josh said at Levin's response time.

@michaellevinlacarta: *Why would I care about another scroll in Italy? I wouldn't be surprised if I had one in my back yard.*

Before she laid her fingers on the keyboard again and there was no turning back, she asked, "Do you have a better idea, Josh?"

He did not.

"Then, let's get Father Fullier to safety and let Yigael worry about the rest."

"Yeah, okay."

@susanlovesantiquities: *Not just another scroll, one the "powers" are fighting over.*

@michaellevinlacarta: *You're bluffing.*

@susanlovesantiquities: *00-1-8452391106*

"Like he's going to text."

Susan's phone *pinged.*

"Whoa," Josh said.

She replied with a photo.

Josh turned her phone in his direction to get a better view. "You took a picture of the fragments?"

"For posterity. Or, in this case, leverage."

Michael Levin: *Herod? Second Temple? This could be a forgery.*

Susan Bauer: *So, verify it.*

Michael Levin: *R U kidding?*

Susan Bauer: *How long will it take you to get to the Vatican?*

Michael Levin: *I basically sit on a stump outside the building.*

Susan Bauer: *I'm going to send you instructions and a script to use with the Holy Office.*

Michael Levin: *I know how to interview the guys in the dresses.*

Susan Bauer: *About a story that hasn't happened? The scroll hasn't been unearthed yet.*

Michael Levin: *Heading to my car.*

Susan turned to Josh. "Call Yigael."

As soon as he picked up his phone from the bed, it rang.

It was Yigael.

CHAPTER FIFTY-NINE

SCRIBE HAD THOUGHT BETTER OF THE IDEA, BUT YESHUA INSISTED on going back into Jerusalem each day to teach. The Roman Legion still watched from a high point, while members of the Sanhedrin cast covert glances their way. Scribe expected the Roman guards to arrest Yeshua at any moment. They listened carefully to what he said. But, apparently, he said nothing they could use against him. However, the atmosphere was far from calm. Scribe could see it in the way the guards walked around looking agitated, as if they expected trouble.

The number of local people, who had welcomed him so joyously on the first day, dwindled. By the fifth night, a somber Yeshua spoke only to his chosen twelve, Mary, and Scribe.

Around the fire eating their meal, Yeshua spoke of his impending doom. He said that his death would occur soon and, when it did, they must know how to conduct themselves.

After the meal, the scribe noticed Yeshua slumped by the fire, alone, and lost in thought. John, seemingly Yeshua's favorite, added more brush to keep the flames lit.

Lost in his own thoughts, Scribe had not the faintest idea what the others were up to, except that Mary was nowhere around. What would happen to Yeshua's followers if he were no more? Could they return to their old lives? Or would that be impossible? What would they do? Where would they go? How strange to think of so many lives resting on the narrow shoulders of one man.

Shishi 12 Nisan

Before Yeshua went to sleep tonight, he asked me to write down that he did not fear death. The agony of this tore right into my stomach.

"I beg of you, Scribe, make sure you note that I see my death not as an ending but a beginning."

"Yeshua, you know that we cannot live without you."

"You will. It will be up to you to continue what I have begun, not in my way but your own."

So, when the others curled up inside their tunics to rest, the scribe took his place against the stump of an olive tree and, with branches from a young willow brushing across his forehead, he logged Yeshua's words.

CHAPTER SIXTY

Bethany AD *33*

Hamishi 13 Nisan

*I begin this writing dazed at what took place this very
evening. Yeshua called everyone closest to him, including me,
to share a meal together. A wealthy merchant had offered us
a large room where we could meet.*

*When his chosen twelve, Mary, and I had taken our places at
a large dining table, Yeshua entered, clad only in a towel
fastened at his waist and carrying a basin of water. The sight
mystified all of us. I noticed everyone glancing furtively at
each other. I could tell they had no idea what was going on.*

*When he stooped down and began to wash each one's feet, I
thought there was a real chance he had gone mad. He spoke
not a word until he finished with all of us.*
*Then he told us that this ceremony, as he called it, symbol-
ized man's equality.*

I could not fathom what he meant by this. How crazy to wash someone's feet. What would he say next?

"We live in separation, one from another, master and slave, teacher and student, owner and worker, and man and woman. What separates us is the way we live, one above the other. However, in God's eyes, we are all equal. If I am your teacher and I wash your feet, you, as my followers, must wash one another's feet."

Then, as he passed the bread, he spoke of it as if it were a part of his body. Did he honestly expect anyone to believe that? I nearly wondered that aloud but, as I looked around the room, I saw everyone eating in reverence, their eyes grave. I looked at my hunk and then at Yeshua. His hair was like black silk under the dim, amber light of the lanterns.

I love you. We cannot exist without you. *I hoped he could read my mind as I reached for my bread and wolfed it down. That is when it made sense. With the bread inside my body, I could hold onto the man, not be apart from him.*

He passed an earthenware cup of red wine, expecting each of us to drink from it. I was the last to partake. A profoundly sacred experience, from which I did not recover quickly. I felt a rush of air circling above me and through my body. My body became heat, and I realized that I had sipped of the blood of Yeshua. I gripped that cup so tightly that when we departed, I unknowingly took it with me.

Yeshua referred to this evening as a celebration. Then he told us he would die within days. How could that be a celebration? Surely, Mary thought it no celebration, for she sobbed openly. He explained that his death will not matter because he will still live in spirit. "The body is but one life, the spirit continues on," he said. He asked us to comfort each other and ourselves by the certainty that he will go to God, who will smile and welcome him, but that his spirit will remain with us.

Mary's sobs grew quieter, but her devastation was palpable. She stared down at her plate, unable to raise her eyes. Her bosom rose and fell as she tried to contain her emotions.

Yeshua went to her and placed a hand on her shoulder. "I shall always be with you."

At his touch, Mary broke into heaving sobs.

Yeshua held her face with both hands as he leaned down and kissed her forehead. Then, he said, "You all must love and look after each other. Remember, I shall never be far away.

"Peter, when you cast your nets into the sea, the drop of water that splashes your face will be the dew of my kiss." To me, he said, "Scribe, when you write, I will be the light touch you feel above your thumb as you dip your pen into your inkpot.

"All of you," he said, "I will be the light that finds you, the bright moon that shines your night into day. I will be with you. Always."

Then, he stood up, turned to one of the lanterns, and leaned into it just enough to set his face aglow. "I feel chilled," he said quietly. "It does grow cold here at night."

CHAPTER SIXTY-ONE

Gethsemane AD *33*

HOW THE SCRIBE LONGED TO LEAD YESHUA OUT OF THIS CITY, TO find a haven. Running away seemed the only practical thing to do. He begged God to hear his prayers and keep Yeshua safe.

A recurring thought added to Scribe's already frenzied state. *Could I, with my scrolls, be the one who betrays him? Might the ones that I wrote at the Temple create his demise? Might these that I have now be wrested from me and used to prosecute him?*

Scribe was so glad to leave that room, the room of anguish, as he thought of it.

They returned to their campsite and lit a fire. Yeshua sat nearest, holding his hands close to it, though the weather was mild. The scribe stared at Yeshua.

"Scribe, put your scroll back in your satchel and follow us," Yeshua said. He beckoned to Peter, James, and John.

Scribe tucked his scroll into the safety of his pack and rose.

"We are going atop the hill for a quieter place to pray."

When they were far enough from the others, Scribe heard Yeshua whisper, "My time is growing ever short." It seemed he did not intend any answer back. Scribe restrained himself from pleading with his master again.

They crossed a valley to Gethsemane, a lovely garden on the hillside of an olive grove. They had all visited here, Yeshua passing through on his way to visit friends in Bethany and his chosen ones coming to unwind after a busy day. The moon was almost full and very bright, so they did not need lanterns, though the scribe was carrying one through force of habit.

"I try to tell myself not to be afraid of what faces me," Yeshua said again, facing the foursome. "I fear it will be painful. But I worry more for each of you. I beg you to find the strength to continue our mission. Do not go back to your lives as they were and forget me. Then I would have died in vain. Promise me, John, you, especially. Promise me."

"You know I will never forget you," John said. "This talk of death, please don't give in to this, Master. Why do we not run off, go back north? Live in Galilee?"

Scribe thought the same thing.

They reached the peak of the hill, high above the city. Yeshua turned to them. "It is too late. I cannot turn back."

The scribe could see lights from lanterns in the buildings lining the streets. They twinkled like stars, but from no sky he wanted to lie under.

"Oh, Father, give me the strength to face them!" Yeshua fell to his knees before them, his hands pressed together. "My body aches and I am tired and afraid. Why did we come here? Why must this happen? I find myself enjoying life now, the beauty everywhere." He shifted his gaze to the tops of the olive trees glowing subtly in the moonlight and then, looking down, ran his fingers through the weeds as if they were a silk mantle. "I do not want to die. There is still so much I have yet to see, so many experiences yet to have. Please, I want to live. I feel my heart beating and I do not want to lose that pulsing feeling. Please, Father?"

It seemed as if the scribe could feel Yeshua's heart beating, pulsing, in rhythm with his own.

Yeshua looked up at them. "I must be left alone now, but please stay close by. I am afraid to be too far from you. Just move a few steps back so I may pray to our Father in solitude."

Scribe paused for a moment. From the top of the hill, he saw the open desert stretched out before them. *Would Yeshua try to escape? He could go to Lazarus's home in Bethany. He would be safe, for a while anyway.*

He wanted to grab Yeshua and shake him, take him across that desert. He would have Thaddeus help tie his hands and feet and then lead them along a path where no one could find them.

Scribe knew this thought was ridiculous. He joined the others and walked away obediently.

James and Peter's faces glistened with tracks of fresh tears.

John sobbed openly. "He does not want to die. Why, why must he ...?

Scribe felt as they did, but it showed not in his demeanor. The temple priests had ingrained in him that one must never show emotions openly.

No one was quite sure what happened next.

Out of nowhere, two soldiers appeared, hooked their hands under Yeshua's arms, lifted him from a kneeling position, and led him away at quite the clipped pace. Right there. On the hill-top. It was surreal.

The scribe and the others had no time to react. Peter, regaining composure, raced to follow them. He returned, devastated, meeting John, James, and the scribe, who had returned to the base of the hill.

"They took him to Pontius Pilate," he said, catching his breath. "We cannot stay here. The Romans will likely come for us, arrest us, and ..." Peter stopped himself, unable to say the words.

John finished his thoughts. "Kill us too. That cannot happen. We must survive to spread Yeshua's word."

They hustled back to the campsite where they rejoined the others. Shock registered on every face when Peter told them what had happened to Yeshua.

Matthew pressed the others to return to Galilee. "A few of us could go," he said.

"It won't be safe to split up." Peter urged everyone to wait until Thaddeus could lead a group back in safety. But a few went off on their own, anyway. It seemed that, in no time at all, their group was falling apart.

Those remaining stayed where they were, at the campsite. For the scribe, not knowing what Yeshua was up against tormented him. Every so often, they'd get an update, the latest being that the soldiers had, in fact, taken him to the house of the high priest.

But Scribe argued that it could not be true. "The high priests would never bother themselves with matters of state during the festival of Passover."

The rumors persisted.

"Let's search the upper city for him," John said. "Let's just go. We have to do something."

"It won't work," Peter said. "We wouldn't be able to pass through the gate without attracting attention." Residents of this exclusive part of the city knew each other well. They would identify any of these men instantly as the ones chosen by the man in custody.

Scribe was numb with fear. He would probably follow any expedition led by John. However, what Peter said, urging restraint, made sense. They must not place themselves in danger. They must live to spread the word. The scribe could see now why Yeshua made Peter the man in charge in his absence.

Finally, John nodded in agreement with Peter's insistence, though he seemed too distraught to think on his own or come up with a better idea. Scribe wondered if John would ever recover.

Scribe thought of last night, of how things could have turned out differently. He replayed alternative scenarios in his head until daylight crept in between the trunks of the trees. No one had slept a wink.

Then, Yeshua was seen leaving the high priest's house with temple guards all around him hurling insults. That was the latest word.

What is Yeshua thinking? Feeling? Where he is now? Whose faces does he see? The scribe could only hope the hearts Yeshua now stood before were not those of murderers. He could only hope they would show him compassion, see him as the peaceful, kind man he was, one who had done nothing to violate their laws. However, the scribe had lived among the high priests. He knew their language. He understood their intentions. Now, he could only hope, and wait.

CHAPTER SIXTY-TWO

CARDINAL LAVOTI HADN'T SLEPT IN DAYS. TO CAUSE HIM EVEN more consternation than his sleeplessness had, the incorrigible Michael Levin had materialized. There he was, sitting in front of him, ankle resting on a knee as if he were watching the World Cup from the comfort of his living room, beer in hand. His presence visibly irritated the cardinal. Yet, he had Levin ushered into his office as if he were the pope on Easter. Something big was up. *But damnation, where's my tea?*

As they waited on morning treats from Father Rinaldi, Michael Levin noted that Cardinal Lavoti looked spindlier than usual but then his thoughts veered to his new source. As a journalist, he had built his career on hints and hunches and a whole lot of legwork. And sometimes, his stories fell apart. But @susanlovesantiquities was proving to be a force as sources go. Still, Levin had only part of the story, but he had enough. And he could have the story of the year.

Father Rinaldi waddled in with a tray.

"That will be all, Father Rinaldi," the cardinal said before he'd even set it down.

And off the priest went, with curiosity piqued. The journalist didn't miss that either.

The two branded a couple of insincere smiles as they reached for their tea simultaneously.

Sitting back, Michael Levin revisited the text on his phone from Susan, cringing at the script she'd written. *Here goes.* "I hear it's 'raining good deeds' at the Vatican these days."

"It usually is," Cardinal Lavoti replied.

"I hear you personally sent a search and rescue team to the South of France, something about a senile priest."

"Excuse me?" the cardinal said. "I thought you were here about a scroll?"

"Oh, yes, I did come to interview you about the first-century scroll that I'm to understand the Vatican has in its possession." Levin understood the Church had no such thing in her possession. "But this story about the old priest is so heartwarming. Too often the world overlooks these small acts of kindness."

Cardinal Lavoti was unsure how to answer. He was not, however, unsure about what was happening regarding the priest. "Oh, yes, I agree," the cardinal said, regaining his footing. "But I'm not a man to brag. It is the job of the Vatican to take care of her own."

Levin took out his phone to record the conversation. "May I? Transparency is vital in journalism."

"As it is in my line of work," Cardinal Lavoti said, agreeing to go on the record, adrenaline surging.

"So, before we move on to what's sure to make front-page *world* news—how the Church talked a private landowner out of an old scroll—tell me, Cardinal Lavoti, how is Father Fullier? It must have been traumatic. So far away from home. Is he recovering here ... at the Vatican?"

For the first time since the release of the encyclical,

Cardinal Lavoti was smiling on the inside. *Ah, a trade. Priest for a scroll. Perfect.* This was better than what he'd schemed up, which had its drawbacks, should the police identify the church thieves and trace them back. This way was cleaner, easier. *My Church will be preserved as she has always been.* He should've kidnapped Father Fullier weeks ago had he known it was going to be this simple. He just needed to make the details of this exchange crystal clear to Michael Levin's people, as surely this guy was just the messenger.

"Mr. Levin," Cardinal Lavoti began, "are you familiar with the Ninth Commandment?"

"I know them all, Cardinal, like Italy's National Anthem."

"Of course, then you know that if you break one, anger will descend on you like King Manasseh. According to scripture."

"I am indeed aware of the power of the Lord. And the killer king, Manasseh."

"Good," Cardinal Lavoti said. He was convinced he'd been very clear about what would happen to Levin if he lied. This was indeed a brand-new day. One that would end with the *Secret Temple Scroll* in the Vatican's possession. "Then, I am delighted to report that Father Fullier is recovering nicely in the mountains. It's so tranquil there."

A crumb but that was okay. "Nothing beats the mountains." Michael Levin stopped the recording and stood. "Thank you for your time, Cardinal. I'm going to let you get on with your busy day."

As Michael Levin walked away, Cardinal Lavoti's blood pressure hit the roof. "Hey, not so fast. Get back here. What do you have for me?"

Levin squeezed his cheeks, having gotten his fix, and pivoted. "Oh," he said, returning to the cardinal's desk. "I almost forgot: a gift." He pulled a bottle of Gallo olives from his jacket pocket. "I hear you're a big fan. You know they're ripe for the picking ... *today*."

As Cardinal Lavoti stared at the jar, Michael Levin could see the machination form in his mind and greed take shape on his face. It was something. That, more than anything, informed Levin that whatever was on that scroll, it was huge. *Maybe a Pulitzer,* he thought.

On his way out of the office, having nodded to Father Rinaldi, Michael Levin sent the voice memo from their meeting to Susan via text. Before the door shut behind him, he heard Cardinal Lavoti roar, "Have the car out front in ten minutes!"

CHAPTER SIXTY-THREE

Ercolano

AT 9:15 AM, FROM HIS HOME OFFICE, DANO PICKED UP HIS MOBILE phone on the first ring. After telling Abba he'd be right there, he placed a call to Mayor Sassari.

"There's a Giordano Gallo on the line, Mayor," his secretary said, shuffling behind him."

"I'm on my way to a meeting, Martina. Take a message."

"He claims an ancient canister was dug up when workers began excavation to update his irrigation system."

The mayor pivoted a hundred and eighty degrees on a heel and headed back to his office. "Giordano Gallo, the olive guy?"

"I would think so, Mayor."

The mayor sighed. "Okay, fine. Get Antiquities on the phone." Per protocol, the mayor had to notify the Antiquities Department of Campania on any kind of discovery.

Antiquities dispatched Leonardo Montalbano, the Vesuvius National Park Museum Curator, to the site. He notified his new department chairperson to join him. In archaeology, two sets of eyes were always better than one when it came to the initial verification of a drudged-up artifact. And, though artifacts were plentiful in Italian soil, when one of importance showed itself, discretion was key, of which he reminded the mayor.

It was no coincidence that a young priest *lingering* at the Antiquities Department overheard the call. At this point, an hour into the trek to Ercolano, Cardinal Lavoti had a "young priest" posted at every antiquity department from here to Sicily, waiting on this scroll to turn up. The young priest reported directly to the mothership with the news, as instructed, to Cardinal Lavoti's delight. He forwarded official instructions to let Father Fullier go. He'd kidnap him again if he had to.

Then, he notified Cardinal Justin Parina, the man in charge of the Vatican library and now Valeri, that he had received a call about a scroll and was heading to Ercolano.

AT ELEVEN O'CLOCK, six professionals of one thing or another circled the bogus grave while a handful of neighbors looked on from outside the perimeter. Dano, the two Mossad agents Nicolo and Abba, Ercolano Mayor Sassari, the Vesuvius Museum curator Leonardo Montalbano representing the Antiquities Department, and his new chairperson stared at the canister peeking out from the soil, each with individual thoughts about who would take possession of it.

Montalbano indicated to one of the construction workers to extract the canister from the trench so they could give it a look-over. Nicolo carefully removed it. Montalbano asked him to dig around a bit while they dealt with this, as there was often a spattering of items. Abba jumped in, shovel in hand to assist, and came up with but three silver coins.

Everyone else went over to a shady area of the grove that had tables and chairs for sorting olives. Montalbano walked the canister to a table, extracted the scroll, and carefully laid it out for all to see. Thirty minutes later, the scroll, back in its canister, was boxed and ready to go to its next locale. Except that Dano didn't know who to hand it to because Valentina hadn't arrived. He was beginning to sweat, thinking about how to stall when a car pulled up. *There she is.*

But it wasn't Valentina, fashionably late. It was Cardinal Carlo Lavoti, with Father Orio Rinaldi struggling to keep up.

Materializing out of nowhere, Cardinal Lavoti got right to it, insisting that the Church receive the item because the Vatican's new lab had the most sophisticated technology to date. "It would only make sense to send the scroll there, all due respect to *Signore* Montalbano."

On that note, Dano's phone rang. He excused himself and took it. "Oh yeah?" He squinted toward the group, eyes landing on one particular dignitary. "Uh huh. Sure."

Leonardo Montalbano, with his protégé, and Mayor Sassari by his side, reinforced his claim to the scroll, declaring, "Such a find belongs to the state. *Signore* Gallo phoned us, and we plan to take possession." Then, he looked at his representatives for backup. The mayor, wide-eyed and open-mouthed, looked like a dog waiting on a treat, but his new protégé chairperson just stood there seemingly lost in space. *The Church really knows how to put a wrench in things. The box was practically in my hands for Pete's sake!* Montalbano was incensed.

Like a border dividing two countries, the table holding the box containing the canister that housed the *Secret Temple Scroll* separated the suits from the cassocks.

Though both sides were salivating, with Dano playing godfather, no one was more curious about its contents than Montalbano's new protégé, Kara Maggi.

Kara recognized the canister—that was for sure. She'd had it in her possession less than twenty-four hours ago. However, she did not recognize the scroll that it suddenly and magically contained—one that pre-dated the second century and that she determined authentic, based on her initial review of the calf-skin and the seal it branded. Her brain was in overdrive, trying to unravel the *hows* and *whys* of Valentina's deceit.

Kara had planned to tell Valentina of her new position as Chairperson of the Board of the Antiquities Department, but her mentor had fled as oddly as she'd appeared and hadn't shown up at the boat caves that morning as the guest archaeologist as planned.

Valentina had to have been desperate for this item to bury the scroll. But how could she have known there'd be an empty canister, perfect for a scroll, waiting to be scooped up on site at the boat caves? Was the woman clairvoyant on top of all her other talents? *And where is she?* And the question of all questions that Kara was trying to unknot was: *What in the world does that scroll say?* Whatever its contents reveal, Valentina was willing to risk everything to get it buried and unearthed the old-fashioned way. Someday, she would find out the real story but, at this moment, though the internet was choppy, she was searching antiquities law on her phone. There had to be a loophole that gave the state the right to artifacts on private land because Kara was determined to leave with that canister.

Dano slid his phone back into his pocket and stepped back into the commotion. To elevate the dramatic tension even more, he took a beat before saying, "This land belongs to me, and here is what will happen next. As a devout man of God, I believe entrusting this canister and its contents to the Church is the right thing to do."

Though the cardinal knew this meant he was dancing with the Mafia, his pointy shoulders relaxed. Father Rinaldi did the tiniest of dances on hearing the news and then wrapped his hands tightly around the box, lifting it from the table and hugging it close.

"Artifacts discovered on this land do not belong to you!" Kara Maggi stated emphatically.

Montalbano clutched his chest. His silent partner had come alive. "Dr. Maggi, I, too, am not pleased about this outcome, but the land has been in his family for more than eighty years. It was deeded to his wife when she turned eighteen, almost three decades ago. It is the choice of the private landowner, having owned property for twenty years or more, to choose to whom these types of discoveries are entrusted. The law is plain. And *Signore* Gallo has made his choice."

"But they've only been married for eight years," Kara said, tempering her anger, moving the fight from her heart to her head.

"In the country of Italy, a man can speak on behalf of his wife and vice versa," Montalbano countered. "And all possessions and property become jointly owned."

"As of the date of the marriage agreement." Kara was not leaving without that scroll.

"I assure you, Dr. Maggi, my wife would be in agreement with me, but I appreciate your feminine ... initiative." Then Dano turned to the clergymen and, with the slightest of bows, said, "Cardinal Lavoti, Father Rinaldi, please report the results accurately and expeditiously. Safe travels."

"Thank you." Cardinal Lavoti said. He and Father Rinaldi started to walk away with the scroll.

"Not so fast." Kara was frantic. Trotting along after them, she held her phone up high and read: *"If a spouse is incarcerated, the State speaks on their behalf, as all contracts tied to their name become null and void."* Circling them, Kara reached out to Father Rinaldi and yanked, however gently, the box out of his hands. "The state will take possession of the artifact. Thank you, Father."

Leonardo Montalbano took a cloth from a pocket inside his jacket and mopped his brow. An alarming side of Kara had popped up out of nowhere.

Kara turned to him, fire in her eyes, knowing, beyond the

ensuing Valentina scandal, this would be monumental for her on so many levels.

He smiled back.

Cardinal Lavoti shot a hateful glare at Dano. *Fix this!*

And that's when a black SUV pulled up, and Dano's wife, Bonnie, got out.

Cardinal Lavoti swallowed his venom and turned to Kara. "Losing is tough but you're young, dear. You'll get used to it." Then, he motioned for Father Rinaldi to reclaim the box.

And off they went, with Bonnie breezing past them right into Dano's arms.

As Kara watched the Vatican leave with the canister she'd unearthed but the day before, one that contained the world's most mysterious scroll, her phone buzzed. She held it up and read the text: *Under the weather. Sorry I didn't text earlier. Raincheck on dinner? Valentina.*

CHAPTER SIXTY-FOUR

Bethany AD *33*

Revi'I 14 Nisan

*He is dead now, and I do not know what to say. Yeshua
suffered for hours before he died, with John, the only one of
his chosen twelve, to stay by his side. None of us has the
energy to talk. We sit here, staring off, fading into semi-
consciousness. I do not remember when last we ate. I think I
have not slept for days. It must be the power of his spirit,
gently pressing my thumb and guiding my hand, for I know
not how I could be scribing otherwise.*

SCRIBE WATCHED AS JAMES CUT JUDAS DOWN FROM THE BRANCH
of an olive tree and cradled his dead body in his arms. He
wished he could feel pity for the betrayer, but none came. He
felt only the wretchedness at the death of Yeshua. As for James,
Scribe tried to lift him away from Judas's body, but he could
not. James, weak with shock, could not sit up or eat. Scribe
hoped he would find the strength to recover.

Sheni 17 Nisan

*Mary reported the most unlikely event to us. I could hardly
believe such a thing, but so overcome by the experience was
she that I walked there and indeed found Yeshua's body gone.
When I touched the spot where he had been placed, it was
warm. This I found strange, for a cold body would not heat
the stone beneath it. Who could have moved him? Why
would his body not remain here? Where could it be? I left
confused and wept, hoping that, somehow, he had managed
to escape death.*

*Then John awoke one morning to find Yeshua sitting comfort-
ably at his side. At least that is what he said. John said he
reached out and touched Yeshua's arm and it felt cool and
soft. Yeshua wore a crisp, white tunic stitched of the softest
cotton. Light seemed to radiate from it.*

*Peter also claimed to see him near a small bathing pond,
washing blood from his body. He said he could hear Yeshua
telling him to be strong and eat to stay healthy.*

The scribe left with Peter and others after seven days, not
certain about their next stage. Scribe planned to stay with Peter
and his wife for a time in Capernaum. They decided to
continue hosting Sabbath services for those who still wished to
listen. In time, perhaps, the number of followers would grow.
Or not. Maybe the scribe would end up back in Sepphoris,
learning another trade.

They would stop in Nazareth on their way north to visit
with Yeshua's family. John would stay and care for his mother,
as Yeshua had asked.

Capernaum AD 33

A LARGE COMMUNITY OF FOLLOWERS, saddened by Yeshua's death, greeted them in Capernaum. They settled in at their old campsite, on a hill high above town, dining in town occasionally with old comrades. The weekly Sabbath services were small, but those who came were faithful and seemed dedicated to spreading Yeshua's message. One thing was obvious: no single one of the chosen twelve possessed the great authority and charisma so readily displayed by Yeshua.

Peter honored the scribe as a valuable member of this new Jewish sect, and, as such, one for whom food and lodging must be provided by the other members. Therefore, Peter offered his home for as long as the scribe would like and agreed to support him with his fishing wages. He was now the official scribe for this new faith community and a servant of the mission.

Capernaum—Shabbat 22 Sivan

I am content here at Peter's place. I spend long days writing in the sun beside the calm shores of the sea. Even though I miss him immensely, I feel prepared and ready to embrace the next stage of my life. I can relax easily, as the priests no longer seek me out. With Yeshua gone, they have no use for me.

I am pleased that James has recovered from the loss of Judas so quickly. He is a soft-spoken man, a gentle and fair listener. In the past, when any of the chosen twelve had questions concerning the law and their own personal integrity, they went to Yeshua for clarification. Now, James seems to have taken his place in the eyes of many. He plans to share stories of Yeshua's early years, stories none of us have heard. I have my pen at the ready.

Capernaum—Shelishi 14 Av

A new, rather solemn fellow has joined us. His name is Paul and, he is a tentmaker. His eyes are grave, almost unblinking when we speak of Yeshua. Although he never met our teacher, he has absorbed all Yeshua's teachings and has an alarming recollection of all he has heard and read. I daresay he should be a scribe, so strong is his memory. Often, when I am writing my scroll detailing Yeshua's words, I consult Paul if I do not remember with clarity. He will respond, without thinking, perhaps only a few words, but those words will bring forth a large reserve of memories I thought were gone. He is a quiet man, often by himself, thinking. He enjoys my company, for he likes to make sure those items in his mind are now on papyrus.

Capernaum AD 34
Hamishi 16 Tishrei

I would be remiss if I didn't mention how often I think of Mary. She seemed to have disappeared after we left Bethany. None of us knew where she had gone or what she was doing. I figured she had simply gone home to Magdala. After all, she has a home and a business there. That made sense to me. I thought it not a bad idea to search for Mary and, then, there she was.

Mary wants to join our community and begin to teach. Truth to tell, she knows more of Yeshua and his teachings than anyone else, but Peter has rejected the idea.

I am beside myself and had it out with Peter. I do not know if

DIANE CUMMINGS & JOHN I. RIGOLI

*I can ever forgive him. I disputed his decision and impugned
his character, calling him out as jealous and acting in reverse
of Yeshua's words.*

He was unmoved and turned her away.

WITH SO MANY scrolls written in Hebrew and Aramaic, James
asked Scribe to begin translating them to Greek and Latin.
These languages were to form the basis for the *new way*. Thus,
the scribe spent his days alone in Peter's house, stooped over
his scrolls, translating Yeshua's words.

The months blurred together, the hot, dry season disappearing in the blink of an eye. The wheat had been cut for
another year, fruit had been distributed, and the trees were full
of ripe olives. Add to that, the joyous news came that Scribe's
sister had given birth to her first child, a boy, named after their
father. Scribe took a time-out to visit his family and meet his
new nephew.

His family welcomed him enthusiastically, just as they had
when he returned home after his years of study in Jerusalem.
After pleasant days at home, the scribe returned to
Capernaum.

CHAPTER SIXTY-FIVE

The Vatican
Present Day

WITH CARDINAL LAVOTI GLOATING AND FATHER RINALDI hovering over the box holding the scroll as if it were a dozen fresh-baked chocolate croissants, they made it back to Rome before five.

Exiting the town car with pep in his step, Cardinal Lavoti determined it was a new day at the Vatican. Once unfathomable, now the scroll, the *Secret Temple Scroll*, was in his possession. It could not sneak up on him like that damned encyclical had. He was now in control. And he'd managed all this without holding the highest, holiest rank. He would celebrate, he decided, with the *Ornellaia* red blend his cohorts had gifted him on acceptance of his position as prefect. He would toast to the world's oldest living reference to Yeshua's words never seeing the light of day.

"Father Rinaldi, into my office with the scroll. *Subito.*"

Following the cardinal as ordered and lost in thought from the exciting adventure, Father Rinaldi ran right into the back of

Cardinal Lavoti, who'd stopped cold on seeing his office was not empty.

The party, it appeared, had started without him.

"Cardinal Lavoti," Cardinal Parina began, "I've heard about all your acts of kindness. Busy bee, you've been this week. I had to actually read about them on Twitter, thanks to a student of Yigael Dorian's."

"An intern, Cardinal Parina," Yigael corrected. "A graduate student who works for Dr. Samuel Gold in Israel."

"An intern," the cardinal said. "Well, she sure is good with the social media. If I weren't in charge of the pope's account, I wouldn't know what was going on in my own backyard!"

Yigael approached the traveling clergymen. "Why don't I hold this for you, Father, while you and Cardinal Lavoti pose for a photo with Father Fullier." As he removed the box from Father Rinaldi's hands, he could feel the cardinal's rage building. After the last forty-eight-hours, nothing could have been more thrilling.

"After the photo op," Michael Levin said, stepping forward, "I'll get that blurb for the article we discussed earlier. Then, we'll be on our way."

"Yes, of course. Saving Father Fullier," Cardinal Parina said, beaming. "It's these acts of kindness the world of Christianity needs more of. The pope is most pleased."

Father Fullier hobbled over and held out a hand to Cardinal Lavoti. "Thank you, Cardinal. Who knows where I'd be without your service?"

The cardinal shook the old man's hand. He hardly had a choice.

The old priest nuzzled in between Cardinal Lavoti and Father Rinaldi for the picture, his smile bright and shining.

The flash went off, blinding everyone but no one more than Cardinal Lavoti, who couldn't shake the shock from this turn of events.

"Cardinal, Father, we have tea and snacks. I thought you might need light nourishment after your journey," Cardinal Parina said. Then he coughed and cleared his throat. "Now, onto that scroll."

Yigael held out a chair for Father Fullier, who took a seat. Then he sat next to him, the box containing the scroll on his lap, as the three clergymen and Michael Levin sat down.

"So, about this scroll," Michael Levin began. "Rumor has it, the document was scribed during the time of Yeshua?"

"You can't be making claims about a document that hasn't been translated, Mr. Levin," Cardinal Lavoti spat.

"Which brings me to my next question: Who will be translating the scroll, Cardinal?"

"The initial overview from the state said it was first century, no?" Cardinal Parina asked to no one in particular.

"It did. And I can tell from my 'initial' overview," Yigael responded, opening the canister and delicately sliding out part of the scroll, "that right there is a first-century seal, Second Temple to be precise."

"My niece and I," Father Fullier said, cutting into the conversation, "We don't have a lot in common with our age difference—you know the young—but we just love sports."

Huh? Yigael whirled around to the old priest, wondering whether "senile" did play a role in the game.

"Good for you, Father Fullier," Michael Levin commented.

"Take a world-class boxer, for example," Father Fullier said. "How do we know his worth unless he has another equally skilled opponent to fight?"

Yigael's smile broadened. *Why, the old rascal.*

Father Fullier continued, "The Vatican may very well have the fastest racecar in the world in its possession, Cardinal Lavoti."

"I believe we do, Father Fullier," Cardinal Lavoti said.

"But still, a driver is needed to prove it," Yigael said, completing Father Fullier's point.

"It's no coincidence Dr. Dorian was in the area," Cardinal Parina said.

"At the very hospital where Father Fullier was being released," Michael Levin added.

Cardinal Parina raised his hands in praise. "It's no coincidence because it's what the Church calls a miracle!"

"They happen every day," Father Fullier added.

"I believe it's a sign," Cardinal Parina went on.

"A sign?" Cardinal Lavoti was beginning to believe he'd burst into another dimension.

"Of course. A sign that the Vatican hire Dr. Dorian to head a commission."

"A *Secret Temple Scroll* Commission?" Yigael interjected.

"I like the sound of that. Yes, a *Secret Temple Scroll* Commission." Cardinal Parina laughed, releasing the joy he felt when the world came together as it should. "Just when we need a driver for our racecar, one walks right into the Holy Office. Can you believe our luck, Cardinal Lavoti?"

"Hardly," Cardinal Lavoti responded, choking out the word.

CHAPTER SIXTY-SIX

Twitter Post:

@michaellevinlacarta: From lost priests to ancient scrolls, it's raining good deeds at the Vatican this week! https://LaCarta.com/michaellevin-itsraininggooddeeds.

It's Raining Good Deeds at the Vatican
by Michael Levin

From the south of France to the heart of Italy's ancient artifact reservoir, the Vatican has been busy spreading goodwill. An ancient scroll was uncovered near the ruins of Herculaneum on Italy's western coast near Mt. Vesuvius. The scroll, excavated from the land of a prominent Italian businessman, has attracted attention in certain quarters of the antiquities' world because of its mention of Yeshua of Nazareth. Slightly worn, its lettering faded but decipherable, the initial scan suggests the scroll is a first-century document and may pre-date the gospels, which, if verified, would make it the oldest text in history that references Yeshua, oldest by decades.

In a near scuffle between the State and the Vatican, the Church was entrusted with the document. Then, in a twist only God himself could have seen coming, the Holy Office, headed by Cardinal Carlo Lavoti, created a commission with famed archaeologist Dr. Yigael Dorian and, together, they hired the renowned archaeological team of Valentina Vella and Erika Simone to translate the scroll. This act, on the heels of buying their research lab, Valeri, which was on the heels of bankrupting them, has been touted both wise and compassionate, and blessed by Pope Julius Africanus.

In news of a more local nature, just hours before this discovery, the Holy Office's new prefect saved an old, senile priest who'd lost his car and his way in the South of France. How Cardinal Carlo Lavoti knew of this "lost soul" is anybody's guess, but he was retrieved and released from *Provence Alpes sur-Colline* Medical Center early yesterday, thanks to the cardinal's intervention. Despite his advanced years, the elderly priest appears to be in good health.

After so much scandal, turmoil, and death in and around the Church in the last year, it's inspiring to watch our Christian leaders do unto others. And, I don't know about you, but I'll be waiting with bated breath to see what Vella and Simone uncover when they translate this scroll.

KARA MAGGI SHUT her laptop after reading the article. Then, she picked up the itemized sheet, a single artifact listed, along with Valentina's name printed next to where she was supposed to sign. If she didn't turn her in and this ever got out, she'd be an accessory to potentially one of the biggest crimes in ancient artifact history. Theft from archaeological sites erases the historical and cultural puzzle these treasures can provide. The moral, historical, and scientific implications of separating an item from where it was found—and thus splitting it from its historical context, its story, and from what it could tell us about how it was used and valued in the past—is criminal and considered unforgivable by many. It's rewriting history.

We are seekers of truth. With no clear answer trumping that echo in her head, Kara didn't know what to do. She'd learned from the first strong woman in her life, her grandmother, Rosa, a holocaust survivor, that when an answer is not clear, patience is the only suitable response.

It'd only been twenty-four hours since Kara had laid eyes on the canister that Valentina used to bury a scroll in Dano Gallo's olive grove, and she felt like she was losing her mind. Doing nothing, it turned out, as she'd been learning as of late, was not easy.

"Okay," Kara said to herself, partly as verification that the answer to this dilemma had yet to materialize, mostly to quiet her mind. Then, she folded up the sheet, put it inside her desk, and left for the boat caves.

CHAPTER SIXTY-SEVEN

Rome

BY MIDWEEK, VALENTINA AND ERIKA FOUND THEMSELVES BACK inside the walls of Valeri.

For Erika, it was a sign that she could put the whole Julia scandal behind her, and never look back. With her head down she got to work, organizing instruments. She turned on one computer and filled the screen with background material, especially the fragments found by Susan Bauer in Dr. Gold's office.

Valentina's breath caught when she walked through the office door. She had never let go of Valeri, still couldn't believe it had landed in the hands of the Church. She refused to consider that once this job was done, the "owners" might turn them out again. She scanned the place, secretly noting whether anything was missing. Running her fingertips over a tabletop, she raised her eyes to a window.

Erika glanced up. "What?"

"The shrubs have grown."

"So they have." Erika shuffled through a pile of papers. *Ah.* "Okay, my friend. I get it. I feel it too."

Valentina deposited her coat on the rack and joined Erika. Let's get to work."

They would be able to filter and manipulate images with the scanning devices they had purchased just before losing the lab. There were topnotch infrared spectrometers and a petro-graphic microscope for more intricate analyses of the day's finds. Results would be immediate, available with no outside lab required. They had envisioned this state-of-the-art facility, manifested it, and then somehow lost it. And here they were, back inside. Home, at least for now.

After reacquainting themselves with the lab, the two scientists turned their attention to the *Secret Temple Scroll*.

They began their work with the scientific description and classification, determining a range of dates within which the scroll had originated. They noted that the document was written in the first half of the first century, perhaps twenty to fifty years before any of the gospels that referenced Yeshua. They further noted the paleography, indicating the scroll was written in Herodian Book-Hand.

As the women rolled the scroll out farther, taking their time, allowing the calfskin to relax, Valentina bent closer. "Er?"

"Yo."

"The scribe who penned this scroll is the same one who wrote Mary Magdalene's story. When she arrived at Julia's villa in Herculaneum."

"Really? That scroll was from the second half of the first century."

"Meaning he would have been a kid when he did this one."

"Maybe the first thing he'd ever written. Fresh out of scribe school." Erika chuckled. "Documenting the life of Yeshua. Can you imagine his good fortune? I'll pull up the Mary Magdalene file." Erika hustled over to her laptop, opened the MM file. She pulled up the sparse images they'd been able to read and save.

She took her laptop to the scroll and compared the two.

"Right on." Erika shook her head in awe of both Valentina and their first major discovery about the *STS*.

"Yigael isn't going to believe this." It confirmed what Valentina had already known in her gut. "He's always wanted to know more about Julia's scribe." After a beat, she said, "You know what I'm wondering?"

"I can only imagine."

"I'm wondering where all the other documents are. The ones he scribed after this one and before Mary Magdalene's. They're decades apart."

"That is the billion-dollar question, Val."

CHAPTER SIXTY-EIGHT

Shishi 12 Sivan

*Factions have begun to form among the followers. Those who
believe Yeshua is indeed the son of God, or God himself, also
believe they are cleansed of their sins by confessing them in
his name. This belief is making temple rituals obsolete. There
is no longer any need for Yom Kippur, our Day of Atonement,
if we can rid ourselves of our sins daily in Yeshua's name.
The chosen twelve and the first disciples to follow Yeshua fall
into this category. We all pray each night not only to God but
also to Yeshua. We are unsure about how to answer questions
from those who cannot so easily let go of the religious teachings of their earlier years.*

*We still celebrate Rosh Hashanah and the days after it, due
more to tradition than to any belief in their significance since
Yom Kippur no longer has meaning for us.*

The changes Yeshua spoke of so passionately are still just ideas. Yet, they are ideas starting to come to life, finally, after three years without his presence.
Our numbers continue to grow.

Peter says the time has not yet come and we must be patient, but those of us still here in Capernaum will have to disperse eventually, with several of us going back to Jerusalem. This is how the word spreads.

CHAPTER SIXTY-NINE

Jerusalem AD 41
8 years since Yeshua's death

Shabbat 17 Iyar

*Life here is frightening. After the recent assassination of the
Roman Emperor Caligula, bloodthirsty soldiers took to the
streets. They are looking for new victims, mainly those who
celebrate the life of a man, a rebel rabbi, crucified some years
back. Though the Romans seem to have forgotten Yeshua's
name, we, of course, have kept it alive in our hearts.*

*Peter and James fled to the north directly following the assas-
sination. Unfortunately, Matthew, Thaddeus, and I had not
moved out of the city fast enough, and we were forced into
hiding. Fortunately, a wealthy Jewish gentleman took us into
his home. Thaddeus warned us not to leave the house, not
even to shop at the market. Such was the state of our lives
until I received word that my father was ill.*

We packed food and water and placed my scrolls into my painted bag, which I carried under my mantle, and stole away in the night.

No problems arose as we passed through the city gates. We followed the Roman soldiers' orders to stay close to the road.

Thaddeus and Matthew searched for a campsite outside Sepphoris, while I went to see Father.

He had died that morning, prior to my arrival.

I should have been home to embrace him, to bring him water. I left my father, left the life I should have led, left everything. And for what? To follow a man who is gone now. My father and I shared blood. We had the same laugh, were of the same height. There was our pale, yellow skin, our matching ginger hair, and we stood like twin statues when Mother used to instruct what to fetch from the market for supper.

Father, you are the life inside me. Forgive me for the life that chose me, forgive me that it was not a life that was lived by your side.

I sit here by the fire on our last overnight. Probably because it has been some time since I have slept outside, I feel jumpy. But maybe it's because I've never felt so alone.

CHAPTER SEVENTY

Corinth, Greece AD *49*
16 years since Yeshua's death

GREECE WAS FAR MORE BEAUTIFUL THAN THE SCRIBE EVER COULD have imagined. Though the climate was pleasurable, and the views in all directions were like a painting compared to the desert, Scribe was not as comfortable as when he was in Galilee. They were three: Scribe, Paul, and Thaddeus. They could not afford decent accommodations in Greece, and the people, though kind, were not willing to take them into their homes. They feared the Romans even more than the Jews did.

The Greeks had cults and worshipped gods with impressive fervor, which Scribe found fascinating. He wondered, under the circumstances, how they could possibly convert them. Add to that, their neighbors were foreigners who spoke dialects the scribe did not understand.

Nevertheless, Paul insisted this was the place to stay. With its vital ports, this city of Corinth was a gateway to the rest of the Empire.

Palpable unrest was growing throughout the Empire, with

talk of expelling Jews from the great city. Rumors were spreading that the Roman Army might soon make an appearance in Corinth, which meant the soldiers could identify the three as the perpetrators of the new movement. They had begun moving their campsite every three nights to stay out of reach. Six months in saw them weary and frustrated with their monotonous routine. By that point, it seemed as if the three had been traveling together since the dawn of time. So many cities, so many crowds. The scribe was not as young as when he had traveled with Yeshua so long ago. (*Could it really be almost twenty years?*)

Like the scribe, Paul had attended the temple school and studied under Gamaliel the Elder. However, he had not learned to write to where anyone could read it, so it was up to the scribe to record the movement's progress.

Then Paul changed his mind about staying in Greece. He decided they would travel to Rome, as it was the center of the Empire's power and, as such, the very place where they must spread Yeshua's word.

It was also the last place Scribe wanted to go, and he told Paul such a trip would be folly.

Paul answered him, saying, "All we have is today, Scribe. And today we live for Yeshua. If we wake up tomorrow, the sun on our faces because Yeshua deems it be so, we do it all over again. Live for Yeshua."

Corinth AD 50
17 years since Yeshua's death

Sheni 25 Sivan

We are in serious hiding now. Five days ago, the Romans marched through the center of Corinth, making it known that they are seeking the band of Yeshua's followers who are proselytizing among the citizens. We scrambled to move our tents far south of the city. The nearest village is a trading mecca, so we are posing as traveling merchants, though we have no product to sell.

Paul talks more often now about going to Rome and helping Peter establish a faith community there. I imagine that walking into Rome will be like entering the den of the devil himself.

If we could establish a base in Rome, we would have a congregation capable of reaching out in all directions. How often I have thought of that and imagined us bathed in luxury, living in glorious homes, with followers bestowing gifts and trust on us daily in exchange for morsels of wisdom. Ha! Those are pipe dreams. The opposite of what Yeshua would want. It is more likely that, in a city like Rome, we will be burned alive or stoned to death for the sake of our beliefs—a frightening reality but one that should sink in, so that being on alert becomes habit.

I just received word that Peter needs me in Rome.

"We live for Yeshua." And so, I must go.

LEAVING PAUL BEHIND, the scribe traveled by boat the very next day to Crete and through the Straits of Messina to Puteoli, then on to Rome, where he discovered that Peter's influence was growing, and baptisms had increased by the hundreds.

Peter had a small two-room apartment in a six-story building that he would now have to share with Scribe. After climbing the creaky, wooden steps, they came to a long hallway where another set of steps led them to the third floor. The hallways were filled with noise from tenants. Peter assured Scribe it was a little quieter higher up.

Reaching the sixth floor, Peter unlatched the wooden door. Scribe could not hide his disappointment. With only one window that overlooked the dusty street, the tiny room was furnished with a makeshift writing desk, a stove, and a short counter, which held two large cooking bowls and a pile of dishes. In the second room were two chamber pots and bedding for two.

Peter pointed to the cooking area. "There is some water in the jug behind the counter. I will let you wash and get comfortable before showing you around." And then he left.

Stripping down to his undergarments, the scribe washed off the dust from his journey. He could not compare this room to the one he lived in as a student, for that entire building was stone, with tall ceilings and big windows to air it out. In this apartment, the outer walls were made of stone, but the inner wall was made of thin wood. The room already seemed musky and thick with the unfamiliar odors left from previous owners. Luckily, the scent of bread and sweets baking from across the street managed to drift into their window, diffusing the unpleasant smells.

Peter took Scribe to the street to show him the nearest fountain, public baths, food markets, and a bakery that sold the best Challah.

"I shall give you a stipend while you live here. You will have to buy your food. "Wealthy citizens around here are interested in Yeshua, and they are supporting us. They agreed on the importance of a scribe here and asked me to request you come."

Scribe was impressed. He did not know Yeshua's reach was becoming such that people were willing to support a small group of his followers. As much as Yeshua despised it, he accepted people's gifts for the well-being of his disciples. Now Peter was accepting gifts to keep Yeshua's name alive.

The first night was the hardest, trying to sleep next to a snoring Peter in a room that seemed airless. Scribe cracked the window, but it allowed little relief. *So much for my aspiration to be an important scribe living in the walled enclave of the upper city,* he thought.

In time, he grew accustomed to the noise and heat of Jerusalem outside the temple grounds. He enjoyed the public baths, the cool breeze generated by the city's Romanesque fountains, the variety of foods available at the markets.

John visited frequently with messages from the "northern people." He and James had opened a part-time school, instructing children from Bethsaida and Capernaum about Yeshua. The school was thriving, and people were moving from Nazareth and Gischala so their children could attend. People who were barely into their teens came asking questions about Yeshua. Scribe was amazed by these youngsters now wanting to know of a man they would never meet. Yeshua's word was indeed alive.

Peter tasked Scribe with writing letters to new communities that were popping up like daisies in a field throughout the Empire. He insisted the new order understand that there was no longer any distinction between Gentiles and Jews, circumcised and uncircumcised, barbarians, savages, slaves, and free, but "Yeshua is all, Yeshua is in all."

The scribe discovered, however, that most people did not intend to abandon their separate identities, their class distinctions, their biases, and prejudices. The idea of uniting under Yeshua was intolerable to them.

And so, his work on enemy ground began.

CHAPTER SEVENTY-ONE

Rome
Present Day

AFTER NEARLY A MONTH IN THEIR LAB, WELL, THE VATICAN'S LAB, Valentina and Erika formulated their summary. They noted that the document was a litany of witness testimony against a rebel known as Yeshua, showing him to be not a holy prophet but a charlatan.

They recognized the *Secret Temple Scroll* as arguably the most significant discovery in the study of Christianity. They also knew that when made public the repercussions would be loud and unsettling. It would be argued as a hoax, even by the most esteemed scholars. But, because of the content, the teachings of the Church would, once again, come under scrutiny. This time the *STS* might not fade quietly into the background.

One evening, after finishing and locking up, Valentina, though exhausted, tossed about in bed. She dozed off for a stint but woke with a startle during the witching hour. As she sat up in bed, she could almost hear the outcry from conservative Christians who placed their faith in the gospels. They might come after her, again, and claim she was a fraud. Valentina should be worried about what a billion Christians thought of her with release of the *STS*, but she was unconcerned. This find had rocked her world in a separate way. It had resuscitated her. The thrill of participating in the scroll's discovery and translating it—there were no words.

With her focus deeply embedded in the *STS*, Valentina gradually put behind her the ill-founded attacks on her character, on her work. She felt whole again.

Yigael had been out celebrating Herschel's birthday. One pint led to another, and it was well after 1:00 AM by the time he arrived home and kicked off his boots. Normally, he regretted checking late-night email, as he'd always respond to two or three that could have waited until morning. But not tonight. There was one sent by Valentina entitled *STS* with an attachment. He downloaded the PDF and printed it.

It was with this copy, in an old armchair in the privacy of his Jerusalem apartment, under the dim light of a single reading lamp amid the darkness, tired, stiff, a little buzzy, and with Abra curled on his lap, that Yigael learned that the author of the *STS* was the scribe he yearned to know more about, the one that had lived and worked at Julia Lucinia's Herculaneum villa. Amazed, he sat relishing the content of his advanced reading sample.

CHAPTER SEVENTY-TWO

Jerusalem – Rome – Vatican City

YIGAEL CALLED TOGETHER THE "NEW" *STS* COMMISSION FOR A web session to examine the contents of the document and decide how to publicize it. Herschel Banks had arrived at Dr. Gold's office. Valentina and Erika were together at Valeri, and Cardinal Lavoti was present at the Vatican with Father Rinaldi and Cardinal Parina. Josh and Susan were in New York where, since she had a dream escort to show off, she was now full of enthusiasm for her sister's wedding. Yigael gave them his word they'd be updated as soon as the conference ended. Before pocketing his phone, he smiled at reading the text from Josh: *Pins and needles.*

In Jerusalem, all eyes were on blank computer screens waiting for Valentina and Erika to join the video conference.

At the Vatican, Cardinal Parina entered to find Cardinal Lavoti and Father Rinaldi challenged over finding the "add video" button.

"Hello everyone," Valentina said, her and Erika's faces taking center screen.

"Hello," Erika added.

"Cardinal Lavoti? Can you hear me?"

With Cardinal Parina's help, the camera was now on, and the microphone was working.

"Can we begin?" Yigael asked.

"Yes, we're ready," Father Rinaldi responded.

Yigael opened, "Very good. Okay, then, we're all set. Valentina has something of some import, so let's get right to it. Valentina."

"The document that Dr. Simone and I have studied over the past month is exactly what it has been reputed to be, and that is astonishing. With no physical evidence, word of the existence of this document, and what it tells, traveled only by voiced communication from very few souls starting in the first part of the first century to now.

"Think of it. What did we know of the 'rumored' scroll? That it was testimony given by Galilean countrymen to High Priest Caiaphas against Yeshua." Valentina paused, hoping everyone would realize what a miracle this find really was. She had yet to reveal her personal feelings about it. After all, she was a Church member. She was a scientist first, though.

"It was written long before the gospels ... during Yeshua's lifetime ... by men who either knew him or heard him speak. So, this is the oldest and only known document of its kind."

"That's impossible," Cardinal Lavoti interrupted. "We all know that nothing about Yeshua was written until twenty years or more after he died."

"That's what we thought. Until now."

"Go on, Valentina," Cardinal Parina said.

"Yes, do go on," Herschel added.

"But how can you be so sure?" Cardinal Lavoti interrupted again.

"The author of this diary has penned the date as the fifteenth year of Emperor Tiberius. It appears at the beginning of the document," Valentina said. "In today's terminology that would be AD 30, just at the time Yeshua was traveling and teaching around the Galilee."

In Jerusalem, there were glances all around.

In Rome, the clergymen sat motionless as statues.

Dr. Gold questioned, "Does the scribe identify himself?"

Valentina nodded toward Erika.

"No," Erika said, "but he studied at the Temple in Jerusalem, and this might have been his first task—to take witness testimony of a rebel for the Sanhedrin, the Jewish Supreme Council."

"That could have been any false profit, a 'rebel,'" Cardinal Lavoti countered.

"If this scribe was tasked with this duty, it sounds like he was paid," Herschel theorized.

"Yes, I would imagine so, as were the witnesses who traveled from all over to be heard. There were more than one hundred accounts of the rebel Rabbi Yeshua, Cardinal Lavoti. His name is mentioned over and over," Valentina said.

Erika continued, "Some accounts were sightings of what they called a false prophet, where they heard him preach about God his father. Others were witness to his miracles, which many referred to as black magic."

"If this young scribe was paid, this means nothing!" Cardinal Lavoti barked. "If the witnesses were paid, this is just plain nonsense."

"Just because this scroll doesn't say what some of us would want it to, does not mean it's not true." Yigael was getting heated. "The gospels, as we all know, were written decades after Yeshua's death. How are they accurate and this, this document that's written *during* Yeshua's life—some of it documented within days *not decades* of him speaking—how is this not accurate?"

Herschel gave Yigael a look to calm down.

"Is there anything else to verify its authenticity?" Dr. Gold asked.

"Yes," Valentina said, knowing this was the big blow. "The hand that scribed this scroll is the same hand that wrote the Mary Magdalene diary we discovered." She and Erika had found Mary's diary with Julia's bones. It had proved authentic.

"Now, I've heard everything!" Cardinal Lavoti leaned into the computer, skewing the size of his head considerably. I'll see this thing buried." He turned to Father Rinaldi and spat, "Turn this thing off." Then he got up and left his own office, putting an end to the web conference and the *STS* Commission.

CHAPTER SEVENTY-THREE

Rome AD *64*
31 years since Yeshua's death

Sheni 16 Sivan

I have been collaborating with Peter for more than a decade, and we have added to the movement thousands of followers who believe in Yeshua's words. The Romans do not hide their animosity, and it is becoming increasingly dangerous here to be known as, or associated with, the followers. Everywhere we go, harsh words are directed at us.

Shishi 29 Av

We have just survived the great fire in Rome, a fire that raged for more than six days. When the smoke cleared, much of the city of more than half a million lay in ruins. Rumor has it the emperor himself, Nero Claudius Caesar, set aflame his own city to get even with the government officials who denied him approval to tear down Rome's basic structures and build ornate palaces in their place.

We followers of Yeshua believe Nero had a dual purpose. He has been arresting, torturing, and crucifying Jews by the hundreds since he came into power fourteen years ago. We think he wanted to rid the city of us. I believe he succeeded, because the fire wiped out thousands of our followers in under a week. Peter and I are okay. Our humble rooms on the outskirts are of little interest to the ruling class.

Revi'i 23 Elul

The Romans arrested and imprisoned Peter today. The soldiers allowed me to visit him because they considered me a mere servant and no threat. During our time together, Peter emphasized how important it was to keep the scrolls safe. He urged me to make haste because persecutions are escalating. He cautioned me to seek my own safety and, above all, secure a hiding place for the documents—the life of Yeshua, his body, his spirit, his work. He referred me to a wealthy woman by the name of Julia Lucinia Aquillia to whom I can turn for help. Apparently, she is of an old Roman family in the senatorial class and has a comfortable home. He said to find her in the marketplace and use the code. He promised she would understand.

SCRIBE STUDIED JULIA AS SHE SHOPPED FOR FIGS AND BREAD, waiting for the perfect moment. Between selecting the plumpest and bluest grapes, she would steal glances about the marketplace. Scribe knew from years of traveling with women how intuitive they were. He was certain Julia knew someone was watching her. Scribe saw her finish her shopping and leave the market. Once she and her servant came to a busy intersection, Scribe crossed in front of her, causing her to stop. She smiled and tried to go around him, but he again blocked her.

Nervous but without choice, Scribe raised his eyes to hers. "We search for peace in our homes."

Julia recognized the words. She leaned in close. "Ah, you are the scribe, the scribe Peter spoke of. You are the one."

Scribe nodded.

"My name is Julia. This is Milo, our house steward. Come with me. I daresay I have been expecting you."

"Thank you, *gveret*."

"I am Julia, please."

Scribe nodded.

Milo fetched the carriage.

Back at her home, Julia gestured for the scribe to sit on one of the benches in the *tablinum*. As he did, a servant entered with a cup of warm, spiced wine. He gratefully accepted it, wrapping his fingers around it.

After the servant left the room, Julia asked, "How came you to be in such a state?"

"I am in danger here in Rome. I have been living with Peter. When he was arrested, I ran and hid in the streets."

"But surely they were after Peter. Why would you be in danger?"

"Though I look it, I am not a servant." His tunic was tattered and filthy. "My presence was kept quiet because the documents I produce are a threat. They must be kept hidden."

"What are you called?" Julia asked him. "What are these documents?"

"Call me Scribe. I need only that. I have a library of scrolls, a record of Yeshua's words."

"You have what?"

"Yeshua's words. I was with him too. I wrote of his speaking."

"What he said? His actual words?"

"Yes."

"By gods! Where are they?" Julia jumped out of her seat.

"In our lodgings. Where I stayed with Peter. I am afraid to go back there. If they find me there, or the scrolls—

"Milo!" she yelled, racing out of the room.

CHAPTER SEVENTY-FOUR

Beit Aghion, Jerusalem

IT WASN'T JUST CARDINAL LAVOTI WHO SLAMMED THE DOOR ON the *STS*. Dr. Gold was skeptical too. *"Is this enough to run with?"* he'd asked Yigael after the conference.

Yigael intended to release the document he'd set his sights on for so long right away, but caution and deference told him to clear it first with the prime minister.

"Yigael, you must back off," David Golman advised. "I don't want to bat against the Vatican. Can you imagine the awkward position Israel would be in should the scroll be released and then discounted as inauthentic?"

"But, David, that scroll has been dissected, scrutinized, and studied by two of the greatest minds in archaeology today. I cannot doubt that it is genuine."

"Yigael, into whose hands has that scroll landed?"

"The Church has it, owns it."

"See what I mean?"

Was the project he'd given so much to about to collapse? He was devastated. To his mind, the world needed to know about the testimonies against the man called—falsely, he thought—their Messiah. But what more could he do? He'd hired a team to steal from a basilica. He'd hired the mob! He'd allowed Valentina and Erika to risk their careers. Again.

The subterfuge, the treachery, the confusion, the expense—what was it all worth? "Is that your final word, David? Is there nothing I can say to change it?" Golman's clenched jaw was Yigael's answer.

The age-old religious arguments had not ended, probably never would. In the meantime, he must still face the music and tidy things up. "Prime Minister, there is more you need to know about our find in France."

"And what would that be?"

Yigael related how they had come to know that the *STS* was housed in the cathedral at Saint-Denis, along with the Second Temple of Jerusalem treasure belonging to Israel.

"So now we have a dicey problem," the PM said.

"Yep. Unfortunately. We want our treasure back, but how do we get it unless we reveal our plot?"

"And just how do you suggest we get out of this mess?"

"Well, obviously, we have to tell the Vatican."

"Handle this," Golman said and pointing a finger at Yigael's burly chest, added, "No leaks. No press."

YIGAEL SET out for Rome and arrived at Cardinal Lavoti's office in the Vatican the next afternoon.

The two settled into high-backed armchairs.

"I didn't expect to see you so soon again." Cardinal Lavoti's face was nearly a picture of composure, which he had tried hard to emanate. However, his tight lips gave away the discomfort he felt when he faced this man.

"Well, well," Yigael said, "things have a way of turning up

DIANE CUMMINGS & JOHN I. RIGOLI

and coming to rights. You never know." He got a perverse satisfaction keeping the cardinal on edge.

"But ... but this is well over. I thought you'd be licking your
wounds."

"Heh, heh. Oh, we've a way to go yet." Yigael grinned.

"You don't say. And just what might that be?"

To the cardinal's dropped jaw, Yigael disclosed where they'd
discovered the *STS*.

"You robbed a cathedral? I don't know quite what ...."

"We found something else there, Cardinal. Part of the treasure stolen from the Second Temple all those years back in AD
70. What do you think of that? Our treasure in your church ...
for 2,000 years. I'll be." Then, in a tone that brooked no misin-
terpretation, Yigael added, "We expect that what belongs to
Israel will be returned to her."

Cardinal Lavoti bristled. *He steals from a cathedral and then
wants to go back. But I cannot deny him. The last thing I want is
attention brought to me should I refuse. I have other entanglements
to dodge.* In the smarmiest tone, he said, "Of course, Yigael, your
treasure has been lost to you for far too long. We will arrange
for you to take possession at the soonest possible time." *At least
I have the damned scroll. Nobody will dare talk about it. Certainly
not those two women. Not now after what I've done to them. The
STS will die with me.*

Yigael had done his best. But this was a washout. He left the
Vatican oddly satisfied except for one thing. Valentina and
Erika were locked out of their lab again.

CHAPTER SEVENTY-FIVE

Rome AD *64*

JULIA HURRIEDLY DRESSED IN HER MAID'S ATTIRE AND HEAD covering and dashed outside. Despite Milo's protests, Julia jumped up on the cart alongside the scribe. "Go." She would get hold of these scrolls, or else.

When they arrived in the scribe's neighborhood, the trio, carrying cloth sacks rolled snugly, stepped into a side entrance and began climbing the stairs. No one paid them any notice. Having glimpsed two guards and shooing away a boy with a ball, they made it to the sixth-floor landing.

"That one." Scribe pointed to an apartment in the passageway. No one in sight. They ran. Scribe shook as his fingers fumbled with a key. Milo snatched the key and unlocked the door.

Inside, they all breathed a momentary sigh.

Julia and Milo's faces fell as they surveyed the profusion of documents lying in disarray.

"Let us get to it," Julia said. They all grabbed sacks and started packing.

Just as they recovered the very last papyrus, a loud banging shook the door. "Open up in the name of the emperor!"

"Get into the other room. I will handle this," Julia whispered. Seeing them looking wary, she gave them her sternest look, and Milo and the scribe hauled the sacks of scrolls into the second room and crouched in the corner hidden from the front door.

Julia opened the door a crack. "Yes?"

"Stand aside, woman. We are coming in."

"Oh, you will not be wanting to come in here."

The soldiers hesitated. "And just why is that? Open up."

"Oh no, it is my moon time. You will not want to come in."

That did it for the Roman soldiers. Even the bravest would get nowhere near a woman during her monthly courses. The soldiers took two steps back and hustled away.

Once they were out of sight, the trio flew down the long corridor. The scribe, showing himself to be surprisingly quick on his feet, kept pace.

Safely back at Julia's home, the scribe found that her maid had prepared him a bath and laid out a fresh tunic. She also had a room ready on the front side of the house. It had a window and a cushioned bed. Worn out, he washed, put on fresh clothing, and collapsed onto the bed.

Julia awakened him with the worst of news.

Shishi 13 Adar

Peter was executed today. I am in despair thinking back to his overwhelming generosity and my closeness with his family. I am beyond defeated. I feel hopeless. How will the teachings go on? How can I go on without his leadership? I will miss him so. God, please help me. Yeshua, where are you? Please, someone answer my cries.

I listen but the only response is the buzz of the night. I will be mindful of Peter's final wishes and not tarry with his instructions. "We live for Yeshua." This I must never forget.

Julia has made the quick decision to leave Rome. She and I will travel before daybreak to Herculaneum. She says we will not be bothered there, and the scrolls will be safe. Milo and Julia's maid will follow with her daughters at week's end.

Julia says her country villa sits on a bluff overlooking the Tyrrhenian Sea. Even in her state of despair over Peter's death, this noblewoman thought to paint a warm picture of the place she would be taking me, to put my heart at ease. I have known her but a minute and, already, she reminds me so of Mary. I feel ashamed to admit it, to be moving on without Peter, but I long for the kind of peace she promises.

THE SCRIBE and Julia left for Herculaneum before dawn the next morning, heading into the city along the Via Claudia. Within the hour, as the sun peeked over the horizon, wagons, veering back and forth, crowded the streets as they delivered their wares to eager merchants.

At the Roman gates, as expected, a guard stopped them. He looked surprised to see a woman steering the horses.

"Where are you going in such a hurry?"

"To Herculaneum. I am Julia Lucinia Aquillia. My husband is the magistrate, Marcus Aquillius. I am delivering urgent legal documents to his offices there. Please pass me through."

"Who is he?" the guard demanded.

"My servant, of course. Now, will you let us through?" It was not really a question, more of a demand, evidenced by her tone and her chin pointed skyward.

Scribe never ceased to be impressed by how women so naturally used the power of their minds over their fists to manage tricky situations.

As they passed through the gates, Julia breathed deeply, relieved. The scribe shook off the memory of Roman soldiers beating him, and they were on their way.

CHAPTER SEVENTY-SIX

Herculaneum AD *66*

32 years since Yeshua's death

Sheni 8 Nisan

Under the patronage of Julia Lucinia, I have settled in at the villa that overlooks the sea. Julia is working with me, helping me organize the older scrolls, the records of Yeshua's life and word, into a library built specifically to keep them safe. The room is constructed to withstand even fire, as the walls are made extra thick with mortar and stone. She hired a carpenter, mason, and sculptor to fashion a door of copper. I've never been so close to something this fancy in all my life. It is art. It should be in exhibition hall.

I am content here and feel safe. But, with Peter gone and Paul mainly in hiding when he's not cooling off in jail, it is up to me to spread the word throughout the Empire. Surprisingly, after first refusing, Julia has agreed to be the messenger for Yeshua's word. She'll take Milo along, of course.

Herculaneum AD *67*
34 years since Yeshua's death

Hamishi 23 Nisan

She never explained what changed her mind, but Julia has been taking scrolls to Rome for months now and has come to no harm. It means Yeshua's word will spread throughout the Empire and further the mission.

Thanks to my days with Yeshua, I knew how to keep Julia and the documents safe on these three-day journeys. We could not rely on a false bottom for the family cart, though it had one. Instead, Milo hollowed out a compartment on the side of the cart and constructed a cover that slides invisibly over the opening. We can hide about a dozen scrolls that way.

Soldiers stop Julia all the time. It always amuses her to see them go straight for the false bottom, rip it up, and find no contraband, simply honey and wine. "Gifts for friends," she always says with a coy look. "Would you like some?"

It is unlikely the soldiers will ever discover it.

Later in the year 67

It is thirty-four years since my master was hauled to his death in Jerusalem. Still, I cannot bear to think of it. And now, Paul, my dearest friend, is dead. After being under house arrest for years, Rome beheaded him. What a horrible end. I will always remember him, and I will remind myself that he is with our beloved Yeshua now.

CHAPTER SEVENTY-SEVEN

Parioli

JUST AS VALENTINA HEARD A KNOCK ON THE DOOR, HER PHONE rang. Thinking it had be Erika, she accepted the call without checking the ID. "Hello," she said as she swung the door open to Yigael, whom she'd been expecting.

"Valentina? Hi."

"Kara," Valentina said, motioning Yigael to shush.

"Valentina, you're not going to believe this," Kara said.

"Kara, I've been meaning to call. But I wanted to talk to you in person and haven't had a free second until, well, recently. I've got nothing but free time now. Can I cash in that raincheck? Let's meet for dinner ... how about it?"

"You need to get down here first thing. And bring Erika."

"Erika? But Erika had nothing to do with—"

"Valentina, my team found a door to a stone vault with perfectly preserved scrolls inside, dozens of them, some of which look as old as your secret scroll."

"Oh, my God."

"There's more."

"More?"

"I'll see you tomorrow." Kara hung up.

"Valentina?" Yigael said taking a seat in her most comfortable chair. "Are you okay?"

Valentina turned to Yigael. "Fantastic news." She repeated Kara's words. Then her face clouded. "But why is she reaching out to me? It's her dig. Especially after I stole her container." *Ouch.*

Yigael stifled a chortle. "Guess we'll find out."

"You coming?" Valentina asked.

"Me pass up a vault full of relics?"

Ercolano

AFTER LOSING the *Secret Temple Scroll* to the Vatican and for several months thereafter, Kara applied her attention to an area where a section of marble had appeared. What that represented was anyone's guess, but with great enthusiasm, she and her team went after it, digging down and around and deep. Eventually, two impressive pillars stood side by side. Cleaning off the muck, Kara's heart nearly stopped when she saw the names chiseled into the stone. *Marcus Nonius Aquillius* and *Julia Lucinia Aquillia.*

After the shock wore off, Kara's discovery proved to her that the Church had indeed bulldozed Valentina and Erika for their discovery of the first-century female bishop. At the least, it proved how real Julia was. She knew she needed to go to Valentina. But, after seeing what the Church did to her mentor, she'd been afraid to risk losing a career that had only just begun. And so, she sat on the information, waiting on clarity or, more aptly, courage. Since then, Kara's team had worked tirelessly to uncover the remains of the Aquillii dwelling. As each day passed and more was revealed, the longer Kara sat on the information, the harder it became to tell Valentina.

Just a few weeks ago, Kara's team found what appeared to be an unusual solid piece of metal on a hill above the boat caves. Whether it was art or a sculpture, they couldn't tell. They dug around it for a few weeks, chipping with hammers and pickaxes, peeling back piece after piece of encrusted lava to reveal a magnificent copper door embossed with a peacock. When that amazing door opened and Kara stepped inside, she knew she could wait no longer.

Kara turned as Valentina and Erika approached. A man tagged behind them. Though weighted by her secret, Kara felt a huge sense of excitement at seeing the two scientists she could now call peers.

Dragged down by her baggage, Valentina stepped slowly past security and waved. "Kara."

"Right here. Come on over."

The door was on display for them, ajar, and catching the morning sun exactly right. Yigael crouched down next to the ladder to get a good look at the recessed structure. "Breathtaking." He stood back up. "Yigael Dorian," he said, holding out his hand.

"This is Kara Maggi," Valentina said.

The man himself. "An honor, Dr. Dorian."

"This is like nothing I have ever seen before. Solid, and looks like it's constructed in an unusual way," Yigael commented.

"To protect whatever is behind it," Valentina added.

"And to respect whatever is behind it. That peacock must've taken months to carve," Erika said.

"Go ahead," Kara instructed with a nod, locking eyes with Valentina.

Two members of Kara's team pulled on the ropes that

secured the door, cranking it wide open. They fixed the ropes to *carabiners* and tied them with a square knot.

Valentina and Erika stepped down a ladder and through the door.

The space inside was pitch black. Just as Erika looked up, Kara crouched down and handed her a flashlight.

When their eyes adjusted to the bright ray of artificial light, they could see stacks of cylindrical rolls along the shelves. They also noted a collection, though smaller, of writings in Codex form. The pages of papyrus bound together for reading side-by-side told the two scientists the books could not be older than first century.

Despite the stale air and thick layer of dust, the room's contents appeared in excellent condition. The room looked undisturbed from the moment disaster had struck.

A small area had already been cleared. Those were the scrolls Kara had seen up close, but the others, including the Codex books, all appeared to belong to the same collection. They were so unified.

"A remarkable library," Erika commented.

Valentina stayed quiet, the truth edging toward consciousness. She went back up the ladder. "Yigael," she said, motioning for him to have a look.

Yigael joined Erika in the vault.

Valentina and Kara stood together, neither knowing where to begin.

"I have something for you," Kara said.

An arrest warrant? Valentina thought but asked, "What?"

Kara reached into a carrier for artifacts and pulled out a fat scroll.

Valentina cocked her head. "What is it?"

"I found this on the desk inside the vault. It was partially open at the top, and there was a stylus and a pot of ink sitting beside it. All in pristine condition, perfect really."

"But what does it have to do with me? This is your dig."

"Ignoring the question, Kara said, "It's a good thing I dropped by that meeting where the Secret Temple Scroll was dug up on that landowner's property. I wouldn't have known otherwise."

Valentina flushed with guilt. "Look, I meant to—"

Interrupting, Kara said, "This scroll is partner, in a way, to your *Secret Temple Scroll.*"

"How do you mean?"

"The handwriting in both matches."

What she was reaching for landed, and Valentina said, "Yes." *Confirmed,* she thought. "And this *is* Julia's villa."

"Come with me," Kara said. The two hiked a short distance west to where the Aquillii pillars stood.

At the sight of them, Valentina stilled, her emotions running too deep to speak. After seconds that felt like minutes and through eyes made blind by tears, she asked in a trembling voice, "How long have you known?" And then Valentina broke down. She fell to the ground, sobbing away the pain from all the accusations, the threats, and the doubts she'd entertained about herself. She and Erika would be vindicated. When she'd recovered her sensibilities, she asked again, "How long have you known?"

"Valentina, I think it's time for us to have that dinner. And I want you to take this. It seems personal, his own story. You should have it now." She handed the scroll to Valentina, whose heart was lively again and giving her tingles. "You're giving me this ... to translate?"

"Only if you can find a stray cannister to put it in," and pulling out a sheet of paper, "and only if you sign right here."

Valentina turned to see Kara smiling.

CHAPTER SEVENTY-EIGHT

Herculaneum AD **68**
35 years since Yeshua's death

Rishon 28 Heshvan

To say I was surprised did not begin to describe my incredulity when she arrived. I was in the library when Julia burst in, quite shaken.

"What is it, my dear? What is wrong?"

"I saw her from my bedchamber window, Scribe, an old woman with long, gray hair in the distance, heading in our direction. I watched as she came nearer. When I opened the door to her, she said, 'I seek the scribe.' She is quite frail. I sent for warm wine."

"Who, Julia? Who seeks me?" I am afraid I was beginning to show impatience and I was sorry for it. But it seems the

338

elderly have little tolerance for the waste of time. "Who?" I asked again.

"Why, Mary. Mary of Magdala."

I left the library swiftly and met her in the atrium. "Mary, dearest Mary, it has been such a long time." I grasped her hands, noting how cold and bony they were.

"Yes," she said simply.

I took her to a small side chamber where we could talk. Julia brought us nourishment.

Mary asked me to record her life story. Of course, I agreed. I had always wanted to know all about her in those old days. I never thought this day would come.

We met each day for the next two weeks. I listened and recorded her recitation of the life she had led. When her story was ending, I knew that our time together would be over for good. And, indeed, when I awoke one morning and joined Julia in the triclinium for breakfast, she informed me that Mary had gone.

That was so like Mary, especially the Mary I now knew.

CHAPTER SEVENTY-NINE

Herculaneum AD *70*
37 years since Yeshua's death

Sheni 16 Nisan

Word has come that Jerusalem was destroyed two days past, on the Tisha B'Av. It is said that the Romans looted the Temple and then set it ablaze with a burning stick. The flames engulfed the structure and then spread into the residential sections of the city. We have heard that Jews escaped through hidden, underground tunnels. The Roman legions crushed the remaining Jews. The city is now under Roman control and soldiers continue to hunt down the Jews who managed to flee.

Is this what Yeshua meant when he spoke about the destruction of the Temple?

"IT IS, MY OLD FRIEND," A SOFT VOICE WHISPERED.
Without forethought, the scribe replied, "Old indeed,

Yeshua." Then he dropped his pen and straightened up in his chair, looking about the room. The scribe sat there for a minute, very still, listening for footsteps. Hearing none, he shook his head, chalking his imaginings up to his age. He got back to his diary.

That night, the scribe awakened from the light of the full moon. Feeling odd and extra awake, he followed its path outside to a clearing. High on the hill, he overlooked Herculaneum and felt what he thought must be a false sense of peace. A quiet, clear night can do that. From behind, he heard his name called. No question this time, it was Yeshua.

The scribe turned, and there Yeshua stood, beneath the moonlight, more beautiful than anything he ever could have imagined, in the crisp, white, cotton tunic Peter had described decades back.

He reached out, but Yeshua raised his hand as a signal to stop.

"I know your longing, Scribe, but, you see, I am here. I have always been here."

"I live only for you."

"You originally felt duty toward your temple assignment. Then, you felt guilty. Then, you gave in and began to document my life as the eyes of your heart bore witness."

The scribe looked down, that messy truth having haunted him for so long.

"I want you to know that it did not matter why you were sent to me. It mattered only that you arrived. I wanted to thank you for that, Scribe, for a life of devotion."

"Thank you, Yeshua, thank you."

"You have felt it was your first record of testimony in Jerusalem that caused my death. I have come to tell you it was not, and you must not be troubled about it further. What happened was set in motion long before we ever met, long before you ever held your first reed pen. You should feel only peace in your heart, my scribe, my champion."

A cloud appeared partially covering the moon and, without its full light, the scribe could see only a sleeve of Yeshua's tunic. He stepped forward to outwit the obstacle. "Stay," he said.

But Yeshua was gone.

CHAPTER EIGHTY

Papal Apartments
Present Day

WEARING DOWN THE PORTUGUESE ARMORIAL CARPET IN HIS office, Cardinal Carlo Lavoti chewed on the Church and all its troubles. He was always stomping out fires, keeping the Church only a half-step in front of her detractors. It was exhausting. He had seized control of, and buried from prying eyes, the *Secret Temple Scroll*, which could have knocked Christianity on its knees. For that, he deserved a vacation! But no. That young, emotional archaeologist, another woman no less, had to go discover that avalanche of scrolls. Now, he was up against an inferno. There was only one place left to turn. Just as he was going to put in a request to meet with the pope, Father Rinaldi stepped into his office, notifying the cardinal that he had, in fact, been summoned.

So, at 5:00 on a balmy summer evening, weeks after the discovery of the copper vault, Cardinal Lavoti entered the pope's apartment library to find not only Pope Julius Africanus but Cardinal Justin Parina, both just finishing glasses of sherry.

From the first, the mild-mannered pope, Africanus, had refused to let slide the hunt for Augustine's killer. He had kept in daily touch with the Vatican's clandestine intelligence service, *Santa Alleanza.* Now he would see his efforts rewarded. But first, he wanted for the errant cardinal to feel the weight of the Vatican descend upon him. "The scrolls are causing a great deal of unrest," he began, "and I wish it to cease."

"I couldn't agree more!" Cardinal Lavoti spoke with enthusiasm.

"I have seen enough dissension for one lifetime ... in our Church." He paused, staring at the cardinal with a stone face. "And dissension is not the worst of it ... you, ah ... know."

Where is this going? Cardinal Lavoti shifted uncomfortably.

"But we will get to that. Dissension within has led to intolerance without. Our Church has not always accepted other religions, but I have had some experience in forbearance, and I think there is room for a more, shall we call it, liberal view of religious differences. I would like our Church to be the catalyst in this matter. It serves us to do so, and it is time."

Pope Africanus was fifty-eight years old and the first Black pope. His first year in office, on the heels of the Julia scandal and the sudden, premature death of Pope Augustine, looked uneventful. Behind the scenes, it was anything but. The wheels were turning, to a point it was not surprising to hear His Holiness say, "I am sponsoring a meeting of leaders from every major religion—Christian, Jewish, Muslim, Buddhist, Hindu, and leaders from smaller denominations. We will dialogue about these discoveries. It is to be an inclusive universal council."

Cardinal Lavoti, looking troubled and threatened, said, "Don't you think it might be premature to give attention to these documents now? After all, they are still under scrutiny by scholars." Then he added, "They could be fake."

Pope Africanus raised a hand. "It doesn't matter whether they are fakes. The time has come to end religious wars."

"But they could damage the Church," Cardinal Lavoti said with a wobbly voice. "What the scribe has to say about Yeshua could make the Church irrelevant!"

Cardinal Parina sat quietly, taking in the exchange.

"That is your limited view, and I disagree. The Church, to go forward, must show openness. The world is changing. New archaeological finds are challenging biblical history every day. As you will have other matters to attend to, I am appointing Cardinal Parina to organize the meetings."

Other matters? This should go to me. It's high profile. I should be out front in this. Cardinal Lavoti hiccupped and clapped his hand over his mouth. "But you can't just—"

"This esteemed role might have gone to you, Carlo, but for your recent ... errors in judgment."

Errors in judgment? What does he know? Cardinal Lavoti's mind reeled, plotting his next course. Erasing one scroll had been a feat. How was he to erase dozens? Trapped in the jail of his own making, he did not notice the six *poliziotti* standing around the library doorway.

Pope Africanus nodded to them, and the officer in charge came forward.

"Cardinal Carlo Lavoti," the officer said, "You are under arrest for suspicion of conspiracy to commit murder, the murder of Pope Augustine."

The cardinal gasped. "No." But he didn't resist as two officers entered the library, raised him up by the elbows, and escorted him out.

Cardinal Lavoti could say goodbye to all those scrolls. It was unlikely he'd ever see them again. "Call my lawyer," he barked to nobody special.

If Cardinal Parina was surprised at the happenings, it didn't show. His expression remained as mild as a leafy breeze on an early spring day.

Pope Africanus got back to the business of what he and Cardinal Parina had been discussing prior to Cardinal Lavoti joining them: Valeri. It seemed bucketloads of euros had been spent on an advanced facility that no one outside of its original owners could use. Not one computer scientist specializing in algorithms could break their codes. Valentina Vella and Erika Simone had taken scrupulous care to protect their software as a trade secret, and they held copyright and patents on all relevant applications. In fact, no one had figured out how to turn their equipment on.

"Give it back," Pope Julius Africanus said to the cardinal.

"I couldn't agree more," he said, feeling relieved.

YIGAEL WAS ECSTATIC, per his prediction, his friends had their lab back. And, by month's end, serving as foreman, he had assembled Professor Jacques Ignatius, Philippe Gaston, Anna-Marie Mannes, and Carol Conners in Paris to begin reclamation of the Jewish treasure from Saint-Denis Basilica.

On a break one day, a Friday, with his heart beating rapidly, Philippe found Gabriella and asked her to dinner at *Au Petit Breton*.

She accepted.

CHAPTER EIGHTY-ONE

Herculaneum AD *79*
46 years since Yeshua's death

Herculaneum—24 Elul 79

*I lead a quiet life, this life of hiding. I write on papyrus or
parchment in codex form now for all my recordings. I doubt
I'll ever roll another scroll. These pages allow me to write on
both sides and they are easier to read. I don't know why I
would put this information into my work, as it will be plain
to see by whomever finds these, God willing. But it's my life,
these documents, and so ....*

*I think of Peter and Paul on waking these days, even though
they have been gone now for so many years. I do not know
why I have felt so caught in the past lately. I must shake
myself free of these thoughts.*

Ah, there is the lunch bell, made soundless by a huge, thun-

derous crash from the east. A multitude of those have drowned out the bell for the last few days.

I would rather stay in the library for a while, but I would never make Julia wait on lunch.

And so, for now, I must go.

THE FOLLOWING DAY BEGAN LIKE ANY OTHER. THE SCRIBE intended to go with Julia and her daughters to market to purchase ink and papyrus for his writings. But, just as the lunch bell tinkled, the house tottered, rocking back and forth as if being torn from its very foundation. This boom was like no other, much worse than the day prior.

On hearing the girls scream, Scribe made haste for the dining area, where he found them locked in an embrace, their cries ringing with fright.

"What's happening?" Julia screeched. She rushed in, her face white with horror.

Scribe had no time for pretense. "Girls, Julia." He turned up his voice a notch. "Go to your rooms. Pack enough clothing for four days. Be quick."

Milo hurried in, took in the scene, at once understood Scribe's intentions, and dashed off in another direction to ready himself for the trip.

With bag in hand, Livia returned to the dining area. "Where are we going?" She tried to still her trembling, with little luck.

"Neapolis. We must get to the boats."

A moment before leaving, Scribe hurried back to the library and returned carrying a single scroll. Julia stuffed it inside a cloth bag, and then, spotting his cup on the mantelpiece, scooped it up.

Scribe nodded his approval. "Yes, they should stay together."

Clutching Yarrow, the family dog, Scribe met Milo outside, and they shepherded Julia and her girls down to the waterfront.

The marina had become crowded with citizens scrambling toward the boats. Scribe urged his charges forward onto one of them. Milo followed. Neither Scribe nor Milo would ever allow these three women to leave home without a male escort. In fact, the law prohibited women from traveling alone.

Julia motioned Scribe aboard.

"The smoke seems to be thinning and heading away." Scribe knew it was not. "I'll be fine here."

Flavia reached for Yarrow, but the little dog yelped and clung to the scribe. "He wants to stay with you."

An hour later, when the boat carrying his beloved Julia and her daughters became a spot on the hypnotic blue waters, a blotch of ink on a new sheet of vellum, the scribe, with Yarrow in arms, thinking only of the scrolls, turned to reach the villa. But he didn't get far.

The smoke in the air thickened, the atmosphere darkened, and an explosion resounded that was so deafening, it muted the screams of the two thousand remaining villagers.

Then, indiscriminately, Vesuvius, glowing red, opened her mouth wide and spewed lava, rock, and ash high into the sky. Barely past the waterline, Scribe fell to his knees. All he could see through the dark veil of smoke was the liquid earth cascading from the clouds onto all sides of the mountain, flowing in thick rivers, burning everything in its wake.

He knew he would die of the poisoned air long before the lava reached him. He scrambled for safety, anyway, toward the mouth of the first boat cave. As he held the little dog tighter, he murmured, "I'm sorry, Yarrow."

Then, he closed his eyes, and, for the last time, Scribe felt the warm hand of Yeshua cup his tired, aging cheek.

EPILOGUE

Ercolano—One Year Later

AFTER THE *SECRET TEMPLE SCROLL* AND THE *ANONYMOUS SCRIBE Collection* were revealed to the world, Valentina, having spent a year preserving and cataloguing them, had time for a real vacation. Her one-month sabbatical didn't have her traveling the world but relaxing in a cottage by the shores of the Amalfi Coast. She had begun a routine of long days spent alone, reading opposing opinions and critiques of her and Erika's work with a sense of detached interest, almost forgetting her involvement in the entire event.

For many years, she wondered whether such a text would appear. The *Secret Temple Scroll* had been written nearly twenty years before any other historical document about Yeshua of record. And the scribe's diary had revealed a personal portrait of the man Yeshua: passionate and driven, whose short life would transform first his homeland and later the world. Even more, it drew the daily life of Yeshua into the imagination of millions as if they, too, had walked with him, alongside the Anonymous Scribe. She thought about what the scribe had written in his diary. The healing, the miracles, if that is what they were, the part about seeing and speaking with Yeshua prior to his death. Was it all true?

And what of this scribe? He had revealed himself as an ordinary man from the Galilee, but surprising Valentina with his reference to rusty hair and pale skin, unlike most everyone else in the region. He was young at the start of his writing, having only just completed his training. He had, as only the young do, a jumble of character traits, at once cocky and arrogant about his schooling and his perceived place in society. He had fallen in love, suffered great loss, and become humbled as he grew wiser and succumbed wholly to his life's purpose.

It was her last weekend, and she felt pulled to the site.

After driving into Herculaneum and parking her Alfa Romeo by the side of the road, Valentina got out and stretched. The sheer size of the mountain dwarfed the small buildings and narrow streets that made up the modern-day village. Vesuvius seemed like a god hovering over, at once protecting and threatening. It was now bursting with vegetation and life, not cooled, black rock, dead and barren, as it had been in those days.

Now, standing in the place where he had lived and worked, it seemed fitting that she should revisit. She strolled through town, absorbing its atmosphere, and stared down at the bay, imagining her scribe walking there. Then she headed toward the boat caves.

Stepping inside, she looked at the skeletons huddled together. In a corner, one of them curled around the bones of a small dog.

She moved away, for this was not a place for lingering, and stepped out of the cave into the near-blinding *sole d-estate*. Sunshine of summer.

He had given his life to Yeshua, to the future of the world, to truth. The scribe had sacrificed his life to the very end.

As Valentina contemplated this remarkable tale, she closed her eyes and could almost feel the hot sands and dry days in Galilee. She could envision her scribe seeing Yeshua for the first time. She would never know his name, but she was alive in his world.

—The End of Book II—

A NOTE TO THE READER

We are more than grateful that you have chosen to read *The Anonymous Scribe*!

We love hearing from our readers - so if you'd like, please follow us on Facebook or join our mailing list at VaticanChronicles.com

ACKNOWLEDGMENTS

Thanks to everyone on the Julia team who helped us get this little baby from Start to Print and beyond.

Noteworthy gratitude to Lisa Cerasoli, an effervescent soul whose get-up-and-go knows no bounds. An amazing scribe and editor.

To our Italy connection, Shaun Loftus, publicist extraordinaire, deep, deep thanks. Her magic has allowed us to reach readers across the globe.

From the UK, much appreciation to our great award-winning, ever-patient cover designer, Jane Dixon-Smith.

Thank you, Cassandra Campbell, for your mellifluous voice and beautiful narration of our story for the audiobook.

ABOUT THE AUTHORS

John Ignatius Rigoli's experiences as both a cradle Catholic and former US Naval officer informed his world view in a rather unexpected manner, opening his eyes to the proposition that those who seek power are the last people who should hold it. John is an unabashed social justice advocate, outspoken liberal, and a patriot – and he sees no dichotomy in this. As a talented and inquisitive amateur historian, John became interested in the stories of the earliest women in the Church, and how they have been erased. Though a work of historical fiction, The Vatican Chronicles takes its inspiration from the real women throughout history who toiled unacknowledged alongside their brothers.

Diane Cummings is a California girl, a UCLA alum, and is currently sweating in Atlanta, Georgia, with the world's smallest Persian cat. Diane has worked as a reporter and news director. Deciding that truth was too much stranger than fiction, she turned in her microphone and press pass and set about applying her passion for writing and editing to the world of literature. Diane has edited or ghostwritten more than fifty titles – and now she wants her name on the cover. The Vatican Chronicle Trilogy has encompassed six years of research, writing, and polishing and she hopes you enjoy Book I – The Mystery of Julia Episcopa as much as she has enjoyed writing it.